ONE
LIAR
LEFT

BOOKS BY EMILY SHINER

EMILY SHINER

ONE LIAR LEFT

bookouture

Published by Bookouture in 2024

An imprint of Storyfire Ltd.
Carmelite House
50 Victoria Embankment
London EC4Y 0DZ

www.bookouture.com

ISBN: 978-1-83525-589-6
eBook ISBN: 978-1-83525-588-9

For Ashley
For a myriad of reasons, but especially one only you know.

PROLOGUE

Stars exploded in her vision, the pain from the back of her head radiating to her eyes, a terrible throbbing that was only second in horror to how her lungs screamed for oxygen.

She gasped for air, clawing at the hands around her neck. Digging her heels into the ground, she bucked up, trying to knock the person off her. He straddled her, his weight forward on her chest as he leaned into his work, his gloved fingers tight around her throat, sinking into her flesh. There was a pounding in her head; her tongue was dry, swollen in her mouth. When she tried to scream, she couldn't get enough air to catch her breath and only ended up wheezing.

He laughed. The rank smell of alcohol and fetid breath rolled over her. Before she could think through what to do next, he leaned down, his thick tongue slithering against her cheek, up the side of her head, into her ear. His teeth closed down on the shell of her ear, a painful shock that caused her to fill her lungs and cry out.

Tears sprang to her eyes, hot and burning, but she did her best to blink them away. She had no idea who this man was, or what he wanted with her, but she didn't want to give him the satisfaction of seeing her cry. When she squeezed his wrists tighter, trying to dig her nails into his skin, her grip slipped against the gloves he wore.

"I've been waiting for this."

The first words he'd said to her since the attack began. She and her friend had seen him standing there, looking lost, thin but handsome, much better equipped to sit in front of the TV all day than tramp around through the woods, and she'd felt bad for him at first, wanted to help him. He'd looked in need of help, and goodness knows she'd needed help before in her life. Besides, it was the right thing to do, wasn't it? Help someone who needed it?

And then he'd attacked her friend.

It happened from time to time, and she knew that, but never in her life had she thought it was going to happen to her. One night in the woods, just one night with her friend and some beer and a lifetime of memories before she moved away and then her friend would be back in her home with her fiancé, and this was how it was going to end?

It didn't make any sense. How was this happening to her?

A strong twist and she rolled under him, digging her elbow into the dirt, her eyes searching for her friend. There, by the fire, her glassy eyes reflecting the flames, her mouth open like she was in the middle of a scream, the side of her head caved in. Like ground beef. Bloody and raw, the huge rock he'd used to attack her, to bash her head in, to splatter her brains across the dead leaves littering the forest floor now lying just a yard away.

If only she could get it, she could—

"Look at me. I want you to see me when I kill you." The man chuckled, and her stomach rolled. Hot bile burned the back of her throat, and she swallowed, tearing her eyes away from the rock and looking at the man even as she still reached for it.

Her fingers brushed against something. Wood. A stick.

Thin, like a chopstick, nothing at all strong or firm enough for her to actually use as a weapon. Still, she closed her fingers on it while keeping her eyes locked on the man sitting on her chest, his rubbery lips wet with spit, a bubble of it forming in the corner of his mouth.

The man grinned at her compliance. "You're a good girl now, aren't you, Jolie? But you weren't back then, were you?" He leaned back. His long thin fingers still rested on her throat, but he released her enough that she could finally breathe properly.

Gasping for air, she filled her lungs, ashamed at how she panted for it, unable to stop herself. It was clear from the expression on his face that he enjoyed watching her as she fought for breath, sucked in little puffs of it, enough to keep her from passing out.

Then it hit her.

He knew her name. How in the world did he know her name? She was sure she'd never seen this man before, but *he knew her.*

That only meant one thing, and that terrified her. He'd followed her. Watched her. He'd been around long enough to know who she was and to call her by name.

He knew what she'd done.

The stick slipped from her grasp.

She sucked in air again, a wave of dizziness washing over her. Planting her hands on the ground, she pushed up, but trying to move him was like trying to move a Mac truck. He leaned forward, rolling his hips against her. Something hard pressed into her chest, between her breasts. He reached down, grabbing her through her shirt, a moan escaping from his lips. There was his tongue again, slipping out from between his lips like it had a life of its own before snapping back into place in the dark cave of his mouth.

"You've been a bad girl, haven't you?" He tsked, one hand

on her throat, the other brushing hair out of her face. The movement felt strangely intimate, and she shivered. "You deserve this, you know? People like you don't just get to live out the rest of your lives pretending like you're not a terrible person, pretending like you're not making the world worse just by being in it."

"Why?" Her voice rasped. Sounded broken. Without thinking, she reached up to touch her throat. It was bruised. It hurt.

The man growled, settling forward on her chest, his fingers clamping around her throat once again. "Don't act like you don't know." He lifted her head up, holding her by her neck, then slammed her down.

Everything went black. Pain radiated from the back of her head, angry and hot. She gasped, or tried, but there wasn't any air now, not even a little wisp of it. He was crushing her throat, and she clawed at his arms, but he wore long sleeves, he wore gloves, and she couldn't get any purchase on his skin.

She'd seen enough CSI shows to know she needed his DNA, needed some way to prove he was there with her, that he—

He lifted her again by the neck and slammed her back down. The edges of her vision went blurry. He swore then leaned closer to her, speaking right into her face, but she wasn't able to make out the words. They dripped with hate, with revenge, but before she could latch on to one and try to decode what he was saying, something pressed up against her skin, cold and sharp, then a fierce bolt of pain shot through her.

Blood soaked the forest floor as fear wrapped itself around her, a thick blanket she couldn't shake loose. Her eyes were unblinking, wide open. Staring. Raindrops hit her cheeks. Her lips. Her open eyes.

The blackness wasn't comforting. It was cold, all-encompassing. She felt herself tilting into it, into that nothingness, and then the fear was gone.

ONE

MONDAY

The Fawn Lake Police Department smelled like hot, fresh donuts.

It was a cliché, cops and donuts, and that drove Freya Sinclair crazy, but with Esther—the woman who had taken Freya in when everything fell apart with her parents—right down the corner always making her treats and her detectives in love with anything deep fried and covered with frosting or powdered sugar, there were sweets in the break room more often than not.

She grabbed the only chocolate-glazed donut right before Candy Ellinger, her favorite detective, managed to snatch it.

"Been spending extra time at the gym, Captain?" Candy teased, grabbing a sprinkle donut instead. "You never have seconds when Esther brings stuff by."

"I don't believe in working off my calories," Freya replied, licking a bit of chocolate frosting from her fingertip. "But I do believe in rewarding ourselves for a job well done. Did you realize we had a one hundred percent close rate for the new cases that came across our desks last month?"

"That's because we have Brad on our team now," Candy

said. She wadded up a napkin and flicked it at him, laughing when he batted it to the floor.

Freya grinned. "Seriously, though, this is good. The town is happy. Chief's happy. I know I'm probably going to jinx everything by saying that, but it's true. We've got this, you guys. I want you two to enjoy the day, okay? Get downtown and walk around, make sure people see you. Chief loves it when we do community outreach, but that doesn't have to be some big event. It can be as little as you two just popping into the shops on Main Street to check on the owners."

"Easy enough." Brad nodded and adjusted his duty belt. After Freya had gotten him moved upstairs, he'd told her how much he loved not having to wear the polyester blue uniform of road officers, although she personally felt the duty belt was going to send her to the chiropractor one day. With a taser, gun, handcuffs, flashlight, rubber gloves, and radio all attached, it put more pressure on officers' hips than most people realized. "I'll start on the east side of the street and work my way down."

"That's fine by me. That lets me check out that new hiking place that opened up this spring," Candy told him, tapping her fingers against the table before nodding. "I've been wanting to look for a new pack anyway, so might as well get it locally instead of ordering it from Amazon or something."

Brad pulled a face. "It's overpriced downtown."

"Sure, but these are our people." Candy hooked her fingers together and stretched her arms over her head, rocking back and forth on the balls of her feet before exhaling and releasing the stretch. "If something goes wrong with my pack, who do you think is going to care more? The people at Harold's Hiking or the corporate drones working their lives away at Amazon?"

"Touché." Brad grinned at her. "On that note, I'm off. See you two later." He sauntered out of the break room, leaving Candy and Freya alone.

Freya popped the last bite of donut in her mouth, flipped

the box closed, and picked it up. "I'm going to take these down to dispatch and see if they want any. Let me know if you run into anything interesting on Main Street, okay? Not that I expect you to, but I'm just going to head to my office after dropping these off."

"Sounds good." Candy eyeballed the box but shook her head. "One question though, and I mean this seriously: is Esther trying to fatten us up?" She didn't have to glance at the trash can in the corner of the room for Freya to know exactly what she was talking about. Five more donut boxes poked up from the open top of the trash can. Esther had been by every morning for two weeks now dropping off treats and checking in on Freya.

"Esther's fine," Freya responded before she realized that wasn't what her detective was asking. She shook her head and plastered a smile on her face, her fingers squeezing the donut box so hard the cardboard started to bend. "She's just checking in on me. Likes to know I'm okay."

There was a beat of silence. "Oo-kay. Just noticed that she'd been coming around a lot with food and thought I'd ask to make sure nothing was going on."

"Nothing's going on." Freya's voice sounded high and tight, even to her ears, so she had no doubt Candy would pick up on her stress. The problem with working with intuitive people who regularly called others out on their lies is that they tended to do that to you too. She turned away, still gripping the box way too tight.

"Okay, sure. Now, when you're ready to tell me the truth about what's going on, just let me know, okay? You know I don't judge. And I'm more than happy to let you chat while I stuff my mouth with French fries." Candy paused, but Freya didn't look back at her. On her hip, her radio squawked, with a dispatcher sending an officer to a wreck at the south end of Main Street.

"Fries sound good," she said without turning around. "I'll take a peek at my schedule, okay? See what time I have free. I'm sure we can work something out." She hurried down the hall and grabbed the door to the stairs, throwing it open behind her. It slammed into the wall, but she was already in the stairwell to head to dispatch, and she didn't bother to turn back.

Dispatch had a completely different feel from the floor she'd just been on. One of the dispatchers was diffusing lavender, and she wrinkled her nose as she pushed through the door.

"Watch the cat!"

"Cat?" Freya looked down, surprised to see a black cat winding around her ankles. Keeping her eyes on the feline, she closed the door behind her. "When did you guys get a cat?"

"We adopted him." Sandra, an older lady with peppered hair, pushed back from her desk, turning to speak to Freya. She had headphones on with a microphone angled in front of her face. "Someone dumped him in an alley last week, and we found him. He's our mascot. We named him Brimley."

"He's a cutie," said Freya, squatting to run her fingers down his back.

"He's better for morale than your tarantula," Sandra said with a grin. "Softer at least."

"He is that," Freya said, stepping carefully over the cat as she offered the box of donuts to the dispatcher. "Here, Esther brought these by for us, and while they're really good, there's only so many that we can eat. I thought that I'd bring them down for you guys to enjoy."

"Thanks," said Sandra, standing and taking the box from Freya. "You know that we're always happy to have some sweet treats down here." She put the box on the table in the middle of the room then walked back to her station.

Another dispatcher, Tom, gave Freya the thumbs up without looking over his shoulder. His fingers flew over a keyboard, and he nodded while listening to the person on the other end of the line. "Tell me how long ago you found them," Tom said.

Freya froze. She watched the dispatcher, waiting.

"Okay, thank you for letting me know. I'm going to pass this information along to our Captain of Detectives right now and send some officers out to meet with you. Are you able to stay there at the scene?" Tom slowly turned around in his chair and pinned her in place with a stare. "You are? That's great. Hold tight and let me pass this on." He reached behind him and mashed a button on his desk.

A chill danced up Freya's spine. It was clear from the expression on Tom's face that whatever he was about to tell her was way worse than anything she could've expected. She swallowed, her fingers twitching in anticipation.

"What is it?" Freya couldn't help herself. She had to know what was happening.

"Bodies." Tom gave his head a little shake before continuing. "Two bodies out in Clear Creek Forest. It's bad, Freya."

TWO

Freya's throat tightened. The shock of what the dispatcher had said hit her like a stiff drink on an empty stomach. She leaned forward, bracing her hands on a table while she tried to wrap her mind around what Tom had just said.

No matter what she did, the words stayed the same. *Two bodies out in Clear Creek Forest.* Even with just that little information, she knew it was going to be bad. People died out there each summer, tipping over waterfalls when they got too close to the edge, but this didn't sound like a waterfall accident.

She closed her eyes and the faces of little girls swam in front of her. Shaking her head, she forced them away.

Two bodies. The words echoed in her brain, and she tried to think of any missing persons reports that had come through.

Nothing. She hadn't seen a single one. They'd just been celebrating how all the cases were closed out. Nothing was left —no missing persons, no reports of runaways, nothing that would make this an easy open-shut case.

"Tell me everything," Freya demanded as she reached into her pocket, feeling for her car keys. "All the details, what you know." Her hand closed around them and she gripped them tight, staring right at Tom.

"You know what I know." Tom held up both of his hands like he was in trouble. His chin wobbled a bit, and it was immediately apparent just how young he really was. Babies working dispatch, babies getting calls about some of the worst things that people do to each other. It was terrible. "That was Roy Waters, up in Clear Creek Forest. He stumbled upon two bodies at a campsite. Sounds bad, Sinclair."

"Where in Clear Creek?"

"Hold on—I'll write it down." Tom spun back around to face his desk at the same time another call came in.

Without missing a beat, Sandra picked up. "Fawn Lake Police Department. What's your emergency?"

"Here." Tom turned and thrust a piece of paper at Freya. She barely glanced at it before turning away. "There are some officers towards that area. I'll give them the information and see if they can get up there, seal the scene."

Thank goodness the police department had jurisdiction of that forest. It backed up to Pisgah National Forest, and if the murders had been in there... well, the job would fall to the National Park Service Law Enforcement Rangers or US Park Police. But Freya and her team could work this case, and she was eager to start.

"Good. Do that. And if you hear anything else about this, give me a call." She paused, one hand on the door. Behind her, Sandra's voice was calm and mellow as she clearly talked someone through a crisis. "I'm taking either Candy or Brad with me, whoever I find first. Keep me updated on what you hear."

"Yes, ma'am," Tom said, but Freya was already pushing through the door.

Adrenaline coursed through her veins. Her hand was slick on the stair railing, and her feet pounded the stairs as she hurried down them. She tore through the lobby and hit the front door at a full run, bursting out into the bright light of the day.

The storm last night had come up so suddenly that most people hadn't even known it was a threat. There had been a slight chance of rain, more of a promise of mist than anything else, but dark clouds had covered the sky, building up on each other like thick layers of black cotton. They hung heavy, pregnant with rain, then the storm had broken, late in the evening, dousing everything in inches of water.

The potted plants outside the police department were waterlogged. A SALE flag across the street at the Tea-rific Tea Emporium hung limp and weatherworn. After the destruction of last night, the sun breaking through the clouds right now felt like a joke, and Freya blinked into the light, looking for either Candy or Brad.

It was entirely possible that they hadn't made it far down the road and would be within sight. Just as she was about to radio one of them, Brad appeared, holding a Styrofoam cup of coffee, a swing in his step. He looked at her, surprised, then gave a little half-wave.

"Decide you couldn't stand the fluorescent lights anymore? I don't blame you. Look at how gorgeous it is today." He swept his arm around his body, encompassing the sunbeams, the water dripping from awnings, the puddles on the sidewalk. Then he turned back to Freya, a huge smile on his face. This slowly slid off as he got a good look at her. "What? Something happened. What is it?"

"Dispatch just got a call about two bodies up in Clear Creek. I want you to go with me."

Brad's expression tightened. His lips thinned and small wrinkles appeared at the corners of his eyes. He gave one stiff nod. "Do you know where?"

"Tom gave me this," she said, handing him the slip of paper. "I know where we're going."

Brad glanced at the paper. "Great. I'll drive."

"And I'll text Candy so she can meet us there."

Twenty minutes later, they had reached Clear Creek Forest. Fully expecting a long day of paperwork, Freya wasn't dressed properly for the hike, but she wasn't about to complain. Briars picked at her pants, and she'd stepped in thick mud. It now coated her right shoe and was seeping in through the stitching around the sole. She could feel her sock sticking to her skin, and chances were good there would be a blister before she reached the crime scene, but none of that mattered.

The air was muggy and thick from the storm, and wet leaves coated the path. More than once, she and Brad slipped on the slick leaves as they worked their way up the steep side of High Ridge Mountain. The going was tough, and her heart was hammering in her chest by the time they finally reached the flatter area of the crime scene. The trail kept going, but Freya stopped, no longer worrying about putting one foot in front of the other.

Thank goodness the victims hadn't gone camping all the way at the zenith.

Her anxiety mounted as she caught sight of the bright-yellow tape fluttering in the wind. It cordoned off a huge area of land, twisting through bushes and tree limbs. Without slowing down, Freya lifted the tape and stepped under, holding it just long enough for Brad to slip under behind her.

She stopped, taking a moment to turn and look slowly around her. High Ridge Mountain lived up to its name. In the summer, there wasn't much of a view thanks to the thick leaves, but right now they were falling and she could see the hazy outline of other mountains. A cold wind whipped through the trees, making her shiver and driving thick clouds directly over-head. Fallen branches and downed logs were scattered in the woods, and this far up, the trail was more of a suggestion than a reality.

She could only imagine what the weather had been like up here on the mountain. It swept in late in the night and had been storming hard, rain washing in rivulets down the mountain, carrying dead leaves and mud into the river. Now even more swollen than normal, the sound of the river was white background noise to the scene spread out among the trees.

A bright-red tent sat to her right, speckled with drops of water sparkling in the weak sunrays that had managed to work their way through the trees. About ten yards away to the left was a firepit, the rocks used to line it mossy and soaked. There was a drop-off even farther to the left where the river currently bubbled and churned. Lined with large boulders, it was a menacing force, one that led straight down the mountain to High Ridge Falls.

Just like the caller had said, two bodies sprawled in the dirt and wet leaves between the firepit and river. A young officer stood off to the side talking to a man in camo, but Freya barely looked their way. Her eyes flicked over them, then she stepped towards the body that was closest. The woman was sprawled in front of her, her neck twisted in an unnatural angle, her mouth frozen open in a scream. Her head had been bashed in, chunks of her skull visible in the dirt. Jagged pieces of bone stuck out from the side of her temple. Flies lifted from the exposed brain when Freya leaned forward to get a closer look.

Her red hair stuck to her cheek and the remains of her forehead. Her one eye bulged, pushed out of its socket by the trauma to the side of the head. Red blood vessels were bright against the sclera. Off to the side of the woman was a large rock. It had been washed clean from the rain, but it had to be the murder weapon. The woman's right arm was thrown out to her side, bright red nails chipped and dirty, her hand pointing at the rock, a silent accusation.

"I need someone to scrape under her fingernails for DNA. If she was able to fight back when she was attacked, then hopefully we'll get a fast match," she said to Brad. "Someone's taken pictures already?"

"Officer Cathy Holbert." Brad nodded at the younger officer talking to the hunter. A camera hung on a strap around her neck, bobbing this way and that as the officer nodded.

"Anyone other than the police, the killer, and the hunter been up here?"

"Not that I know of." A pause. "I don't think many hikers or campers come this far up."

"Yeah, and hunting in a national forest isn't exactly legal, even if it were deer season. Glad he stopped and called us." Freya glanced up, really looking for the first time at the hunter. It was possible she'd seen him in Over Easy, the locals' favorite breakfast place, but when hunters dressed in camo and pulled their caps down over their ears, it was difficult to tell them apart. No orange safety vest, which means the man was much more interested in going undetected than making sure he wasn't shot by another hunter.

So he'd been up here poaching. Not hunting. Freya filed that away.

"Scrape her nails," she repeated. "We need to get that test started stat." Turning away, she focused her attention on the crime scene. Talking to the hunter who'd found the two women was important, but first she wanted to familiarize herself with the crime scene.

She took in the doused campfire and the tent. It was closed, the tent flaps zipped tight against the rain. It was possible the killer had gotten into the tent and taken something, but it was impossible to know for sure without getting forensics involved. Her team would check the tent and look for prints. Still, no personal items were spilled on the ground. The only thing that

kept the scene from appearing like a happy camping trip were
the two bodies.

Freya walked over to the second body and crouched down
to get a better look. She took in the woman's long dark lashes
resting on her cheeks, how her hands had been arranged on her
stomach. The woman would look almost peaceful if it weren't
for the few bits of mud that had splashed up on her that the rain
hadn't washed away. None of her clothing was out of place,
although it was now plastered to her body, and her hair was
stuck to her face. It was dark and long, spread like spiderwebs
across her skin.

While the redhead looked like a rag doll a child had tossed
onto the floor, this woman looked like she'd been carefully
posed. There was a red scarf wrapped around her neck, the
ends of it tucked neatly under her body.

She frowned.

The killer had obviously taken time to make sure this body
looked its best, though they couldn't do anything to prevent wet
leaves and mud from splashing up on the body.

"This was put here post-mortem," she said to Brad, who had
kneeled next to her. "Whoever the killer was, they acted on
impulse with the other woman and took their time with this
one."

"It's different," he agreed. "Maybe he cared for this woman.
Maybe she was important to him and the other woman was
collateral damage."

"Maybe." Freya sucked her teeth. "To know that for sure,
we'll need to find out who the two women were. That will help
clear up why they were treated so differently."

She hesitated then pulled a pen from her jacket pocket.
Carefully she tucked the tip of it under the scarf and lifted. For
just a moment, the scarf stuck to the woman's neck.

"Come on," she muttered, angling the pen up a bit more.
Finally, the scarf slipped free from the woman's neck. It had

been fluffy before the rain, but now the soft yarn matted together, hanging like a dead rat from the end of her pen.

Black embroidered initials towards the end of the scarf caught her eye. *V.O.* Freya wasn't much for fashion but could easily see a young woman like this wanting personalized clothing. She'd bet it was the woman's initials.

Twisting her hand from right to left, she angled her head to look underneath the scarf. The other woman had died from blunt force trauma. It hadn't been a painless death and Freya was sorry for that, but this woman had suffered just as much, if not more.

"Her throat was slashed?" Brad's voice was low, and she nodded.

"Cut wide open." The dead skin around the cut was white and cold, the edges already curling away, but the gash in the woman's neck was a deep red, angry and dark.

Freya spoke quietly. "So the killer cut this woman's throat, but instead of leaving her like he did the other victim, he wrapped her neck up with a scarf."

"Was he hiding the injury?"

Freya shook her head. "I don't think so. Look at her hands, arranged on her stomach like this. She looks peaceful, posed. Nope, this was not him hiding what he did. I highly doubt the killer would be ashamed of what he's done. This was a present."

THREE

The morning sun slanted down through the trees, playing across the ground. A lizard scampered across the leaves before finding dark refuge under a fallen log. Freya ignored how good the sun felt on her shoulders, how it chased away the chill of the damp woods and death, and instead focused her attention on Roy Waters standing in front of her.

Dressed in camo, with thick work gloves poking out of one pants pocket and a knife strapped to his other thigh, Roy looked intimidating. Freya considered getting a closer look at the Bowie knife Roy wore but knew that even if the man was the killer, he would have taken steps to clean it off before calling the cops.

Besides, most murderers wanted nothing to do with the police. They actively avoided calling the police for anything, so even though Roy looked nervous as he stood in front of Freya, it was doubtful his nerves were because he had just killed two women and then alerted the police to his crime scene.

It probably had to do with the poaching.

No, Roy wasn't a murderer. The haunted expression in his eyes told her everything. He was just as bothered by what he'd found in the woods as she was.

"It's just that we're hungry," Roy said, spreading his hands out in appeal.

Freya looked at them, taking in all the details that she'd turn over and over in her mind later when she'd gone home for the night. Roy's hands were delicate, fine-boned. When she was younger, she'd labored over piano lessons. No matter how hard she tried, her teacher would sigh and tell her mother that her hands were like bear paws, useless on the piano.

If the women had been choked, she wouldn't look twice at Roy. He didn't look like he had the hand strength to kill those women. But he could easily gut deer, and smashing a woman's head in with a rock wouldn't be too hard for someone accustomed to fighting for his life like Roy was. It was important to remember that.

"I lost my job," Roy said, dropping his voice in shame. "I've been looking for another one, but it takes time. Not many places are hiring right now."

"So you came up here to poach?"

Roy closed his eyes for a long moment before answering. "I have a daughter," he said, his voice tight. "Trish. She can't live on just instant ramen noodles like I can. She needs meat; she needs to be able to go to school and focus, and she can't do that if she's hungry. I know it wasn't right, but I didn't feel I had a choice."

Freya didn't respond. She knew—everybody knew—that people sometimes made the trek up into the national forest to hunt when they were hungry. It was just one of those things that happened in a small town. Everyone looked the other way, and when someone's luck changed and they could afford a hunting license again, or could afford to buy meat at the store, they stopped what they were doing.

"I wouldn't do it if I didn't have to." Roy reached out for Freya, then dropped his hand before touching her. The way the man struggled to meet her eyes told her more than any words could. "And then I found those poor girls. I knew calling it in might get me in trouble, but what was I supposed to do?"

"You did the right thing. You're not going to get in trouble for the hunting. When you leave here, I want you to go by Food Mart, pick some things up. Tell them I'll be by later to pay the bill."

"You don't have to—"

She waved her hand, clearing the air between the two of them. "Don't worry about it. Now, tell me exactly what you saw."

A long exhale. "I was tracking a buck through the woods, and it burst through into this clearing here. I stopped following it as soon as I saw the red of the tent because I didn't want to scare whoever might be camping up here. I didn't think people camped this far up into the woods, to be honest. That's when I saw the first one."

"The redhead?"

"Yeah. She didn't look... right. I wasn't creeping up on them, I swear. I just thought something might be going on. So I called out. They didn't answer. I thought maybe they'd gotten drunk and were sleeping it off, but why sleep on the ground when there was a perfectly good tent right there? And the fire was out. It was chilly this morning when I got out here, and you heard the storm last night. None of it made any sense, and I thought about turning around and going back down the mountain, but I didn't. I just kept thinking... what if it were Trish up here?"

Freya nodded but didn't say anything in case he clammed up.

"I went closer to check on them, and that's when I could tell they were... well, you saw them. But there isn't any cell service up here. I had to hike back down the mountain to call you guys. I hadn't brought my truck up here of course." He paused. "Didn't want to scare the deer."

"You didn't see anyone else? Nobody who looked out of place?"

"Just a few campers. The hard-core types, who think staying out in a rainstorm means they're better than others. You know the type. I think most people probably went home due to the storm or just didn't stay out last night. How many people camp until Monday morning? Most people have jobs to get to." He spat the last sentence like it was bitter in his mouth.

"You did the right thing." Freya put her hand on the man's shoulder. Roy flinched. "Calling us, getting help? I'm not going to write you up for the poaching, Roy. Go to Food Mart. Please. Get some groceries and make sure you pick out something special for Trish. I bet she'd like some chocolate. Don't be too proud to take help from someone, alright? Tell them to bill me."

"I'll pay you back."

"Fine." Freya knew he wouldn't. "That sounds fine, Roy. Now why don't you head on out of here, get something to eat, warm up. There's no reason for you to stay out here the rest of the day. We can take it from here."

Roy nodded. Freya watched as the man ducked under the yellow caution tape and disappeared silently into the woods like a shadow.

She glanced down at her watch. Time was ticking. They needed to get to work.

FOUR

Leaning against a thick red oak with rutted and rough bark, Freya watched the scene play out before her. Her hip ached after the trek up the mountain. Officers worked the crime scene, moving like they were part of a choreographed dance. They catalogued everything, taking pictures of each angle of the scene. To her right, the two women were loaded into body bags. The zippers were loud in the quiet of the early morning. Briseyda Hernandez, the head paramedic, oversaw the operation, her arms crossed, her keen eyes not missing anything.

For a moment, Freya watched her, then turned to where Briseyda's team of paramedics had finally prepared to carry the bodies down the trail. It was a long walk down the mountain, and they moved slowly, carefully picking their way through the wet leaves and tree roots as they carried the body bags.

"Do you think we should follow the bodies down the mountain?" Brad asked, coming to stand by Freya. He glanced around them at the fluttering caution tape, the disturbed ground, the officers still clustered around the Jeep.

"I'm thinking." Her voice was short. After a moment, she continued. "All these trees, all these places to hide and run, and it didn't look like the women had even tried to save themselves. Maybe we'll get something on the fingernail scrapings, but I'm not holding my breath on that."

"So he overwhelmed them—that's what you're thinking? Took them completely by surprise?"

"Even if they saw him coming, he could have overwhelmed them. It's happened before." Freya turned her head away from Brad, wanting to ignore the question in his eyes.

She knew how quickly someone could be thrown to the ground, how fast they could have the breath knocked out of them. She'd been in high school the last time she'd been here in these woods and seen someone attack a woman, seen a man crush her to the forest floor. Freya had intervened, all 130 pounds of her.

And the woman had been fine, but that wasn't always the case.

What were the chances that it was the same man hunting women in the woods again? He'd be much older, but that didn't mean he'd have changed his ways. It didn't seem likely that it was the same guy, but Freya tucked the thought away, like a note in a pocket, to pull out and examine later.

Moving carefully, stepping so silently that she barely disturbed any leaves, she walked the perimeter of the yellow caution tape. Officers had been all over the scene already, looking for any sign of where the killer had come from and which way he'd left.

They'd all come up empty-handed.

"Tell me what you see." Brad was right at her side, eager as ever. He glanced at Freya's face before squinting and looking deeper into the woods.

"Okay. Let's see." She paused and exhaled hard. "We got screwed with that rainstorm. If it hadn't hit last night, then we'd have an easier time looking for any evidence, but since everything is washed away, we need to think outside the box."

Brad frowned.

She continued. "During the summer, the ferns and poison ivy take over up here, right? There's hardly enough room to shake a stick, let alone hike up the mountain if you don't stay on a trail. Those plants are dying back now, but they're still lush enough to get crushed if someone were to come through here."

"I don't see any paths."

"Exactly." She made a fist and smacked it into her open palm. She led the way away from the campsite, leaving the sounds of the others behind them. "That tells me he was smarter than that. He didn't just stroll up here, crushing plants in his path. They got beaten down with the rain, but they're not crushed like someone walked on them."

"So how did he get up here? It's not like there was a report of a helicopter or anything." Brad grinned, but the smile slid from his face when his joke didn't land.

"There." Freya didn't point, but she sounded triumphant. "Right there." She pulled her walkie from her hip and pressed the button. "Candy, do you copy? I need you up at the campsite."

A momentary silence, then a bit of static. "I met the bodies coming down the mountain and was going to head to the ME with them."

Lance Jones would need time to find any clues left on the bodies, and Freya would have to visit him later, but she knew time was ticking. She needed to get a move on.

"That can wait. Come now, Candy. I want you and Brad to see this."

"Roger that."

Brad shifted, scrubbing his hand down his cheeks in frustration.

They stood silent for a few minutes before Candy arrived.

"I'm here! Don't start without me." She burst between the two of them, her cheeks bright red, a camera in one hand, a bottle of water in the other. Without preamble, she thrust the bottle at Freya and then took a step past her, peering into the thick woods like it was a fortune teller's crystal ball.

Freya uncapped the water bottle and took a swig while she watched Candy. The younger detective scanned the ground, looked up into the trees, then finally turned to her, her free hand planted on her hip and a puzzled look on her face.

"You don't see it?" Freya asked.

"No. You know I don't. Don't make me suffer any more than I already am." She wheeled on Brad. "Did you see it?"

"He didn't." Freya pointed, taking Candy by the shoulder and turning her back around. "Look again. But don't just look at the trees, look *through* them. You too, Brad. I want you both working on this."

"Okay." Candy exhaled with a puff, then turned towards the woods. After a moment, she turned back, squinting at Freya. "He didn't leave a path. That or the rain washed it out... but nobody knew that storm was coming. Even the paper this morning mentioned how it snuck up on us."

Freya nodded, shoving her hands into her pockets. "Keep going."

"So he couldn't have known the rain would help him out, unless he's an armchair meteorologist and somehow knows a lot more than the news did. Which means he had another plan, one that didn't involve him leaving a trail up the mountain and then down again when he was done."

"And?"

"He needed another way to cover his tracks and to keep anyone from knowing he was even here. The river wasn't swollen last night like it is right now because of the rain, but that doesn't mean it wasn't loud enough to drown out any sounds he would have made coming through the woods."

"Good. The river is key."

Candy nodded, clearly a little frustrated. "Yeah, I see that. I just—"

Bingo. Freya saw the moment Candy realized exactly what had happened, like someone had yanked a chain in her mind and flicked on a lightbulb.

"He came up along the river! He didn't just use the sound of the water to hide the fact he was walking closer to them; he used the river itself. Look at the huge rocks along the sides of it. When it hasn't rained a lot recently, these are going to be exposed. They're flat river rocks, most of them pretty smooth. Walking on them now would be—"

"Suicide, yes," Brad interjected, getting excited as he caught Candy's train of thought. "But last night it wouldn't have been too dangerous."

Both of Freya's detectives beamed at her.

"Unfortunately, we're going to need to wait for the river to go down a little bit before it's safe to walk on those rocks," she said. "Why don't you two walk along the side of the river—take a look? I don't know what you'll be able to find, but I'm sure you'll see something."

"What about you?" Candy was still glowing with the excitement of their realization. "You're the one who figured it out. Don't you want to walk the river and see if you can find the path?"

"No." Freya held out her hand to Brad. "Keys please." After they were dropped into her waiting palm, she shoved them in her pocket. "I'm heading to town to talk to Lance. See what kind of profile we can build up on this guy." Her stomach rumbled, but she ignored it. Today wouldn't be the first time she'd skipped a meal to really concentrate on a case. "You two can fill me in on what you find when you get back."

She turned to leave when an officer ran up to her. "Captain? We found a driver's license tucked under the victim's body." He gestured behind them. "Jolie Marin." He paused. "She's victim number two, with the slit throat."

"Jolie?" Freya shook her head, thinking of the scarf wrapped around the woman's neck. "Are you sure it's a match?"

J.M. vs. V.O.

It was possible the scarf belonged to the other victim. Who knows why the killer would have wrapped it around her neck? Or it could have been a hand-me-down. A lot of people shopped at local thrift stores, and the victim may not have cared about someone else's initials on the scarf.

The officer paused. His eyes flicked from Freya, to Candy, to Brad, then back to Freya. "I'm sure. Here." He thrust an evidence bag at Freya, who took it, smoothing out the plastic to get a better look at the ID inside.

The woman smiling up at her looked happy. Her hair was freshly styled; lipstick stained her lips. Even though she was a far cry from the woman she had just seen, it was obvious they were a match. Jolie Marin was dead.

So who in the world was the other woman?

"Good work," Freya said, giving him back the ID before turning to her team. "Ever heard of her?"

Brad and Candy shook their heads.

"Me either. On second thought," Freya said, making Candy arch a brow, "call me as soon as you complete your search. We need to work this as quickly as possible. Make sure to dust the tent for prints and anything the killer might have left behind if he entered it."

"You don't think this was an isolated incident." Candy shot Freya a look. It was a dare.

Freya paused before speaking. "The killer clearly knew what they were doing if they came up along the river, which tells me they knew the two women would be here. So even if it is an isolated incident, it wasn't a crime of opportunity. Someone planned this out."

FIVE

Walking faster now, Freya made her way back to the campsite, skirting around the fluttering yellow tape. It would stay up either until an officer came to remove it or something in the woods pulled it free. By spring, the campsite would be reclaimed by the forest, and it would be like nothing had ever happened.

Brad's car started up without complaint, and she felt her foot grow heavier on the gas as she flew towards town. She zipped past the diner where she would have loved to stop and get a sandwich, tore into the hospital parking lot, and pulled into the first space she could find.

It was the first time she'd caught her breath all morning. She dialed dispatch, leaning her head against the headrest while the phone rang. Sandra picked up, and Freya relayed her request.

A search for a missing woman with the initials V.O.

Freya told her not to limit her search to the Fawn Lake area but to look for women in their twenties and thirties in surrounding counties. After Sandra confirmed, Freya hung up, took a deep breath, and hurried across the parking lot.

She was halfway to the front door of the building when her phone pinged.

Hope rose in her that Candy and the rookie had some information for her, but it was quickly dashed when she saw Chief's message on the screen.

I need an update, Freya.

"I need an update, Freya," she muttered, slipping the phone back into her pocket. "Right."

Hurrying now, she rushed through the hospital and down the set of stairs to the morgue. It only took her a minute to don a white robe and net cap so her curly hair was out of the way, then she pushed through the door, blinking in the bright lights.

It had to be bright downstairs so Lance could easily see to work. It took her a moment to orient herself.

"My favorite captain," Lance called, throwing her a wave. "Come on over here and see what I'm working on."

The sharp scent of antiseptic burned Freya's nose, but even though it was strong, it didn't completely cover the smell of blood. The morgue smelled clean—and filthy. Fresh—and desecrated.

Even when the blood was cleaned up, the bodies were stowed away; even when the cleaning staff had just been through, the place smelled like death. Hidden death, covered-up death. But death nonetheless.

"You knew I couldn't stay away for very long." Freya glanced down at one of the women. The redhead, her brains still spilling out of her skull. Under the fluorescent lighting she looked pale green. "Please tell me you have something."

"I only just got started. These ladies pulled me away from breakfast. Cold pizza." Lance gestured over at the plate of half-eaten food, smears of tomato sauce visible on the paper plate, then turned back to the women. "But you can be here with me while I start making my observations. Nothing is official yet of course, so don't go back to the office and start running your mouth about all the things I'm about to say."

Freya nodded. She needed Lance to start talking. He was the best ME they'd ever had in Fawn Lake and was never wrong with his first impressions. The sooner he got to work, the sooner she would have a few more clues to find the murderer.

"The victims are two women, both in their twenties." Lance held a small recorder by his mouth as he spoke. "The first victim had her head bashed in. Death is by blunt force trauma and is consistent with this, but there are no other marks on her body. So far there is no evidence of sexual assault."

She exhaled hard. If the killings weren't sexually motivated, then what happened up there at the campsite? She had a very good feeling Jolie, the second victim, had been the intended victim, and she couldn't wait to hear what Lance had to say about her. She'd had her throat slit, then been arranged. The first woman seemed like she'd been in the way of the second.

So the killer had removed her.

"Victim appears to be in good health, the only injury the trauma to her head. I will search her body for DNA, but after the storm we had last night, there is a very good chance any DNA left behind was washed away."

Exactly what Freya was afraid of.

She pointed to the second body as Lance pulled the sheet up over the first. "We have an ID on this victim."

Lance nodded. "Good. Name?"

"Jolie Marin."

Lance turned away from her to Jolie's body and removed the sheet covering her. "The second victim, Jolie Marin, has scrapes on her body consistent with being knocked onto her back. There are contusions on the backs of her legs, her buttocks and her back, as well as scratches on her hips. Lividity suggests the body was on the ground for approximately twelve hours before being discovered and moved. The cause of death is a lacerated throat." Here he paused and lightly touched the flaps of skin on her neck with a gloved finger. Freya moved closer, wanting to see exactly what Lance saw.

"The wound is ragged. Rough. The skin wasn't sliced so much as it was torn open by a serrated knife. Besides that, the victim appears healthy, but I'll know more about other damage to the body including sexual assault and the overall health of both victims at the conclusion of the investigation."

The click of Lance turning off the recorder was loud in the quiet room. He covered Jolie with the sheet and stared at Freya, his head cocked. "Does that give you anything to go on?"

"Not really. No sexual assault?"

"On the first victim, no. If you look at her," Lance said, turning and sweeping the sheet off the body once more, "there's no damage to her except for her head. It was brutal, but fast." He paused. "Some suffering, but nothing like her friend here. No marks on the breasts, hips, or the inner thighs. Jolie, however... that's another story."

He replaced the sheet. Freya waited patiently while he tugged it up to cover the first woman's face, then turned and pulled the sheet off the second woman again. The difference was immediately apparent, even to someone who hadn't gone to medical school.

"She has scratches on the hips. Deep ones, like it was a battle with whoever attacked her." Freya pointed it out, walking closer to get a better look. "And... look at this." She pointed again, keeping her gloved finger from accidentally touching the body.

"Good find." Lance grabbed a clipboard and made a note, then came around the table to stand next to her for a better look. "See how the bruising on her ear is so consistent? Even? What do you think made that?"

"Teeth." She didn't have to guess. She knew without a doubt what had made those little marks on Jolie's ear.

"Excellent. You might have a future as an ME if you keep it up. I'll swab for DNA, but that storm last night was brutal. One other thing I thought you'd like to know. Jolie has a tattoo on her inner wrist. I noticed it when she was brought in, and I'm not saying I'm hip to all the tats kids get nowadays, but I've never seen anything like it before."

"Let's see it." Freya waited as Lance took Jolie's hand, pulling her arm out from her body. When he twisted her hand, her inner wrist appeared.

"Have you ever seen a tattoo like that?" Lance asked.

Freya already had her phone out. She snapped a picture of the tattoo, then enlarged it on her screen for a better view while Lance placed Jolie's hand back at her side.

"Well, I use lingo I'm pretty sure went out of style twenty years ago, so I'm not really the person to ask, but no. Does it look legit? Or like a stick and poke?" She turned the phone for Lance to see the enlarged photo.

"Hmm. It's so faded that it's hard to tell what it was originally. Numbers, I think. I've seen a lot of tattoos doing this, and you can always tell when a professional did the work and when someone got drunk and took a needle to their skin. This is the latter—I'd bet on it."

"Are you sure those are numbers? They're so blurry." She blinked hard to clear her vision and stared at the tattoo again. "This is why I don't have tattoos and I'm not interested in getting one. Lose weight? They look like crap. Gain weight? Again, crap. Sometimes they just look like crap because they weren't done correctly." She paused. "But this does look like a five. Look."

"Yeah, I definitely think those are numbers." Lance was next to her now, and Freya shifted the phone over for him to see.

"Month, day, year. Don't you think? With little dashes between them?"

"Maybe, yeah. I can see it. So she has a date on her wrist. People only do that when they want to commemorate something important. Like a birthday, an anniversary, a death date." She paused, tapping the phone against her chin.

"What are you thinking?"

"I want to know the meaning behind it. Figure out what the date is, which would be a lot easier if it weren't so dang blurry. We can see the first digit, but the others are blobs." She drummed her fingers on the counter. "The problem with date tattoos is they're usually incredibly personal. Can't overlook the fact that it could be something as insignificant to us as adopting a dog or her dog dying. Just because it was a big-enough deal for her to tattoo the date on her body doesn't mean it was really important in the grand scheme of things."

"See? This is why you get paid the big bucks." Lance grinned at her, then gestured at Jolie. "I'm going to get to work unless you need anything."

"I'll show myself out. Thanks, Lance."

He nodded and looked back down at his clipboard, furiously making notes. He was fast diving into his job and would only surface again when he'd finished. It was one of the things the entire police department liked about the man. He was thorough, driven.

But his silence meant Freya was now alone with her thoughts.

The tattoo was interesting. She needed to figure out what the numbers were, what the date was. Once she had that information, she had no doubt she'd be one step closer to solving Jolie's murder.

But it wasn't the tattoo that really gave her pause. It was the marks on Jolie's ear.

She knew what had caused the bruising, not because she'd

seen it in a book, not because she had an amazing imagination, and not because she was able to quickly guess via context clues what had happened to a victim.

She knew it was teeth that had caused the bruising because she'd seen it before, in the only murder she'd failed to solve in her entire career.

SIX

Heat from the early-afternoon sun warmed Chief's office. The chill in the woods that had chased the residents of Fawn Lake into their homes early this morning was gone and now Main Street crawled with people. News of the double murders hadn't yet reached the town's gossip mill, although that was sure to happen anytime now.

"It's the *same perp*," Freya told Chief, leaning forward a bit to make her point. "I'm not sure what the motive is, why he targeted these two women, specifically Jolie, but it's definitely him. He's back."

"And you think that because of the bruising on the ear?"

"Not just bruising. It's not like she was hit with something and developed these bruises. They're *bite marks*. They're his calling card. How many cases have we worked where the perp attacked the victim like that, leaving bite marks on the ear?"

Chief didn't respond. He didn't have to.

"Just one," she said, filling in the blank for him. "Just that one case and now this again? He's back."

"It's been ten years. You do realize that, Freya, right?" Chief cleared his throat. "Ten years since you've seen any sign of this killer, and yet you're immediately convinced he's back? What makes you think it's not a copycat? Or just an accident? People bite ears in the heat of passion. Remember Mike Tyson?"

She didn't smile.

The previous case had been before Chief's time. He'd gotten the job here in town just eight years ago, and so while he'd heard stories about the one murder she hadn't ever been able to solve, he hadn't seen first-hand the detective's frustration at not being able to find the perp.

"This wasn't an accident. And we never released that detail to the public. The only people who know about the bite marks on the ear are the people here at the department, the Fawn Lake Killer, or someone he told—"

"Who then became a copycat." Chief heaved a sigh and adjusted his tie. Every day he came into his office dressed like he was going to lead a parade in DC. His brass shone as much as his shoes, and his uniform was starched to within an inch of its life. "Look, just because they didn't get the clue from us doesn't mean they didn't get it from someone. Ten years is a long time for a murderer to go underground. *Too* long. When's the last time you heard of someone killing and then waiting a decade to do it again? Sorry, I'm not convinced."

Chief picked up a pen and tapped it on his desk, staring at Freya while he did so.

She straightened up in her chair. "Okay, say it's a copycat."

"It's a copycat."

She glared at him. "Who? Who does a killer trust to tell? We never caught him. He never went to jail for his crime. So there isn't any way he confessed to a cellmate. I don't know about you, but I wouldn't trust anyone with information like that."

"People make stupid mistakes. They tell each other things they shouldn't. If the bite marks are the same—"

"Which they are."

"—then you can focus on it being the same killer, but don't zero in on it too much."

Freya sighed. "I just know it."

"That doesn't cut it in this department."

"Listen," she said, putting herself on thin ice. Chief's nostrils flared. No man in uniform likes being told to *listen* by anyone, especially one of his subordinates. Especially by a woman. "If it's the same guy, I can prove it to you."

"Yeah?" Leaning back in his chair, Chief crossed his arms on his chest. His eyes were locked on Freya, measuring her. Judging her. "And how do you plan on doing that?"

"There was another detail that wasn't released to the public." She flipped open a Manila folder that she'd brought from her office. This was her last bit of ammunition, and she couldn't let her shot miss. No matter what other success she'd had in her career, catching this murderer was something she had to do.

Chief took the piece of paper she was holding out. He read it quickly, his eyes flicking back and forth across the page as he soaked in the information. While she watched him, some of the anxiety she felt disappeared. It wasn't abnormal for Chief to dismiss people right out of hand if he didn't agree with what they were saying. The fact that he hadn't done that yet boded well for her.

"Where did you get this?" Chief flipped the paper over like he expected there to be something written on the back. There wasn't. It was just a photocopy. The original was in a page protector in evidence, locked up where nobody could touch it and where Freya knew it would be safe.

"He sent it to me after his first killing."

"To you personally?" Chief's eyebrows flew up. "Why?"

She shook her head. "You think I haven't asked myself that over and over again? If I could figure out that one piece of the puzzle, then it would be that much easier to solve the case. I was a nobody back then, so why would the Fawn Lake Killer reach out to me rather than one of the more experienced officers working the case?"

Because there were other officers working the murder. Or, at least, there *had* been other detectives working the case before Freya had received this letter in her mailbox. After that happened, they'd all stepped back. Everybody wants to catch the bad guy, but nobody wants to put themselves directly in the line of fire.

With that letter, she had been placed in the killer's crosshairs. As soon as everyone had realized that, she'd stood alone. She shook her head to clear her thoughts. That was the old department. It didn't work that way anymore.

"He was mocking you." Chief handed the paper back to her, then sighed. "Okay, now I can see why you're taking this personally, but that doesn't mean it's the same guy... What did you call him again?"

"The Fawn Lake Killer. His first victim was a woman who had gone swimming in the lake. Michelle Hawsey. It was late in the evening and everyone else had left. A family with little kids found her the next morning, her throat slit, her body arranged on the dock like she'd just been sleeping. She had the same bite marks on her ear."

"So you're telling me that you should be getting a letter from this guy, since it's the same person?"

"Exactly."

"Fine. How long did it take for it to show up in your mailbox the last time? Assuming this is the same perp, which I still don't think it is." He crossed his arms and stared at her.

"It was there that evening when I got home from the department, but there's no way to know when it was delivered. It's not like I have a lot of neighbors."

That was an understatement. When the letter had appeared in her mailbox, it was the first and only time Freya had ever wished she lived in town near other people. She liked living out in the boonies by herself, liked the long drive on curvy mountain roads she had to take home from work every evening. At first, when she'd got the job, she'd told herself she would use that time to clear her head before she made it home.

But that wasn't how life worked.

Some cases never left you. They were waiting at the bottom of your second beer, or tapped you on the shoulder when you were watching a movie. The Fawn Lake Killer was one of those cases. No matter how she tried to forget about it, the memory wouldn't leave her alone.

She'd spent all day at Fawn Lake when Michelle Hawsey had been found and had been exhausted by the end of it. Even though it wasn't her case, she'd still been there as support. Since she hadn't known about the letter until later, the other detectives hadn't pushed the case off on her yet. Her fingers had cramped from all the reports she'd been writing and her feet had ached from being on them all day. All she'd wanted to do was go home, drink something, and pass out. Still, out of habit, she'd stopped at her mailbox.

It had never crossed her mind that she'd need to wear gloves to check her mail. She'd pulled out the usual suspects—bills, pizza deals, pleas for money—and tossed them onto the passenger seat. Without thinking, she'd slipped her finger under the flap of the thick envelope and pulled out the single sheet of paper.

It was creamy, like the heavy paper used for wedding invitations. By the time Freya had realized what she had in her hands, it was too late to search it for prints, as she'd grabbed it and held it in half a dozen different ways trying to figure out exactly what it was. Her prints were all over the paper, completely obliterating any the perp might have left behind. It was something she'd berated herself about for ten years, and it had made her as uncompromising as she now was when it came to collecting evidence.

"Do you think the letter could be there already? If it's really the same killer?"

Chief was humoring her, but who cared? Freya would willingly endure the man's laughter if it meant she got what she needed.

"I think it's a little early, but I'm willing to drive out there and see."

"I'll send an officer."

"No, I'll go after I check up on Jolie's apartment; we have her address from her ID. I just knew you'd want an update before I drove out there. I have Brad looking her up, trying to find out everything he can about her personal life." The words spilled from her lips before she could stop them. At the questioning expression on Chief's face, she explained herself. "I need to go check my mail myself. I want to make sure the evidence is handled correctly."

"You don't think an officer can do that?"

"I do. I just—I need to go. I'll talk to Jolie's landlord and get a warrant, then go to her apartment. After that, I'll check my mail."

Chief waited until she had put her file back in order and made it to the door before he spoke again.

"Tick tock, Sinclair. We still don't know the name of one of those two women. Or who the killer is."

Freya bristled, but she refused to take the bait. "We will. I'll figure out who they are."

But she had to hurry. The longer she stood in Chief's office, the greater the chance the killer could strike again.

SEVEN

After calling Jolie's landlord, getting a warrant, and grabbing Candy from her office, Freya drove to Jolie's apartment. It was easy to obtain permission to enter from the landlord, but there was one thing better than verbal permission. A warrant. That way, if any executors of Jolie's estate came forward, they couldn't claim their rights had been trampled on. A warrant was basically a get-out-of-jail-free card, and she loved them. The one allowing her access to Jolie's apartment sat in the backseat of her Jeep.

She pulled up to the apartment, and the two women stared at the building.

"Not the nicest place, is it?" Candy mused.

Freya had to agree. The front windows were dirty. The entire building, in fact, had a green film growing on it. A good pressure wash would do wonders to clean it up, but not all landlords cared enough to put in the effort.

"Not really." Freya turned to Candy. "You ready for this?"

"So ready."

The two women got out of the Jeep, Freya making sure to hit the button on her fob to lock the doors. "Remind me why we don't have a key to the place." She twisted the door handle. Locked.

"Because Marcus Hill—that's the landlord of this lovely establishment by the way—is out of town. His exact words were 'I'm not coming home for a week, but you're welcome to get in there if you don't break the door,' so I guess we have to hope she kept a key outside somewhere. It would be great if we could just grab her house key from evidence, but that's not going to happen."

Freya sighed and cupped her hands around her eyes and peered in the window. Someone in Jolie's family would have to come and clean it out or the landlord would take care of things, most likely by renting a dumpster and hauling things off. Officers were trying to notify family, but so far they hadn't been able to reach anyone. Perhaps the women weren't due home until today so nobody had yet realized they were missing. Or maybe neither of them were close with their family. Freya certainly understood that. Either way, she would find out.

"Nothing under the mat." Candy stood and wiped her hands on her pants. "I really don't want to have to break down the door and deal with Mr. Hill."

"Me either." Freya stretched up and ran her hand along the top of the doorframe, but all she found was dirt. Turning, she looked up at the exposed rafters in the porch roof. "If we can find a key, then we can lock the door behind us and won't have to worry about someone else getting into the place. Boost me up, would you?"

Candy kneeled, and Freya stepped on her leg, grabbing the rafter above her head and pulling herself up.

"Oof. I bet Jolie kept a ladder for this purpose if you want to look around," Candy said.

"No, just give me one second." A grunt, and Freya stretched to reach.

"Are you single-handedly keeping Esther in business?"

"Hush, you, or I'll stay up here longer than I need to." A thick layer of dirt and dead flies covered the top of the rafter. Freya grimaced and patted down the dirt. "Got it," she cried, grabbing the key and stepping off Candy's thigh. "Good teamwork."

"Put me in for a commendation."

Freya grinned at her, then slipped the key into the lock. The door swung open but complained the entire time. She flicked on the light then paused in the door, letting her eyes adjust to the bright light.

The room she was looking into was filled with boxes. Some were stacked high by the front door, a teetering tower that looked like it would come crashing down the moment someone slammed the door too hard. Others sat on the sagging brown sofa. Some of them had kitchen utensils poking out of the tops; a few were tightly sealed up so Freya couldn't see what was in them.

She and Candy stepped into the room. "Ooh, looks like she was moving out," Candy said.

"Sure does."

A half-zipped duffel bag was in the middle of the floor. Strappy shoes poked out of the top, the spike heels looking like something that belonged on stage.

Freya pulled her phone from her pocket and called Brad, who answered on the first ring. "You were next on my list of people to call," he said.

"I love to hear it. Listen, Candy and I are at Jolie's apartment and are going to dig through it, see if we can find any reason why someone would kill her."

"I can help with that; I've been looking her up. Found her social-media account."

"Let me guess: she was stripping." Freya eyeballed the strappy shoe and reconsidered. "Or hooking."

"You got it. No Facebook, so I had to dig into Instagram, but that's where I finally tracked her down."

"And?"

He exhaled hard. "It doesn't say exactly what she does for work, but I have two eyes. It wasn't hard to figure it out. She has... loads of followers. It would be a nightmare to sort through them, try to find anything meaningful there."

"Okay. Good work." Freya exhaled hard. "Thanks for finding that. I have to go; we need to see what we can find in her apartment."

She hung up and walked around the apartment looking for any other clues as to who Jolie really was. The difference in the two women's murders wasn't something she could overlook. Whoever had killed the two of them had got rid of the first victim like she was just an inconvenient problem but had taken their time with Jolie. One was business, one was pleasure.

No, with Jolie it wasn't pleasure. It was *personal*.

Freya yanked her phone from her pocket and dialed Brad again. "Hey," she said as soon as the call connected, "I want you looking at all the comments on her social media—see if you can find out who Jolie pissed off. I don't think this was a random crime. Let me know." She hung up and looked at Candy. "The killer took his time with her."

Just like he took his time with his first victim ten years ago, Freya thought. Michelle Hawsey had been Jolie's age when she'd died. Was it really possible it was a copycat killer? Or was it the same murderer simply back to make a point? The bite marks on the ear were all too familiar. She couldn't overlook that.

"You're thinking something," Candy said, narrowing her eyes at Freya. "Spill."

"Okay, hear me out." Freya started to pace back and forth through the living room, being careful not to knock into any boxes. "You know about the Fawn Lake Killer, right?"

Candy nodded.

"Do you know that he bit Michelle's ear when he killed her?"

Candy's eyes widened. "What? No."

"Yeah, that wasn't ever released to the news, so unless you'd searched out the file, I didn't think you'd know. Anyway, Jolie has the same bite mark on her ear."

"So it's the same guy."

"That's what I'm thinking. But it doesn't explain a few things. Michelle was attacked by herself and was the only victim. And she was killed by the lake, which is a much easier location to get to. Hiking up the mountain to kill her seems..."

"Driven."

"Driven, yeah. A driven killer is definitely one of the worst types. And one that strikes again, maybe because they're afraid of being forgotten?" She shuddered.

That conjured up the mental image of her parents, but she pushed the thought of them away. In her experience, all killers wanted to be known. As much as they wanted to remain free and out of jail, the allure of bragging was too much for most of them.

"So it looks like the Fawn Lake Killer on the surface," Freya said, speaking slower now. "But there are some differences I can't ignore. Michelle was a crime of opportunity, a crime of passion. But what happened on the mountain felt personal. Not at all opportunistic. Planned, like we said." She turned to Candy. "Did you and Brad find anything else up at the crime scene?"

"Nope. Whatever might have been there was washed away in the storm. It's clean as a whistle, which just means we have to work harder to solve this."

"We've got it." Freya looked around the apartment as she spoke. "This guy is smart. Or lucky, but we're coming for him."

There was one thing she knew that she was pretty sure the

murderer didn't realize. Every time the murderer showed himself, every time he made a move, it produced evidence. That evidence might not look like much at first and might not be enough for some people to hunt down a killer, but Freya was confident.

She had to be, because either the Fawn Lake Killer was back or he'd trained someone else to pick up where he'd left off. She wished she knew which it was, but she kept vacillating. Something had made a killer take the lives of two women. Freya had to find out what that was, and then she had to do whatever it took to stop him from striking yet again.

Candy was silent. The two of them walked slowly through the apartment, their heads moving as if on swivels.

Esther called and Freya tapped the side button on her phone to ignore it. A moment later, her phone pinged. Esther again.

Come by—I need to see you.

Guilt washed over her as she slipped her phone back into her pocket.

Freya ignored the kitchen and instead walked into the bedroom. The bed wasn't made, the sheets and blankets half-puddled on the floor. She barely glanced at them before walking to the bedside table.

When her phone rang, she swiped her thumb across the screen without paying attention to who was calling. "Captain Sinclair," she said. A cream notebook sat next to a half-empty glass of water. There were six lipsticks on the table, an empty condom wrapper, and a handful of change.

"Sinclair, I need an update."

"Chief." Freya grabbed the notebook and flipped it open. "I'll have an update for you soon." As soon as she saw what was written inside, her heart flipped.

"Good. I'm waiting." He hung up, and she pocketed her phone before calling out to Candy.

"Just found a financial tracker. Can you believe people still use these things? Lots of cash deposits. Looks like we were right about those shoes out there."

Candy appeared in the door, brandishing a phone. "I'll see your bank book and raise you not one but two phones." A grin spread across her face. "One is dead and looks like it takes an ancient charger, but I have a box of cords under my bed. After you get us back to the department, I'll swing by my house and pick it up. The other phone is locked, but I can try to hack it when we get back." Her face fell. "It's an iPhone though, one of the older touch ID ones, and those are darn near impossible to get into, but I'll do my best. Please tell me there's information in that book about who was paying her."

"Nope, but don't worry. I know who to talk to in order to get some answers, and she goes on shift this evening." Freya shut the book and tucked it under her arm. "Let's go."

Before Candy could say anything, Freya's phone rang again. She juggled the notebook to answer.

"Freya, I have something you might find interesting." Shayla Dalton, a patrol lieutenant, sounded hurried. "I heard about Jolie Marin."

"What do you know?" Freya gestured to Candy, who stepped closer.

"Well, let me just say I've known Jolie for a long time. Part of it is from work, part is from our families living close to each other when we were little. Anyway, I know where her mom is. I don't have her number, but I can give you her address in Taylors if you want to swing out there and talk to her. Give her the death notification."

"I'd love to chat with her. Will you text me the information?"

"You got it. Talk to you later, Freya."

There was a click, and Freya shoved her phone in her pocket.

She needed to swing by her mailbox and look for a letter. But talking to Jolie's mom? That had to come first.

Even before Esther.

"Change of plans," she said, leading Candy from the bedroom. "I'm dropping you off at the department so you can get your phone charger. I'm going to talk to Jolie's mom. I still have a few hours before I can talk to my next person anyway. Load up—we're out of here."

EIGHT

Wanda Marin sat on her front porch in a chipped rocking chair, a lit cigarette dangling from her fingers, a scowl on her face. She'd watched as Freya pulled up to the house, her expression never changing, then waited until Freya was standing on her porch to speak.

"I didn't do anything. Why are you here?"

"Mrs. Marin?" Freya waited until the woman gave a curt nod, then continued speaking. "I'm Captain Sinclair from the Fawn Lake Police Department—"

"Fawn Lake?" the woman cut her off. "You're out of your jurisdiction. Even I know that."

Freya nodded. "I am; you're right. I'm sorry to drop by out of the blue, but I'm here to talk to you about Jolie." She glanced at her chest camera to ensure it was recording. Just in case.

"Jolie?" The woman's face changed. A smile appeared and she leaned forward to tap her cigarette on an ashtray. "What did she get into now? Is she in trouble?"

Freya hesitated. "Mrs. Marin, I'm so sorry to come here and tell you this, but Jolie was found in the woods this morning. She was killed."

The smile slid off the woman's face. Her lips tightened, and she closed her eyes, shaking her head. "You're wrong. Not Jolie."

"Mrs. Marin—"

"No, you listen, Captain. You're wrong. It's not my Jolie."

Freya fell silent. Everyone processed grief in their own way, and Jolie's mom had to work through what she was feeling. It wasn't fair for her to try to rush her.

"Jolie was doing some stupid stuff," she said, pinning Freya in place with a stare. Freya nodded, and the woman continued. "But she's turned a leaf. She's getting out of Fawn Lake, starting fresh in a new town. I told her she couldn't keep... keep living the life she was and be a productive person."

Freya thought about the hooker shoes packed in a box. "I was in her apartment earlier, and it looks like you were probably right. I saw a bunch of shoes packed up like she was getting rid of them."

Bright spots of color appeared in the woman's cheeks, and she nodded, then took a drag of her cigarette. "Exactly. Those stupid shoes. Her stupid ideas for making money." She blinked hard, fighting back tears. "I told her if she didn't get her act together that something terrible would happen eventually, and she was. She was getting it together. Moving. Getting a job. She got a new job, Captain. She was changing her life." Her voice broke.

Freya reached out and took her hand. "I'm so sorry to have to come here and tell you this. I can't imagine how terrible this is to hear. It sounds like Jolie was making a huge change for the better." She paused, waiting for a response.

"She was." Another shaky drag on her cigarette. "Do you want something to drink?"

"No, thank you," Freya said, and the woman nodded in response. She pushed out of the rocking chair with a groan and went inside. A moment later, she was back, a bottle of beer in her hand.

"Tell me what happened. Was it a John?" Her voice shook, and she took a sip of her beer while Freya responded.

"I don't get that impression. She was camping with a friend and they were attacked. Beyond that, we don't have any information, but I needed to come let you know and find out if you knew anyone who would want to hurt her."

Again Mrs. Marin lifted the bottle to her lips. When she lowered it, the beer was half-gone. "Jolie wasn't always a good girl," she finally said. "But everyone has a past, right?" She looked at Freya for confirmation; Freya nodded. "She was so good in school, always with her close girlfriends, never dating. Then when she graduated and some of them moved on, went to college, got married, she just... was lost."

"It's hard to be left behind."

"Exactly. She got left behind." Mrs. Marin kept nodding. "My Jolie... she just wanted to belong, and even though I've never stopped loving her, I don't think it was enough. She wanted more love. More from people. More than I could give her."

"Hence the hooking."

"Doesn't hurt that it was good money." Mrs. Marin drained her beer and set the empty bottle down by her chair. "That's what she told me anyway. I never would have gotten involved in something like that." A heavy sigh, and the two of them sat in silence.

"What do I do now?" Mrs. Marin took a shuddering breath. "Without Jolie? Or for her? I don't even know where to start."

"Her body is in the morgue, and you'll be able to claim it." Freya didn't mention her brutal death. No reason to do that to the woman, not when she was already struggling to process what had happened to her daughter. "But right now, I want you to tell me everything you can about who she was involved with. Was there anyone she was afraid of?"

Mrs. Marin shook her head. "We didn't talk about her work beyond her telling me what she was doing and me telling her to stay safe. I think you can imagine I didn't want to have that conversation with my daughter. Maybe if I'd been willing to, she would have told me if she were in trouble, but I can't think about that now."

Freya reached out and patted her hand. "I know this is hard. I'm sorry to have to ask you these questions right now, but I need to do everything in my power to find the person who killed her." She paused. "We found her phones. They'd be property of her estate now, but if we could get your permission to look through them—"

"Do whatever you need. I just want you to find whoever did this to her."

"I'm doing everything to make that happen."

"Did she suffer?" Mrs. Marin sucked in a breath. Her eyes went wide, glistening with tears.

"I don't think she did." Freya wasn't sure if she was lying to herself or the woman sitting next to her. "I think it was over so fast."

"Good. She got in trouble from time to time, but that doesn't mean she deserved to suffer."

"Nobody does."

A car drove slowly down the road. Neither of them spoke. It was Freya who finally broke the silence. "Do you know anyone with the initials V.O.?"

Mrs. Marin didn't immediately answer. Finally, she shook her head.

They held hands for another minute, then Freya pulled her phone out. She flicked through her photos until she found the one of Jolie's tattoo, then held it out for Mrs. Marin to see. "Does this date mean anything to you?"

The older woman rocked forward in her chair to get a better look at the photo, then immediately leaned back. "That was on Jolie?"

"Yes, ma'am."

Mrs. Marin exhaled slowly. "I've never seen it before. I never wanted tattoos. They're trashy. Told Jolie I thought that, and she agreed with me. We're not the tattoo type."

"It looks like it wasn't professionally done." Freya still had the phone out for the woman to look at, but Mrs. Marin's eyes were studiously locked on Freya's face.

"Captain, I've been honest with you about Jolie and what she did for work. Why would I lie to you about a tattoo?"

Freya didn't know. But she couldn't shake the feeling that it was important.

NINE

Freya's mouth was a tight line as she pulled up to her mailbox. There weren't any other cars on the road, as perfect as that would have been. Seeing the killer driving away from her mailbox would have been too easy, and that simply wasn't the way life worked. Maybe in a movie, but not here. Not today.

She moved slowly as she got out of her car, her ears straining, listening for any sound. A snapping twig could be the killer watching from the woods. Anything could clue her in, and she refused to move so quickly she missed it. Her hand rested on her open car door until finally she opened the mailbox and reached inside, her gloved hand carefully closing around the stack of mail there. Leaning against the hood of her car, she flipped through the envelopes, her heart sinking a bit more with each one she read.

There was a furniture sale downtown at Brunson's. Chicken was on special at Food Mart. That reminded her she needed to go pay for Roy's groceries, but that would have to wait.

Heat warmed the back of her neck when she reached the bottom of the stack.

"Come on," she muttered, flipping through the pile again, faster this time. It was here—it had to be. There wasn't any way it wasn't the same killer. Somehow, the man was back. He'd hidden out for a decade, biding his time, just waiting until Freya felt she could finally breathe again, but no.

There was nothing. The letter she knew had to be there wasn't. Exhaling hard, she shoved the mail back into the box and slammed the door shut. Maybe she'd just come too early. Maybe she needed to wait a few more hours and come back to check again.

A wry smile twisted the corner of her mouth. In her heart, she knew it wasn't too early. The letter should have been there, but it wasn't, and that meant it wasn't coming.

Why not?

She hopped in her Jeep and threw it in reverse, yanking the wheel hard to turn out onto the road. Before she could make it more than half a mile back towards town, her phone rang, the sound loud through her car's speakers.

Freya hit the green button on the screen to answer the call. "Candy, talk to me."

"Where are you?" Candy sounded breathless, and Freya's stomach turned.

"I was at my house for a second. Why? Is everything okay?"

"Someone just called because their fiancée is missing. She went camping over the weekend with—get this—another woman, and she hasn't come back home. He was freaking out. I want to get out there and talk to him, but I figured you'd want to go with me."

"You know I do. I'm not too much farther out." Freya pressed down harder on the gas. "Did you get all of the guy's information? I want to pick you up and go."

"I've got it." Candy took a deep breath. "Freya, there's something you should know about who we're going to go see."

"Hang on," Freya said. "I've got another call coming in.

Lance. I'll be at the PD in just a few minutes, so make sure you're outside and the two of us can head out right away."

"Freya, wait—"

Freya tapped a button on the screen to switch calls. "Lance? Tell me you have something for me."

"Hey, Freya. Do you have a minute?"

"About five." She tapped her brakes and rolled through a stop sign. They were optional when there was an emergency, weren't they? Maybe not officially, but still.

"The second woman—Jolie—with the cut throat?" There was a soft rustle, like Lance was looking through papers as he spoke. "You're going to find this really interesting. Her tongue is gone. Cut out."

Freya tried to wrap her head around what the man was saying. It was so unexpected that it took her a beat to find her voice.

"Cut... *out?*"

"Yep. Looks like it was the same knife that he used to slit her throat. She would have been unconscious within a few seconds, so that's a small mercy."

"Mercy." Her throat felt tight, and she was suddenly too aware of her own tongue.

"I haven't finished the rest of the exam," he said, pulling her thoughts away from how physically uncomfortable she suddenly was, "but I'll let you know as soon as I have more answers, if there are any to be found."

"Thanks, Lance. I really appreciate you giving me the heads-up on this. Talk to you in a bit." As soon as he said good-bye, she hung up.

Just two blocks to the police department. This time, when she reached a stop sign, she came to a complete halt and tapped on her phone screen.

Ringing filled the car.

"Hey, Freya." Brad sounded wired. "Candy filled me in that

we've got an ID on the second woman. She's outside waiting on you."

"Good." Freya could already see her detective out front; Candy was rocking back and forth on her heels, looking antsy. "Listen, I just talked to Lance and one of the women had her tongue cut out. I know the two of you walked around up there and looked for anything out of place, but I want you back up there. Candy said you didn't find anything, but it's worth another look."

A sharp intake of breath. "Of course. I'll head up there now."

"Call Holbert and take her with you. She was on top of it this morning, and I want you to take another set of eyes. And it's safer that way."

"Ten-four. I'll call her now."

She pulled up next to Candy and hung up on Brad. Candy opened the passenger door and slid into the seat.

"Where to?" Freya was already backing out before Candy was buckled in.

"Listen, before I give you the address—"

"Candy. Address."

Candy blushed and rattled it off. "If you don't know where that is, it's—"

"In the same neighborhood as the Jernigans," Freya finished for her. "I remember where we're going. Now, what did you want to tell me?"

"It's who called, Freya. He's her fiancé. The second woman is Millicent Woodward."

"Okay." Freya was barely listening. "What's the fiancé's name?"

"Steve Petit."

Freya slammed on the brakes.

TEN

A long warm shower last night had chased away the chill that had settled into his bones as he'd walked back through the woods. Now he was taking himself out to lunch to celebrate a job well done.

Over Easy was close enough to the police department for him to keep an eye on what was going on there. Maybe, if he was lucky, he could even catch a glimpse of Freya. He closed his eyes at a red light and allowed himself to imagine the frustration etched on the woman's face. These murders would be enough to put her over the edge. It was a thrilling thought.

Tomorrow morning his handiwork would be on the front page of the paper. He broke into a grin and covered his mouth. Pulled into a parking space.

He looked up, hoping to be lucky enough to catch a glimpse of a harried Freya Sinclair hurrying past, but the sidewalk was disappointingly empty. He'd hole up inside later too, but not for a while. After he ate, he had one more stop to make.

ELEVEN

Freya pulled into Steve Petit's driveway and killed the engine. The house looked freshly painted: the red-brick home was now white. Trends would come and trends would go, but paint on brick was probably a nightmare to get off. Was it Steve or his fiancée who had pushed for the reno?

The flower beds in front of the house were immaculate, with an explosion of colorful mums tucked in beds of new mulch. A few orange pumpkins were artfully tucked here and there in between the flowers, and there was even a bale of hay with a scarecrow perched on top.

The Petits Freya knew—thought she knew—wouldn't have cared this much about their front yard. Nor would they have decorated for a holiday, especially this early. Then again, it wasn't like she and Steve were that close. Freya had beaten the crap out of his dad for trying to rape someone in the woods, but that was as far as their shared history went, and that hadn't exactly inspired a bosom-buddy friendship between the two of them.

Charges had been pressed; Steve's dad, Robert, had been convicted and done time in jail; and then got out, got a job, and pretended to be a respectable member of the community. He'd thrown himself into raising his son, Steve, trying to make up for the time he'd missed with his kid while he was doing time.

And the town had moved on. That was one thing a lot of people didn't realize about small towns: when you do something wrong, you need to be prepared to live with the consequences, but only until someone else messes up. No matter what you've done, there's always someone out there preparing to do something even more stupid to take the attention off you.

And as for Robert, he'd grown up a little after he'd gone to jail. He'd finally married Steve's mom. Tried to settle down; worked at the plant in town. And since then, Robert and Freya had done their best to avoid each other. It had worked out just fine, but there was no reason to believe Steve still wouldn't hate Freya for showing up on his front porch.

No matter. She had a job to do.

Ignoring the growing pit in her stomach, she glanced at Candy. The two of them were parked behind a BMW and next to a Range Rover that looked like it had just been driven off the lot. The BMW had a dealer tag on it, the careful block lettering stating the tag would expire in just a few weeks.

"We'll want to check to see if he financed that or if he paid cash," Freya said to Candy, who nodded.

"You think he was planning on paying for it with Millicent's life insurance money?"

"I think a car like that costs a lot, and if it belongs to Steve, then I want to know about it. We can radio dispatch after we leave here to find out everything possible about this guy. I especially want to know when he got this car and how exactly he can afford this house."

"You think he's like his dad?" Candy asked, eyeballing her.

"The apple doesn't fall far from the tree, Candy."

They got out of the car, working their way past the decorations to the front porch.

"It can," Candy mused, "but not often. And sometimes, even if it falls far from the tree, it's already rotten. Is that the case here?"

"I think we need to give him the benefit of the doubt," Freya said. They were on the porch now, and she rang the doorbell, listening as the chimes sounded through the thick door.

Candy nodded her agreement. "We don't even know if his fiancée is one of the women up on the mountain. Besides, if he is the same as his father, then we'll get to the bottom of it."

The door swung open. Steve Petit, his eyes red, his cheeks covered with a day's stubble, stood in front of them. Without thinking, Freya glanced down at her watch. Wasn't it a little early to be drinking?

"Mr. Petit, I'm Captain Sinclair, and this is Detective Ellinger. Do you mind if we come in and ask you a few questions?"

Steve braced his hand on the doorframe, whether for support or to stop the two of them from entering his home, it wasn't immediately obvious.

"Oh, thank God. Millicent's missing. Can you find her?" He blinked at the two of them, tears welling up in his eyes.

"Mr. Petit, why don't you tell us what made you call us to report her missing." Freya kept her voice calm.

"Millicent, my fiancée, was supposed to be home already, and she isn't. I told her not to go camping with Jolie, that just because they were friends in the past didn't mean they needed to stay friends now. They're nothing alike." Frustration dripped from his words, and he scrubbed his hand down his face.

Freya glanced at Candy, whose eyes were wide. "I understand, Mr. Petit." She looked behind him into the house, but there was no sign of his father. "And we'll do everything we can to find Millicent, but we need more information from you. Where did they go camping?"

"Up in Clear Creek somewhere, but Millie wasn't clear on the location."

"Did Millicent not choose the location?"

"No, Jolie did. She chose everything—even went so far as to come by and pick Millie up so nothing could ruin her plans." He scoffed.

"You don't like Jolie."

He shook his head. "Never have. She's a terrible influence. Jolie's the kind of person who'd steal drugs from a little old lady."

"That's a strange thing to say about your fiancée's friend," Candy said.

Steve turned to her and blinked but didn't respond.

Freya leaned forward slightly, trying to get a better look at the man's eyes. Had he been using drugs as well? Or just drinking? "Tell us more about their plans. When did they leave? When did you think they'd be back? Who drove?"

"They left Saturday night, and Millie was supposed to be back late last night for work this afternoon. She'd never miss a shift at the hospital. Millie... she loves her patients. Loves taking care of them. She's amazing, always staying late to keep an eye on someone who isn't doing well, checking in on them first thing the next shift. She's a hero, the type of nurse you want when you're in the hospital."

Candy raised an eyebrow. "But you didn't report her as missing until this morning."

"I know." He exhaled and ran a hand through his thick hair. "Believe me, I know how it looks. But you don't know Jolie. She's always been able to get Millie to do stupid things. Honestly, even before they left, I had a good feeling they'd stay another night. It's just how the two of them used to be when they got together."

Silence.

Freya crossed her arms. "What were you doing last night?"

"Work." He took a shuddering breath. "Although now, if I'd known she wouldn't come home on time, I'd have gone out looking for her."

"Work on a Sunday night?" Freya raised an eyebrow. "Those aren't enviable hours. What do you do?"

"I work in a law firm."

"You must have a big case coming up to have to work the Sunday night shift. What law firm?"

"Does it matter?" Steve narrowed his eyes at Freya. When she didn't respond, he continued. "I work at Jernigan, Smith, and Prasil. Why are you asking me all of these questions? Millie is missing and we need to find her."

"Mr. Petit," Candy began, but he cut her off.

"You're acting like I'm the problem here, but I'm not. It's Jolie. She isn't a good influence."

"You said that." Freya glanced at Candy. "Mr. Petit, do you have a picture of Millicent?"

"Of course I do." He leaned back into the house, and Freya watched as he yanked a photo off the wall. He handed it to her, still in its frame.

Steve and a gorgeous redhead grinned out from the photo. She was in a long dress, he in a suit. Behind them, a huge balloon arch stretched across the photo, the sky a clear, bright blue.

"We were at a wedding a few months ago," Steve said. "That's where it was taken."

Candy's eyes flicked over to Freya. A look of understanding passed between the two of them.

"Mr. Petit, you might want to sit down. Maybe we can come in and talk."

"Oh God, you know something." He groaned, closing his eyes. "Is Millie okay? Just tell me if she's okay. I have to know."

"Mr. Petit, two bodies were found in Clear Creek Forest this morning. The car parked in the hiker and camper's lot was registered to Jolie Marin. We found her driver's license but nothing identifying the second woman." She paused, letting the words sink in.

His legs gave out, and he slid down the doorframe. "Not my Millie," he said. "Please tell me you're wrong."

Freya squatted next to him. "Mr. Petit, I know this is hard, but we're doing everything we can. Did Millicent take her purse with her? Her ID? Anything?"

He was already shaking his head. "No, she left everything behind. Since she wasn't driving, she didn't need it, and I didn't want Jolie to have access to her cash."

Freya and Candy locked eyes before Freya spoke again. "Mr. Petit, we need to take this picture and see if we can identify your fiancée. I promise you'll get it back."

He nodded without opening his eyes. "That's fine."

"Does Millicent have any identifying marks? Tattoos? Birthmarks? Any jewelry she wouldn't ever go without?"

"No birthmarks." A heavy exhale. "But she does have a mole on her inner thigh. And she left her engagement ring here so it didn't get lost."

Candy squatted next to Freya and put her hand on his shoulder. "Do you want us to call anyone for you? I know this is terrible, Mr. Petit, and there's no reason you should be alone."

He shook his head. "My parents are inside. I'll talk to them when you leave."

Robert Petit was in the house.

Freya felt the hairs on the back of her neck stand up. She hadn't come face-to-face with the man in years but knew they'd recognize each other instantly.

"Thank you for talking with us." Freya pressed her card into his hand. His fingers closed around it, but he didn't look at her. "We're going to go, but we will be in touch about Millicent."

He nodded.

Freya paused. "Do you know anyone with the initials V.O.?"

Steve turned to her, his gaze glassy. "V.O.? No... no, I don't."

"Thank you. We'll be in touch."

The two detectives hurried to the car, Candy calling dispatch for information about the BMW's temporary tag as Freya backed down the driveway. The response was immediate: the BMW was registered to Steve's mom, Jayne.

"Now what?" Candy turned to look at Freya, concern written on her face. "Jayne's probably up to her eyeballs in debt with that car, but at least it leaves Steve out of it. What do you want me to do now?"

"I'm going to drop you off and head to talk to Lance, see if we can get a positive ID on Millicent. You heard who Steve works for, right?"

"Yep, Jackson Jernigan himself. Why?"

"Call over there—see if he was really working last night. Unless they have a big case coming up, I can't imagine he'd be pulling that kind of weekend shift. Something's really wrong with this picture. After I talk to Lance, we're going to have to call Steve in for an official ID. And get your charger. We need to crack into Jolie's phones."

"Got it." Candy fell silent for a moment, then cleared her throat. "It's always the husband, or so they say."

Freya shook her head. "Not necessarily, but I do think he knows a lot more than he's letting on. I don't think he would kill Millicent, but it's obvious he's not exactly torn up about Jolie being dead. But why? What did she do that was so terrible that he would hate her so much?"

TWELVE

"Did you ever find the tongue?" Lance yanked on a drawer and pulled out a huge tray with a body on it. Without waiting for Freya to respond, he flipped back the white sheet covering the dead body.

"Nope. I sent a detective and an officer up there earlier. Got a text from them a while ago that they'd crawled all over the mountain and hadn't found a thing." Freya handed the photo of the happy couple to Lance. "I'm assuming it'll show up when I least expect it."

"Is this our unknown victim?" Lance turned the photo upright then held it up to the face of the redhead. "Could be her."

Freya stepped next to him to take a look. If she closed one eye and squinted, ignoring the way half of the woman's face was missing, she was pretty sure it was Millicent. "Millicent Woodward. Her fiancé said she has a mole on her inner thigh. Do you mind?"

Lance yanked up the end of the sheet. "Saw it earlier," he said, pointing. "Is that enough for you to positively ID her?"

She nodded. "I really wanted to avoid making Steve ID her if possible."

"I agree, but he'll want to see her. Most men do; they think they can stomach what's going to be underneath the sheet. I don't know of many who are glad they did it though. Sometimes it's best not to know what your loved one looked like at the end."

"He'll want to see." Freya knew it beyond a shadow of a doubt. "And we're confident about the ID for Jolie, so that's a relief."

Lance flipped the sheet over Millicent and slid her tray back into the wall. "Jolie looks like her photo. Much easier to ID. Do you think there's family or friends who will want to come by and verify?"

"I talked to her mom and told her Jolie's body was here, but I'll have an officer call and give her the option. Honestly, I don't know if she'll want to see her daughter like that. According to her, Jolie was doing everything she could to turn her life around."

"It's a shame." Lance shook his head. "But work talk: I found some things. Millicent was killed with the rock you found. There were small chips of it embedded in her brain matter, so it's pretty clear how she died. But besides that, she was untouched. No other bruising, just the expected lividity. Remember?"

"I remember."

"But Jolie is an entirely different story."

"Don't hold back on me now."

"She fought back and was beaten. I found scratches on her arms in addition to the lividity on her back. Nothing on her inner thighs, no skin under her fingernails, although there was dirt, like she'd tried to get purchase on the ground. No bruising on her arms or face. She didn't go quietly, but once he slit her throat, it was over quickly. It's a small comfort, I guess. She suffered, but she didn't have to live through that."

"And you didn't find any traces of fluids?"

"Nothing. He didn't rape her, if that's what you're asking."

"Okay." Freya tapped out a rhythm on her thigh as her mind raced. "The Fawn Lake Killer raped Michelle Hawsey, but he didn't wear a condom."

"Might not be the same guy."

She nodded but didn't respond. She'd been so sure it was the Fawn Lake Killer.

But what if she was wrong?

"You're thinking something." Lance had wandered over to the counter and now poured himself a cup of coffee. He held up the pot in question to Freya, who shook her head.

"Yeah, I'm thinking a lot of things." She walked over to him and leaned on the counter while he doctored up his coffee and took his first sip. The grin that spread across his face was almost enough to make her forget that the coffee was probably brewed hours ago and was thick as sludge.

"About the Fawn Lake Killer?"

"Well, yes. It just fits. Scratch that. Part of it does. The parts that don't, though, are making me question everything." Freya groaned and pressed down hard on her temples. "And I'm wondering what in the world is taking Candy so long."

She tapped on her phone. Candy picked up on the second ring.

"Freya, I was just about to call you." She sounded breathless.

"You're on speaker with Lance. Please tell me you were able to speak with the law office about whether or not Steve was really at work last night."

"Sure did. I spoke to them, told them what I needed to know, and they said they'd get back to me."

"Neither confirming nor denying." Freya shook her head. "They have to know that makes him look guilty. Okay, that's something to keep on them about."

"Yeah, who knew a bunch of lawyers would do everything possible to keep from giving the police any information. Want me to start a warrant to get it?"

Freya grinned. "Do it."

"Consider it done. Were you able to confirm Millicent's ID?"

Freya glanced at Lance, who gave her a sad smile. It didn't matter how many dead bodies you ID'd, it was still hard to put someone's name with their corpse, to know their life was over, to have to prepare to tell the family.

"Yeah. This is Millicent Woodward. I'll have to swing by Steve's house and give him the news." It was literally the last thing she wanted to do, but someone had to tell the man, and calling him to let him know over the phone wasn't appropriate. She didn't like his father, but he still deserved common decency.

"I can have Brad do it. He's here filling out some paperwork, but he said he'd be happy to help however you need."

"Good, thanks for taking care of that for me. I'll head there in a few minutes to give him Millicent's picture to take with him."

"Perfect. And I talked to dispatch. No missing women fitting your age range with the initials V.O. They had one missing woman, but she was in her fifties, and our victim definitely wasn't that old."

"It was a long shot. Thanks for following up with that, I'll see you in a few."

Freya was about to hang up the phone when Candy spoke again. "Oh, and Freya? Be prepared. Chief was muttering about a press conference. He's on edge with this one."

"Freaking wonderful." Freya hung up and shoved her phone into her pocket before grabbing the photo from the counter.

"Oh, but you do so well on TV." Lance took another sip of his coffee. "You'll be fine."

"Easy for you to say, hiding down here in the basement like a gremlin." Freya grabbed his coffee and finished it, almost gagging on the swill. "Holy crap, Lance, that stuff will kill you. The caffeine is not worth it."

"That's because it's for gremlins." He grabbed his cup back and turned to refill it. "I'll be tuning in with everyone else, Captain. Let me know if you find the tongue."

"You'll be my first call. Thanks for your help." She hurried up the stairs and out to her Jeep. A cold breeze blew through the parking lot. Shivering, she pulled her jacket tighter around her body.

All she could think about was a missing tongue. A blurry stick-and-poke tattoo of a date.

And why one of two killings had been so personal.

THIRTEEN

The sun slipped lower. Freya's shadow stretched long on the sidewalk in front of her as she walked across Main Street. Her stomach gnawed at itself, on strike because she hadn't had anything to eat since breakfast.

She needed to see Esther, make sure she was okay, then it was time to see Chief. She'd already dropped Millicent's photo off with Brad and sent him to talk to Steve, freeing her up to talk to Esther and Chief.

The Fawn Lake Killer was back and had murdered again last night, or so she thought. And if that was the case, how could Freya be sure she'd catch the guy this time when she'd failed to before?

She was ten years older now, had ten more years of experience under her belt. That had to count for something.

Frustration rushed through her, hot and silent, and she turned left off the sidewalk, not through the open door to the bar that would have pulled her into its warm embrace a few years ago but into the bakery.

"Freya!" Esther stood behind the counter, white curls escaping from her hair net. She'd been helping a young couple, but they now trundled past her, a box of something baked held tight like a present. "I haven't seen you in here in months. Where have you been hiding?"

"It hasn't been that long, Esther." She leaned on the counter and inhaled deeply. Cinnamon and vanilla swirled together, the scent spicy and delicious.

"Weeks then. Okay. Days."

"Try this morning." Freya made herself smile through the worry. "You called and I couldn't pick up earlier. Is everything okay?"

"I miss you. The problem is that I keep coming to you, so I guess that's why you're not swinging by here." Esther threw her hands up and then wiped them on her apron. "You need something sweet, I can tell. Bad day? Did you already finish the donuts I brought by?"

"You heard the news?"

Esther nodded. "Not the full story yet, but people are starting to talk." She grabbed a flat box, flipping it and folding it into shape before grabbing tongs and sliding open the bakery case doors. Moving quickly, she filled the box, layering cookies on top of each other until the lid barely shut. Then she took a sticker that bore the name of the bakery, Parker's, sealed the box, and slid it across the bakery case to Freya.

Freya watched Esther carefully the entire time. Was she unsteady on her feet? Did she look more frail than she had last week?

"Well, there's that," Freya said, tapping the box without taking it. "The detectives and dispatchers loved the donuts by the way. Thanks for bringing them by."

"I'll always take care of you. Well, as long as you let me. Talk to me. You look like you have the weight of the world on your shoulders and don't know what to do with yourself."

"It's a long story."

"It always is. I have time."

Just looking at the woman standing across the counter from her got Freya thinking about when she was younger. She'd been a jerk, like a lot of teenage girls, and put Esther through hell, fully expecting her to turf her out at any moment. But she never had.

Esther had been there for her the day she'd wrecked her car, wrapping it around a tree outside of town after leaving a boy's house in a hurry, and then been there later when she'd taken her oath as a police officer. She'd bandaged Freya's fists when she'd come home from the forest after beating up Robert. Freya had put on a lot of weight since then, most of it muscle, but she still felt like the young girl Esther had always taken care of when she stood across from Esther like this.

There was nothing tying the two of them together, no official paperwork that said Esther had to look after her, but the woman had never faltered.

"You have time, but I don't. I have to solve these murders before the killer strikes again." Freya opened the box and popped a mint chocolate chip cookie in her mouth. Minty and sweet, her favorite. "Unfortunately for me, eating cookies isn't going to get it done." She glanced up sharply at Esther. "Everything okay? You called and then texted."

Esther blinked at her. The blank expression on her face made Freya's stomach flip. This was what she'd been worried about. The nagging feeling that Esther needed more help than she could give her ate at her.

But what had happened over the summer when Freya had mentioned a home nurse coming by Esther's in the evening to keep an eye on her? A huge argument, one Freya never wanted to relive but couldn't stop thinking about, especially when she was trying to fall asleep.

All she wanted was to take care of Esther the way Esther had always taken care of her. But Esther was making it difficult.

She was forgetting more and more things, and then the argument over the summer...

"Oh, yes, I remember now." A soft laugh. "I'm fine, Freya. I just needed to see you."

"I'm alive," Freya said with a smile. When she went to grab the box to leave, Esther stopped her, reaching out and resting her hand on her arm. Freya was surprised when she looked down to see how old it looked, how thin her fingers were, the age spots on her skin. There had been the fall this spring, but how was it possible Esther was getting so old, so quickly?

"Darling. I worry about you out there, running around after killers, putting yourself in danger. I know why you do it."

Freya sucked in a breath, then ran her hand through her hair. "You think I'm doing this because of Mom and Dad." Her voice was flat.

"Aren't you?" Esther peered at her. "If you're honest with yourself, Freya, isn't a lot of why you push yourself so hard to make up for what they did? Maybe to prove to yourself that you're not like them, not even a little bit?"

Freya shook her head. "I can't think about that. But I know it's the Fawn Lake Killer. It has to be him. There's only one problem."

Esther waited, her hands clasped in front of her, her eyes locked on her. She'd wait like that until Freya was ready to continue, and so she took a deep breath.

"He hasn't sent me a letter. Last time it was in my mailbox waiting for me after he killed his victim. There wasn't anything today." *So maybe it wasn't him.*

Esther leaned forward. "What did the letter say?"

Again, Freya ran her hand through her hair. They'd had this conversation before. She knew she'd told her what the letter said, although admittedly that had been years ago.

Maybe Esther had just forgotten. Maybe her memory was going. That wouldn't be too surprising, not at her age. Especially not after the fall. I mean... how old was she? Pushing eighty. Esther was at the age where most people were slowing down, accepting more help. It would certainly reduce some of the stress Freya felt if she didn't worry about Esther from sunrise to sunset.

"*Dear Freya,*" she said, repeating it from memory, "*I hope this letter finds you well. She wasn't going to make it, not after I got my hooks into her. I wish you could have heard her scream. There's nothing like it, and you'd find out if you gave it a shot. Catch me if you can, although I doubt you'll be able to.*"

"Grisly." Esther shivered. "You didn't release that to the public, did you?"

"Not a chance. It's in the file, but unless someone stole it and passed it out, nobody aside from the department and the murderer would ever know what it said."

"But you haven't gotten a second letter, so the chances are good it's not the same person." Pleased with her deduction, Esther crossed her arms on her chest. "No second letter, not the same guy. What do you say about that?"

"I say... I hope you're right." Freya didn't have the heart to tell her about the bite marks on the ear. It was an unreleased detail and, besides, Esther was older now: the last thing she needed was to hear all the gruesome details. "Anyway, I need to update Chief. He's probably about to come out of his skin." The doorbell tinkled behind them. "And you have more customers."

"Well, will you look at that? I'm always surprised when people come back for more."

"You shouldn't be. You're the best baker in town."

"Correction: I'm the only baker in town." Esther held up a thin finger and wagged it back and forth. "Let me know how it's going, won't you, dear? In fact, why don't you come for dinner—unless you have someone waiting for you at home. Maybe my neighbor?" Freya rolled her eyes, and Esther laughed, then continued. "Fine. I'll make meatballs."

"I'd love to, but I really can't sit and have a meal with this case still active. I wish I could, Esther, but I have to find who killed them. But I'm glad I came by to see you. I miss you." Moving with purpose now, Freya grabbed the box and closed its lid.

"I miss you too, darling. I'll put some leftovers in the refrigerator for you. You have to eat, so make sure you come by and get them. That's me meeting you in the middle, by the way." She wiggled her fingers at Freya, who turned and hurried out the door, exhaling hard as it closed behind her.

The sun had set even more. It was still afternoon, but the light was getting weak. Ducking her head against the cold breeze, she hurried to the police department.

The trip up the stairs was fast, and soon she was standing in Chief's office. The cookies in her hands felt out of place, but she didn't want to go into her office to drop them off. Without being asked, she sat, flipping the cookie box open, and putting it on Chief's desk.

"Well?"

"Brad Williams is looking into Jolie, searching for any social-media accounts, and he just went to deliver Millicent's death notification to her fiancé Steve. Candy found two phones. She had to swing by her house to get a charger because one is dead and is then going to try to hack into them. One's an iPhone though, so you know how that will go."

Chief nodded.

"And now I'm going to call in a favor from someone who will probably know Jolie. I just have to hope she'll be willing to talk to me."

"Good. And you still think it's the Fawn Lake Killer?"

"I don't have proof, but it feels like him." Freya took a deep breath and waited. When Chief didn't immediately respond, she continued. "I'm going to work the case looking for all suspects, while keeping in mind that I've seen something like this before. There are just too many similarities to ignore the possibility."

Chief sighed. "But you don't have a note. There was a note before, and that was key for you to know this was the same guy."

"Right, but it will turn up. I know it will."

"I don't think it's him," Chief began, but that was as far as he got.

Footsteps pounded down the hall, and Freya turned around, angling one arm over the back of the chair as she stared at the door.

Candy burst through it, her eyes wide. Skidding to a stop in front of Freya, she waved a piece of heavy paper in her face.

"I got a letter."

FOURTEEN

One look at Candy's face told Freya all she needed to know. The younger detective didn't need to say another word, didn't need to show Freya the paper clutched in her hand for her to understand that she was right; it was happening again. Only this time, the killer had reached out to someone else.

Freya half-stood, grabbing Chief's desk for support, then forced herself out of her chair. Chief stood too, his chair scraping against the floor, but she didn't turn to look at him. She was focused on Candy. On the letter in her hand.

Candy was holding it together, but barely. Her face was pale, her cheeks bright pink. There was a furrow between her eyebrows that wasn't normally there, deep enough to look painful. Her fingers were tight, like claws, as they clutched the paper.

She wasn't going to let it go. Freya recognized the same emotion flowing through her that she had experienced herself when she'd received her letter.

Only Candy was handling it better. Maybe she'd learned from Freya's mistake. Maybe she'd watched more *Law & Order* than she had. Or maybe she was just a smarter cop. Whatever the reason, Candy's letter was already in a protective plastic sleeve. It caught the light from the overhead fluorescent bulb and seemed to shine.

"May I see it?" Freya's throat was tight. Chief was next to her, having hurried around his desk faster than she'd expected. He peered over her shoulder as the detective took the letter from Candy, holding it in both hands to keep it still while she read it.

Only she didn't need to read it. It was the same thing, the same words; everything, right down to the punctuation, was an exact copy of the letter she had received. She grimaced, closing her eyes. There was sound out in the main lobby of the fourth floor, but it was nothing more than a distant hum to her.

She couldn't focus on anything other than what she was holding in her hand.

"Was it in—"

"My mailbox, yes."

Candy reached for the letter. Freya had to concentrate to let go of it. Handing it over felt monumental, final, like she wouldn't ever see it again. She knew she was wrong, knew it would be entered into evidence and kept with the rest of the case file while detectives worked on finding the murderer. But still.

"He's back." The words felt heavy in Freya's mouth. Just saying them was serious, like she was accusing someone of something. She rolled them around like heavy stones, then spoke again. "He's *back*, Chief."

Chief didn't answer.

From outside the office, someone laughed. Candy winced.

"Why would he send it to me?" For the first time since Freya had met her, Candy sounded worried. Her voice was airy, light, like it was being carried away on the wind. She reached up and touched her throat, her fingers grazing her skin. "Why not you? He knows you. He sent it to you last time. Why would he change his plans now?"

"Because he's messing with me. Just like he did when he singled me out from all the other officers ten years ago. He knows we work together, knows we're close. This is all a game to him." Freya's voice was robotic. She dug deep to find the words she needed to try to explain what was going on. The Fawn Lake Killer, whoever he was, was one of the most important people in her life. She'd never admit that to anyone of course, never admit the embarrassing amount of time and energy she'd spent thinking about the killer. Even when she wasn't at work and wasn't supposed to be worried about the job, there was always part of her searching for the killer.

Throughout her career, she'd thought that if you focused and worked hard enough on what you were trying to do, you'd succeed. That hadn't been the case here, and now the killer was moving on to someone else. The game had changed.

"But why?" Horror filled Candy's voice. "You're back, Freya. You're not going anywhere. So why would he drag me into this unless there was something else he wanted?"

Candy's life had just changed. She'd realized it, but she had no idea how bad it was going to get.

"I'm not going to leave you to handle this on your own," Freya began, but Candy cut her off.

"That's what happened to you. Everyone abandoned you to deal with it on your own." Her eyes flicked over to Chief, like she was just remembering he was standing there listening.

"I'm here." Freya reached out, taking Candy's hand in her own. The younger detective swallowed hard. "Listen, just because he sent you the letter doesn't mean you have to try to handle this on your own, okay? Trust me. We've got this."

"Who else knows that it's the same guy?" Chief asked.

Freya slowly turned to look at him. "You believe me now?"

Chief didn't immediately respond. "The letter is pretty convincing."

"Glad to hear you're on my side." Freya had to fight to keep the bite out of her words. "As for who knows about it? You, Candy, Brad, and me." She ticked off their four names and held up four fingers. She paused. "And Lance. I talked to him about how similar the cases are."

"Good." Chief nodded slowly. "The last thing we want is panic. If people catch wind of the killer coming out of retirement, then they're going to freak out. You have to catch him. Fast. Before he kills anyone else. We don't want the papers to spin this how they like to. Get this guy off the street and make sure he doesn't have any chance of ever getting out of prison."

Of course. It was all about public image and what people would say about him. While Freya and Candy were consumed by a need to catch the killer to protect the people of Fawn Lake, Chief was more worried about what people in town would say about him as the chief of police if the perp wasn't caught and put behind bars.

"We're on it." Freya squeezed Candy's hand. "This guy isn't going to get away with it again."

Freya was finally going to be able to exorcise her demons.

Chief nodded. "The press is going to be all over us, so I need you two laser-focused on this. And Brad Williams too. Do you have any other open cases right now?"

"This is it. Top priority," Freya told him.

Chief grunted in response and lowered himself back behind his desk.

"Let's go to my office," she said to Candy. "I'll fill you in on everything I know. Get you up to speed. I want you to know this case inside out, better than you know yourself."

Candy managed a weak smile. It was only then Freya noticed her wet pant legs. They clung to her, soaked up past the knees.

"Sorry, I slipped." She blushed. "I ran into my house to get my charger and stopped at my mailbox. It was muddy by the side of the road, and I lost my balance."

Freya nodded.

"When I found this, I knew I needed to get back here as soon as possible. I figured it wouldn't matter that my clothes were wet."

"You're fine." Candy had to be uncomfortable in her damp clothes, but she was right. The two of them needed to get started right away. Freya glanced at Chief. The man's face was stony, impossible to read. Gesturing with her chin, she directed Candy down the hall.

When they were settled in her office, she took the letter from Candy and put it on her desk. It sat between the two of them, a reminder of her inability to solve a case a decade ago.

"You need your head in the game," Freya said, putting her hand down on the letter to cover up the words. She ripped her gaze from it and stared at Candy. "You're my partner on this, and we're not letting this guy get away again. Do you understand?"

A nod. Candy swallowed. "You think we can catch him? After so long? Why would he suddenly resurface when it's been so many years? What is it about right now that inspired him to come crawling out from under his rock again? I know you said you thought it was the same guy, but, honestly, I didn't think it made any sense. None of this makes sense."

"No, it doesn't, but you're asking good questions." Freya stood. "Wait right here—I'm getting everything we have on this guy."

There wasn't a lot of information on the Fawn Lake Killer. Freya signed the box out of evidence and carried it back to her office. Candy was still staring at the letter when Freya entered.

"Hey," she said, snapping her fingers, "head in the game. That letter? It doesn't mean he's going to hurt you. It means he wants you to play his game. So you know what? We're going to do just that."

"Yeah, and how do you suggest we do that?" Candy took the lid off the box and reached inside, pulling out Freya's matching letter. Side-by-side, the two of them were almost carbon copies.

"We find him. We nail him to the wall. We make him pay for what he did. He's a few steps ahead of us right now, but we've got this. Take care of the letter first. Dust it for prints, see if you can find anything on it we can use. Then you'll get in Jolie's phones. There has to be something, okay? While you work on that, I'm going to call in a favor."

"Okay." Candy exhaled and dug back into the box. "Let's find this guy."

After a moment, she glanced up at Freya. "Who are you calling for a favor? An old friend?"

"Not exactly a friend." Freya grabbed her car keys and glanced out the window. It was growing dark—and fast.

Time for her to go.

FIFTEEN

Brad barreled down the hall before Freya could make it out of her door.

"Please tell me you have something good," she said, stopping to talk to him.

"I've been digging deeper into Jolie's Instagram and thought you'd want to see it. Take a look." He held his phone out, and Freya paused. She really needed to go, but she took the phone from him, turning it around to see what was on the screen.

"xxxUrLocalGrlxxx?" she asked, reading the username. "You're right, that doesn't seem like the handle of someone who's just posting pictures of fall leaves and hikes in the mountains."

"Yeah, because she's not." Brad moved beside her to look down at the screen as well. "Take a peek at her profile and you can see the photos I was looking at."

Freya scrolled through the posts, holding her finger on one from time to time to enlarge it. Jolie posed dressed in lingerie and high heels. Every facial expression was suggestive, every way she turned her body to the camera was carefully chosen to leave little to the imagination. It was surprising that Instagram allowed the shots. Most of them were more suitable for OnlyFans.

"It's hard to tell from the shots, but they all look like selfies," Freya finally said, handing the phone back to Brad. "Seems like she was working solo, doesn't it?"

"Yeah. That's what I was thinking too. I dug through her comments like you wanted, but there really isn't anything helpful there. They're all what you'd expect from the type of men who follow these accounts, but none of them seemed dangerous."

"Drat. Okay. I appreciate you doing that. If there were any comments that were borderline, I want you to dig a bit more into the person who left them."

"Will do." Brad pocketed his phone. "Do you think she met a client, and it went south? He could have followed her up to where she and Millicent were camping and killed her there in retaliation?"

"That could be it," Freya said slowly, "but I don't want to assume it is. Normally a John gets angry and beats a girl up. It's a flare of anger, then he acts out. Following her like this? It's not the same. And Candy got a letter. I'm still leaning towards it being the Fawn Lake Killer."

"She got a letter?" Brad sounded surprised and looked past Freya. "You okay?"

Candy had risen from Freya's desk, where she'd been making a call, and moved towards the door. "No good prints on the tent," she announced, "just ones from the two women. And I'm fine. As fine as possible, I guess. It sure makes it seem like it's the same guy, doesn't it? The letter, I mean."

"It seems like he's back." Freya closed her eyes to think for a moment. "The Fawn Lake Killer. A John. Or Steve. There's nothing like a jealous fiancé to put an end to someone's life."

"Or an angry father," Brad offered.

Freya stilled. "Robert is a possibility. But to kill your son's fiancée as well?" Her voice trailed off.

"You said yourself he had an anger problem when he was younger." Candy crossed her arms and leaned against the wall.

"I did," Freya said. "We can't discount him. But I don't want to assume it's him."

"Jolie was bruised," Candy pointed out. She stood at Freya's side. "Johns do that when they're angry, but they normally act in the moment."

"Right. And she wasn't battered. No broken nose, no bruising on the face. It was more like she fought back than like she was beaten on purpose." Freya shook her head. "It doesn't feel right. Unless..." She grabbed her phone and dialed Lance's number, tapping the screen to put it on speaker.

The phone only rang once before she heard the ME's voice in her ear.

"I was about to call you, but you go first."

"Jolie," Freya said. "Was she battered?"

"You mean bruised around the face? She didn't have any bruises covered up with makeup, if that's what you're asking. Why?"

"Just checking." Freya chewed her lower lip. "Why were you calling me?"

"I have someone you'll want to check out."

She arched an eyebrow, and both Candy and Brad leaned closer so they didn't miss a word. "Tell me everything."

"It's some guy, Nathan Caldwell. I don't know anything about him, but apparently he's come to the hospital a few times to try to get down here into the morgue. The nurses at the front desk keep running interference on him."

"Nathan Caldwell," Freya repeated, walking back into her office. She sat down at her desk and ran her finger across the trackpad to wake up her computer. "Is he there now? We can be there ASAP."

"No, he's not here right now, so don't rush over. But I gave your name to the front desk to call if he shows up again. Hope that's okay."

"It's great. I'll look him up in the system. See who this guy is. Thanks, Lance. Go get some rest."

"I could say the same thing to you. Talk to you later, Freya."

There was a click, and she put her phone down on her desk, her fingers flying over her keyboard once she opened The Last One. The app, which only law enforcement had access to, afforded her more information than most people knew. Name, current address, past addresses, phone number, known associates... it was a veritable gold mine when it came to researching someone.

The only thing the app couldn't do was tell her exactly where the person she was looking for was currently hiding.

"Okay," she said, sitting back in her chair, her eyes on her screen. "Nathan Caldwell, age twenty-two. Last confirmed address was in South Carolina." She frowned. "Way south in South Carolina, a four-hour drive away."

"So you think he's homeless?" Brad offered, and Freya nodded.

"Maybe living in his car or crashing on a couch. That makes sense to me. He has an expired driver's license. A few drug charges, one for domestic violence. He's also been charged with public intoxication in the past. I wouldn't peg him as someone you'd want to meet in a dark alley, although he probably spends a fair amount of time in them. Look at him." She turned her screen for Brad and Candy to see.

"He's a young George Clooney," Brad said, surprised.

"Remember, this was a few years ago, but yeah, he's attractive. Or was. That's what I keep coming back to. If this is the guy who killed them, he'd have to somehow get them to trust him. Remember the crime scene? The women didn't run, and whether that's because they couldn't or because they were taken by surprise, I don't know. But if he took them by surprise then part of it was probably in how he looked."

"Someone dressed in rags and smelling like a barn isn't going to elicit the same level of trust as someone in a suit."

"Exactly." Freya exhaled and ran a hand through her hair. "But if he cleaned up..." She shook her head to clear her thoughts. "So this guy has been trying to get into the morgue. Maybe he's feeling bad about what he did. Maybe he wants to check his handiwork before he leaves town."

"Maybe he wants to make sure he killed the right person," Brad said.

Freya snapped her fingers and pointed at him. "There are a lot of possibilities. We need to find him."

"I'm on it." His stomach grumbled.

"First you need to stop and grab something to eat."

"I'm fine. I'll get some coffee and hit the road to look for this guy. There are a few places the homeless like to hang out, so chances are good I can find him there or at least run into someone who knows him if he's been living on the streets for a while."

"Sounds good, thanks." She turned to Candy. "You're on phone duty."

Candy nodded. "Honestly, though, I don't have a lot of faith in cracking the iPhone. Apple stands by their customers, saying it's for their benefit that law enforcement can't hack into them, which is a bunch of crap. But the Samsung? As long as the phone isn't damaged and will charge, I'll get into it tonight." She paused. "I'm hopeful, Freya. But I want to be honest with you: the Samsung is really old, and the charger port looks like it had something shoved in there."

"You're the best—just try, okay? We all have our marching

orders. Keep me updated when you find anything. This guy doesn't deserve another night out of jail."

Now that Jolie's mom and Brad had both confirmed that Jolie was hooking, Freya was even more convinced of who she had to talk to.

SIXTEEN

On sky-high stilettos, Diamond strutted over to Freya's car. Her tight black leather skirt rode up with every step she took, but she didn't make any effort to tug it back down. Her red top was cut low, the black lace of her push-up bra on display. Long blonde hair streaked with bits of gray hung around her face. She needed to get to the salon to have her roots touched up, but Freya figured that was more expensive than she could afford on a regular basis.

Stopping a few feet away from Freya, she tapped her foot before holding out a hand. "Smoke?"

"Don't have any." Freya shifted her feet. She had been leaning against her car, keeping an eye out for the woman she wanted to talk to. Diamond had been working the streets since Freya was on patrol. She clearly didn't remember Freya busting her a few times for solicitation when they were both younger, but she figured they'd both aged a lot since then.

"Then you want to take Miss Diamond on a date somewhere?" Diamond leaned forward, grinning at Freya.

"Maybe in another life, Diamond. But no, I wanted to ask you about a girl who might've worked the streets. Her real name was Jolie, but I don't know what she went by when she was working." Turning her phone so Diamond could see the screen, Freya showed her a picture of Jolie all dolled up for a night on the town.

Like it burned her, Diamond took a step back. "Why are you asking about her? You a cop?"

"Detective," Freya said, putting the phone back in her pocket. "Come on, Diamond, I just need your help. She was murdered."

"And you're here to bust me? I was just being friendly." Another wary step back. She was going to bolt.

"No, I'm not. Listen," Freya said, running her hand through her hair, "if someone is targeting prostitutes, then you need to be careful. Help me get this guy off the street."

When Diamond didn't immediately answer, she pushed a little harder. "You help me and I'll take you to Over Easy, get you something good to eat. What do you say? No pressure, but any information you have could help save lives. Maybe even yours."

Diamond's eyes flicked from side to side like she was looking to see who might be watching the two of them. Even though she hadn't said anything, her discomfort from simply talking to Freya was obvious. "You've bought me food before," she finally said, and Freya nodded. "When that guy beat me up."

"I did." Freya shrugged. "Nobody deserves to be on the receiving end of that. Let me buy you food again."

"A full breakfast," she finally said. "And something to go for when I get hungry later. But we better hurry—they'll close soon, and the only thing I want is waffles."

"You got it." Beeping her remote to lock the car, Freya gestured for Diamond to walk with her. Diamond hesitated a moment but then followed. "I could go for something to eat too, so this is perfect. Breakfast for dinner is my favorite."

Diamond didn't answer and refused to speak the entire way to the cafe. It was only when they were inside Over Easy, tucked away in a back booth away from the prying eyes of people in the other booths, that she put her hands on the table and stared at Freya.

"Was she one of the girls killed up on the mountain?" she finally blurted.

Freya took a sip of the coffee that Penny, the waitress, had wordlessly given them as they sat down. Not all the details of the case had been released, but she had to get Diamond to trust her.

So she nodded.

Diamond exhaled hard, then turned to Penny to order her food. Freya listened to her order a full waffle platter with sausage instead of bacon as well as another to go. She asked for the same, just one, and then waited while Penny sashayed off to the kitchen to put in their order.

"Do you think she knows what I am?" Suddenly uncharacteristically modest, Diamond tugged at her top.

"Penny? Maybe, but I don't think she cares. I know I don't. Listen, Diamond, I need answers, and I need to catch this guy before he hurts anyone else. Help me out, okay? Please?"

Diamond took a deep breath and put her napkin on her lap. Pulling her coffee mug closer to her, she played with the handle, turning the mug around. It made a scraping sound in the sugar spilled on the table, and Freya winced.

"Okay. Yes. Jolie was hooking. But she didn't do it on the streets like the rest of us. She only got her clients online. She thought that made her better than us." Diamond spat out the words like they left a bad taste in her mouth. "Nobody really liked her. She was Miss Fancy Pants; she didn't work in cars, only in hotels."

"How long was she working?"

She shrugged then took a sip of her coffee before ripping

open a packet of sugar and stirring it in. Freya took a deep breath and waited. Diamond wasn't in control when she was working, but now she got to feel like she had the power. She'd eventually give Freya the information she wanted, but only when she was good and ready.

"Not long, I guess. She caused a ruckus when she showed up because she tried to tell a few girls how to do their jobs better." She laughed a brittle laugh; shook her head. "Like she could teach any of us anything. But I haven't seen her in a week or so. She usually takes a cab downtown to the Amos Hotel and then leaves a bit later."

Penny arrived. "Here's your food. Anything else you need?" Her voice was cheery and bright, a far cry from Diamond's.

"Can you just leave the coffee?" Diamond gestured to the full pot in the waitress's hand. "I'm going to need a lot more of that before I leave."

Penny slid her gaze over to Freya, who nodded. Smiling, Penny put the coffee pot on the table before walking away. Diamond grabbed it immediately, topping up her mug before doing the same to Freya's. It smelled a little burned, but they didn't care.

"Any idea where she was heading when she moved? I heard she was leaving town." Freya took a bite of sausage, the hot grease exploding in her mouth. She hadn't realized how hungry she was. It was the same anytime she was working on a big case —she found herself needing to eat all day just to keep her energy up during the hunt. All too often though, she didn't have time to refuel.

"Don't know, don't care." Diamond inhaled her food. She was skinny, her collarbones sticking out. From the way she was shoveling it in, it was pretty clear she wasn't staying this skinny on purpose.

"Do you know the names of any of the men she was seeing?" It was a big ask, one that could easily backfire on Freya.

One of the laws of the street was not to ever name names. Men wouldn't come back if they thought they weren't going to be able to stay anonymous, and they'd just as soon go somewhere else to find a girl for a few hours. Still, the fact that Diamond didn't seem to have any love for Jolie made her pretty confident that if the woman had a name, she'd spill it.

She was wrong.

Stabbing her fork through the air at her, Diamond laughed. "You're trying to get me kicked off the street?"

Holding her hands up like she was surrendering, Freya shook her head. "Just trying to find this guy. What if he stops by your corner tonight? What if one of your friends accidentally goes with him and they don't make it back? I know you don't want to risk losing a client, but trust me, this guy isn't one you want to have."

The two of them were silent. Diamond dragged a bite of waffle through the last of the runny yolk on her plate and popped it in her mouth. While she chewed it, she stared at Freya. Finally, she swallowed, washed it down with the last of the coffee, and wiped her mouth surprisingly delicately on the napkin. This she tossed on the plate, which she then shoved over to the edge of the table to make it easier for Penny to clean up.

The Styrofoam container of her to-go meal squeaked in her hand when she picked it up. Long red acrylic nails bit into the white box. Freya looked down at them, noting how sharp they were. If Diamond were attacked, at least she would have some way of defending herself.

"I know one of the guys she saw because I used to see him too," Diamond said. Her voice had gone quiet, and she refused to look Freya in the eyes. "I stopped seeing him because he had started to get violent when he was upset. Yelled at me. Called me names. Hit me. I haven't seen him in a while though. Big guy, tattoos up both arms."

"Did you report it?" The question flew out of her mouth before she'd had a chance to think about what she was really asking.

Diamond laughed derisively; shook her head. "No. He promised to kill me if I did. Anyway, I don't remember his name, so I doubt it will help you. It's been a while since I've seen him." She turned to leave.

"Can you describe him? Or, look—I have a photo on my phone if you'd take a look and see if you think this is him." Without thinking, Freya stood, grabbing Diamond by the shoulder. Diamond jerked away, dropping the Styrofoam container of food. The lid popped open, and the food all spilled out on the floor.

"Oh no! I'm sorry, Diamond. Let me help—"

"He looked normal." Diamond's teeth were gritted, her eyes dark. People in the restaurant had turned to look at the two of them, but Freya didn't care. She couldn't take her eyes off the woman in front of her. "Like, J. Crew normal. Short hair, strong jaw. Like any guy you would see in church, at the bank. Maybe a lawyer, I don't know. Big hands." She reached up and put her hands around her own neck then clicked her tongue. "Good luck."

Before Freya could stop her, Diamond turned and practically ran out of the restaurant. Penny was on her way over with a mop and trash can, and she glared at the woman's back as she fled.

Freya was rooted to the spot. Diamond hadn't taken a look at Nathan or Steve's photos, but from what she'd said about the man Jolie was seeing?

Both Nathan and Steve fit Diamond's description of the potential killer.

SEVENTEEN

Freya was halfway across town when her phone rang. Swearing, she tapped the screen on her console to answer.

"I'm a bit busy, Candy," she said by way of greeting. "What's going on? Did you get into the phone?"

"Still charging, or trying to at least. I think it might be a lost cause, but I'm not giving up yet," she said. "But the real reason I called is because you have a visitor."

Freya groaned inwardly. With her luck, it was going to be Chief, wanting to know exactly what the case status was. Again.

"Who is it?"

"Esther." Candy's voice took on a softer quality. "Freya, you —you need to get here."

Freya's mind raced as she tried to think why Esther would be in her office. She had been bothered when Freya said she wouldn't come for dinner, and that probably hadn't sat right with the older lady. But it wasn't like she could turn her back on the case, not when she felt like the pieces were finally starting to slot together.

"Is she okay? I'm following up a lead." She kept driving. There was a voice in the back of her head telling her that she should stop the car and turn around, but after talking to Diamond, she needed to go to the Amos Hotel.

Someone there might remember Jolie. And since it was doubtful they'd be as afraid of her as Diamond was, she could get them to look at the pictures of Nathan and Steve on her phone. If she could just pin down who Jolie had been taking to the hotel, then maybe she'd have an easier time solving the case.

But Esther wouldn't stop by if she didn't need something.

She hesitated, her foot lifting off the gas.

"Freya, I know you're busy, but trust me, you need to get back to the office." Candy's voice had an edge. "The killer reached out to Esther."

She rested her foot on the brake pedal. There was a curve ahead of her, and she let her car handle it while her mind raced. *This couldn't be happening.*

"*Freya.*"

"I'm coming." She slammed on the brakes, then pulled into the parking lot of a defunct gas station and yanked the wheel hard to the right, whipping through some fallen leaves that scattered as she drove through them. "I'm coming. Get her some coffee or water or whatever she needs and I'll be right there. Give me a few minutes."

Sweat prickled her skin. What she wouldn't give for a drink right now. But that wasn't the answer. All that would do was make everything grind to a halt.

She couldn't afford for that to happen.

She pressed down even harder on the gas.

By the time Freya made it up the stairs to the fourth floor, sweat had started to pool on her lower back. Forcing herself to slow down, she took a deep breath and then walked into her office. Candy and Esther were sitting together on one side of her desk, both of them holding steaming mugs of coffee.

"Esther," Freya said, lightly touching the woman on the shoulder before going to sit behind her desk.

Esther took a deep breath and looked at Freya. "I'm sorry to interrupt your day like this," she began. "It's just... I received a package at the bakery."

"From the killer? Are you okay?" Freya forced herself to slow down, to take a deep breath. There were bright spots of color on Esther's cheeks, so even though her skin was pale, she still looked like she'd just gotten in from a run. Something bad must have happened to have her shaken up like that.

"I'm fine." Esther reached for Freya, then let her hand fall back into her lap. "I'm fine. Detective Ellinger here has taken good care of me. But you need to see this."

It was only when she gestured to the box between the two of them that Freya even noticed it. It blended in with everything else on her desk, and she reached for it before stopping herself, grabbing a pair of gloves from her top drawer, and snapping them on.

Candy's mouth was set. When Freya made eye contact with her, she gave a little nod.

Freya pulled the box closer and lifted the lid. She took it completely off and set it to the side of the box before leaning forward to peer in.

Even though she hadn't been expecting it, she knew immediately what it was. Sucking in a breath, she closed her eyes for a moment, then looked again.

The tongue was sitting on a cushion of black velvet.

It looked fake, like it was plastic and bought from a prop store for Halloween, but it was the real thing. The end of it where it had been cut from someone's mouth was ragged. There was dried blood on the velvet that had crusted the fabric. The tongue lay there, limp and swollen, a dead piece of meat, and Freya swallowed.

It had to be Jolie's.

"Where did you get this?" Ripping her eyes away from the tongue, she stared at Esther. Maybe she'd found it on the street. Maybe it was an accident. She didn't want to believe that this was happening, that Esther had gotten dragged into this.

"It was in my deliveries. Wrapped in paper and addressed to me. I know it's late, and I'm sorry to be a bother, but I don't know when it arrived. It was a crazy day at the bakery, and it could have sat there for hours." She leaned over and pulled some brown paper wrapping from her purse. "I brought the wrapping to show you, but I've already touched it, I'm sorry. I don't know what good it will be for you."

"You're not a bother." Freya locked eyes with Esther. What she wanted to say but couldn't stuck in her mouth. She wanted to tell Esther that she'd do whatever she had to in order to keep her safe. She wanted to apologize for dragging her into this. For putting her in danger.

But the words wouldn't come.

"Candy?" All Freya had to do was say the detective's name and the woman hopped right up. In a flash, she was back in her office with an evidence bag. After snapping on a single glove, she plucked the paper from Esther's hand and tucked it in the bag, sealing it up and putting it on her desk next to the box.

"Did anyone say anything to you? Did you see anyone, hear anyone? Anything out of the ordinary?" The questions were rapid-fire.

Esther blinked against the onslaught, then shook her head. "I'm sorry, Freya, I don't... It was just there. I didn't see anyone. I opened it, thinking it was something for the bakery. When I saw what it was, I..."

Her voice trailed off, but Freya didn't need her to finish her thought. She could only imagine how terrible it had been for her.

Air. She needed air. The tiny window behind her desk never let in enough of it, and right now she needed to clear her mind. She stood and stumbled away from her desk. "Stay right there, okay?" she said, pointing at Esther.

She didn't even make it to the stairs before Candy was next to her. Her detective stepped in front of her, holding her hand to her chest to stop her. "Freya. You can't leave right now."

Freya exhaled. Laughter reached her ears. Someone down the hall was laughing. How dare they? How dare they find anything humorous when Esther had just been targeted because of her case? It was one thing to accept danger for herself, but this was different. Unacceptable.

"It's one thing for me to be targeted. Or you," she said, remembering that Candy had been the one to get the killer's second letter. "But Esther? To cut out Jolie's tongue and send it to her? That's too much. That's personal."

"I know. We'll keep her safe. We'll put a detail on her, make sure officers watch her house. But you can't leave her alone in your office right now, Freya. She's scared. We'll check the paper for prints, okay? See what we can find."

"I know. It's just—" Her voice broke off. Something wasn't right. A shiver ran down her spine as she tried to catch the fleeting thought before it got away. "The tongue. Did it have a piercing?"

Candy eyeballed her. "No. Why?"

"Did it have a hole like it had a piercing at some point? Recently? Like someone pierced their tongue and then took it out?" Brushing past her, Freya hurried back down the hall to her office. Her head pounded.

"Freya, what in the world?" Candy followed her down the hall.

Freya burst into her office, and Esther turned to look at her, concern written all over her face. It felt uncomfortable, but she managed to give the older woman a smile before pulling her phone from her pocket, swiping it on, and navigating to Jolie's

Instagram. Candy was right behind her and peered over her shoulder at the screen.

"Look at this selfie," she said, tapping a picture to enlarge it. "It's from the day before the camping trip."

"She has a tongue ring." Candy's voice was flat.

"And this tongue never had one. Look." Grabbing the box, Freya held it up, turning it this way and that to get a better view of the tongue. It was swollen, and smelled, but it had never been pierced. "There's no hole, and I don't think it would close up that quickly even if she'd taken it out." Putting the box down, she turned her attention back to her phone and scrolled through Instagram, her finger flicking against the screen to move through the posts as quickly as possible.

Freya stopped; stabbed her finger onto a photo to enlarge it. "Look. Last year. She got it then, so it wasn't new. The hole would definitely still be there."

Candy didn't say anything. She didn't have to.

"Freya. What do you mean?" Esther's voice shook. She wasn't looking at the phone. Her eyes were locked on Freya's face. "What's the big deal about a tongue ring?"

Freya sighed and locked her phone again, slipping it back into her pocket. She took a deep breath, counted to ten, then finally looked at the two women staring at her. "This isn't Jolie's tongue. He's killed someone else and now he's rubbing it in."

EIGHTEEN

In the end, Brad took the tongue to Lance at the morgue. As much as it pained Freya to help Esther into Shayla's car, she couldn't take her home right now, to make sure she was okay, to wait with her. Candy was still trying to get the Samsung to turn on. After checking with dispatch about any new missing person's reports, Freya knew she couldn't wait around any longer.

She needed to go to the Amos Hotel.

Two dead women. One missing a tongue. Another tongue showing up.

And nobody had reported anyone else missing.

Freya's head ached as she drove across town; her eyes felt dry, like sandpaper, and her hip burned. It was only because of the adrenaline coursing through her that she was able to stay awake.

This side of town was quiet. Most of the action was downtown, with the tourists and most locals sticking to the streetlights that illuminated Main Street. Amos Hotel perched on the edge, right between the downtown area everyone loved and the other part, the one considered *on the other side of the tracks.*

Even though the name conjured up some mental image of a towering hotel where tourists would stay, sipping hot tea in the morning and retiring in the evening to perfect bed service, the reality couldn't be more different.

The building was squat. It hunched over the cracked parking lot, the streetlights continually out, the bushes in need of a trim. Junker cars populated the lot, and while it was possible to stay at the Amos for an entire vacation, it was much more likely to find visitors only booking rooms for an hour or so.

It was a problem. No matter how many times the police had tried to clean it up, shining a light on the problem only scattered the hookers and Johns like cockroaches. As soon as attention was directed elsewhere, the hotel opened its doors again, only the most sordid individuals daring to set foot on the stained carpet.

Freya parked right in front next to a beaten-up pickup truck that was splattered with mud. She got out of her Jeep and listened to the music coming from rooms on the left. A few people stood in a group in the parking lot, one of them casting nervous glances her way.

Never mind—she wasn't in the market to bust someone for dealing pot. Any normal night, she'd stop, take their drugs, break it up, but not tonight.

After double-checking that her Jeep was locked, she walked up to the main double doors, rubbing her hip to work out the ache. The crowd behind her kept talking, a loud laugh almost making her turn around. Instead, she threw open the door and stepped inside.

Concrete floors covered in thin stained carpet stretched away from her. Bright lights made it feel like it was daylight. Some rap music came from a speaker behind the desk, and that was where she headed.

A man in front of her leaned on the desk talking to the

clerk. They were laughing, and it wasn't until Freya cleared her throat that they turned to look at her.

"Sorry about my friend here," the clerk said. "I'm Gary. What can I do for you?" He smoothed his hands down his shirt and threw Freya a lazy grin.

"Not a problem. I'm Captain Sinclair; just wanted to stop by and ask you a few questions about someone who used to come here regularly." She pulled her phone from her pocket and flicked through to find a picture of Jolie.

Gary took it from her and glanced at the photo, then offered it to the man next to Freya. "I'm not much help because I usually work days, but Trent here just quit... what? A week or so ago? And he worked nights. What do you think, Trent? Do you know her?"

Freya turned to the man who was now holding her phone. He was tall and thin, the two friends the perfect odd couple. Gary could stand to lose forty pounds and had chubby cheeks, while Trent looked like he spent all his free time on the treadmill; his sharp jawbone looked more appropriate for a photoshoot than working in a seedy hotel. His jacket hung from his shoulders, while Gary's work polo was tight across his chest.

"Well?" Freya itched to take her phone back but forced herself to wait.

"It's hard, with so many people coming through here all the time." Trent used two fingers to enlarge the photo. "Maybe she looks familiar, but honestly, people become a blur when you've worked here so many years." He handed the phone back to her.

She pulled up a picture of Steve. "What about this guy?" This time she didn't let go of her phone, just showed it to the men, who both shook their heads. "Okay, this one?" She flicked to a photo of Nathan and got the same response. Desperate now, she pulled up a photo of Robert.

"I'm really sorry," Gary said, leaning over the counter. "But like Trent here said, people blur together."

"That's fine." It wasn't, but she wasn't going to get anywhere with them. "Is there anyone else who works here who might be better with faces?"

Gary sucked his teeth. "People tend to come and go. Trent and I are some of the longest-standing employees. Well, *I* am." He chuckled, and Trent joined in.

"What about Lorna?" Trent asked, and Freya turned to him. Man, he had dark circles under his eyes. The guy needed a good night's sleep. *Like I can talk.*

"Lorna?" she asked.

"Lorna Reed, sure." Gary snapped his fingers. "Come in tomorrow afternoon if you want. She should be in then. Nice girl—she might be able to help you."

"I'm really sorry we're not more help," Trent added. "Hope everything's okay with the people you're looking for."

"It's fine." Freya closed her eyes and took a deep breath. "Thanks for your help. You two have a good night." She turned and hurried to the front door. Outside, the group had dispersed, but the music was even louder.

In her Jeep, she called Candy for an update.

"The phone that works is an iPhone, like I said. I've reached out to Apple and I'm going to issue a search warrant to them to try to get into the phone, but don't cross your fingers. The Samsung is still dead, Freya. I'm so sorry."

"It's not your fault. And you know what? Don't worry about the search warrant; I've thought of something else." She twisted the key in her ignition, letting the Jeep roar to life. "Go home. Rest. It's... what? Almost eleven? Get some sleep, Candy. I'll see you in the morning."

"Try closer to midnight. Are you going to get some sleep?" Candy sounded exhausted. "I'm not going to bed unless you are."

"I am. I'm going to call Brad and make sure Lance has the tongue, then tell him the same thing. We've exhausted our leads right now and we need to be fresh when something else comes in. Go home, Candy. That's an order." She hung up before Candy could object, then called Brad.

"The tongue's dropped off," Brad said in way of greeting. "I had to call Lance to come back out and check it into the morgue but he was happy to do it. Well, as happy as you can imagine. Said to tell you good catch on the tongue ring, but he's still going to look for sign of a piercing in the morning."

"Thanks. I'm going to home to rest. So is Candy. I need you to do that."

"Thank God. I'm actually halfway home, I was going to grab a Red Bull and head back out, but I could sleep. Thanks, Freya."

"No, thank you. And call Shayla, will you? Let her know I appreciate her help but I'm a little too tied up at the moment to thank her myself. I'm going to call Esther, then crash."

"Ten-four. Hey, just so you know, Shayla stationed one of her officers outside Esther's house for the night. Said she knew you wouldn't get any sleep worrying otherwise."

A lump formed in Freya's throat. "Thank you. I want an officer there twenty-four seven."

"Everyone loves you, Freya. I'll make some calls, tell them that's what you want, and see to it. See you in the morning." He hung up.

She heaved a sigh and pulled up to a red light. Traffic in town was almost nonexistent this late in the evening. Her eyes burned, and she resisted the urge to rub them. Even though she was exhausted, there was a very real possibility she'd get in bed and her mind wouldn't let her rest, but she'd have to deal with that once she lay down.

A few touches of her screen and ringing filled the Jeep.

"Freya, are you okay?"

"Esther, I could ask the same thing about you." She was on the home stretch now, almost to her house. Relief washed over her, both because of hearing Esther's voice and because she just wanted to rest.

"I'm fine, darling. You don't need to worry about me. That Shayla is a lovely woman and looked through the house before she left."

"There's an officer outside your house, okay? Just for a while, until this settles down. We can't have you be a target. Just ignore them, Esther. Stay in the house."

"I'll do my best. Get some rest, Freya. I'll talk to you tomorrow."

Rest. Yes, she needed that. Freya drove the rest of the way on autopilot.

Just a few hours. That's what she needed to be able to function. Her to-do list for the morning raced through her head.

Once home, she collapsed in her bed and tried to calm her thoughts, but her mind kept racing.

She needed to find out who the tongue belonged to. Talk to Lorna from the Amos Hotel. Right now, she couldn't do anything about Nathan showing up at the morgue, but if the hospital called, she'd have to drop everything and hurry over there. Then there were the initials on Jolie's scarf. Those bothered her too.

That line of thinking made her think about Wanda Marin.

Jolie's mom had been convinced Jolie would never get a tattoo. There was just something about it that didn't sit right with Freya.

She had to know more about it.

NINETEEN

TUESDAY

Freya woke, stretched underneath her flannel sheets, and for just a moment was blissfully unaware of what had happened the day before. It was early, her room was still dark, and the radio was tuned to a country station to wake her up. Dolly Parton sang about the problems of working an office job as Freya swung her legs out of bed and planted her feet on the rug.

She yawned, reached over, and clicked on the lamp. For a moment everything was blurry—and then it snapped into focus.

The two dead women. Someone sending Esther a tongue. The letter Candy received. Her complete and utter belief that it was the Fawn Lake Killer back after ten long years.

Groaning, she dropped her head into her hands and squeezed her eyes shut. "This is why you became a cop," she muttered to herself, pushing herself to her feet and stumbling to the bathroom. A quick cold shower would help wake her up even though she would hate herself while under the water, and in just a few minutes she was getting dressed, much more alert than she had been when she'd first woken up.

After checking her phone to make sure she hadn't missed

any important updates about the case, she made toast and ate it standing at the kitchen sink. A quick flip of the sprayer rinsed the crumbs away. She downed a hot cup of coffee and some painkillers to keep the ache in her hip at bay, brushed her teeth, then was out the door with her keys clutched in her hand.

Family pictures still hung on the wall along the staircase. The dining-room furniture was draped with white sheets, ones Esther had helped Freya put there to protect the furniture when she'd moved out of Fawn Lake.

The smart move, the one everyone had wanted her to do, would have been to sell the house. And although she and Esther had talked at least a dozen times about doing just that, in the end, Freya couldn't do it.

It wasn't that she wanted to live in the house where she grew up. She didn't want to eat off the same dishes she had as a little kid. She didn't want to walk past the door to the basement where everything had happened.

But when she'd left Fawn Lake, she'd given up her apartment. And when she'd been ready to move back... well, real estate in a cute mountain town is hard to come by. The house was there.

Waiting.

Freya hadn't ever run from anything in her life, and she wasn't going to start now, not when the thing in question was a house. Esther offered for her to move in, but she didn't. She'd had a host of reasons not to.

She didn't want to put Esther out. She didn't want to wake her by coming and going at all hours of the night. Though if she was honest with herself, part of the reason she hadn't moved in with Esther was because she had to face what had happened in the house.

Living there, as hard as it was, felt like the best way to stand up to her demons. To her parents.

Her house was far enough away from town that the city lights weren't visible. The dark around her house was impenetrable, so thick and heavy that it seemed to settle around her, at times not only blanketing her but choking her. She took a deep breath as she turned the key in the ignition. Her car roared to life and she glanced at the time before reversing out of her driveway—5:07.

It was a long drive to the police department, and her mind raced as she drove. As she pulled up to the building, she forced herself to relax her grip on the steering wheel. Her hands were cramped from squeezing it so tightly, and there was a throbbing in the back of her head that would only be silenced with a hit of caffeine.

She was early enough that she beat most of the staff in, including Kathy, the desk sergeant who handled walk-ins, and she waved her key card at the door to open it. The dispatchers and some overnight officers would be the only ones at work this early.

Pounding up the stairs to the fourth floor, she reached for the door, but it swung open first. Instinctively, her hand flicked to the gun on her hip, but she stopped herself. Anyone on the fourth floor wasn't going to be a danger.

"Freya." Brad took a step back. His eyes were wide, and she could see dark circles under them. The cowlick on the side of his head made it clear he hadn't showered this morning. He held a huge travel mug in one hand, and she could smell the dark coffee.

Her mouth watered.

"What are you doing here so early this morning?" Freya pushed past her detective and let the door slam shut behind her. Her eyes flicked around the fourth floor. A soft glow came from the break room, but there weren't any lights on in any of the offices yet. "Didn't you get any sleep?"

He laughed and shook his head. "Not really. It was hard to

shut my brain off, if I'm honest. But I probably got about the same amount you did."

"Good thing it's not a contest." She gestured at the mug in his hand. "That doesn't smell like the swill we brew up here on the fourth floor."

"This is from Over Easy." He held the travel mug up as if that would prove it. "They're not open yet, but I banged on the door and they took pity on me."

"They're good people." She ran a hand through her curls. "I ran into a dead end at the Amos Hotel last night. I'm going to see Lance about getting into Jolie's phone unless there was some headway last night."

"You mean Candy."

"Nope. Lance." Freya gave him a smile. "Forensics trickery. Trust me."

They walked down the hall to her office. She turned on the overhead light, banishing the shadows. A skittering sound from the tank on her credenza turned her head, and she watched as Cinnamon scurried into her hidey-hole. Leaning forward, she peeked in at the spider, then turned back to her desk.

"Since I couldn't sleep much last night, I poked around Steve's Facebook," Brad said.

She nodded, pleased. "You're the new social-media maven, you know that? Go on."

"You'll love this." He put his coffee on her desk and produced his phone. "I found some pictures of him and Millicent at a party. Jolie's in a bunch of them but always off to the side, like she didn't quite fit in."

"That makes sense. He made it clear he didn't like her and didn't want Millicent to go camping with her."

"The question is: would he kill her?"

Freya eyeballed his cup of coffee. "Hmm. You can dislike someone and not want them dead." She walked out of the office to the kitchenette, motioning for him to follow her. She needed caffeine.

Brad waited and watched as she measured out the ground beans, added water, and finally started the coffee maker. When the two were facing each other again, he replied, "True. And taking his fiancée out at the same time? That's the part I can't seem to get on board with. He hated Jolie, that much is clear, but from what I saw, he seemed"—he groped around for the word—"unwilling to get his hands dirty."

"Huh. Fair enough."

"But if he hated her that much, or thought she was going to hurt Millie, thought she might bring him down, he might have been willing to handle things himself," he said, leaning against the counter while she worked. "Stop her from hurting his fiancée; stop her from even being in their lives."

"Whoever killed her didn't just stop her; they punished her."

"What do you mean?"

"He bit her ear." Freya's back was to Brad when she spoke.

"Wait, what?"

"Her ear." Triumphantly, she grabbed a coffee mug and turned back to Brad. "There were bite marks on Jolie's ear, just like there were on Michelle Hawsey's a decade ago."

"Lovely," Brad murmured. "So what are your thoughts on this? The killer clearly walked through the woods and the river to get to the two girls. Steve... well, does he seem like the type to do that? Do you really think he could be the Fawn Lake Killer?"

"He was a wreck when I saw him yesterday. But no way is Mr. Boat Shoes going to pull on waders and go slogging through the forest to kill two women. I don't see it. But Michelle was killed ten years ago, and that would put Steve in his mid-twenties at the time of her murder." Freya paused. "He would be young but not so young he couldn't overpower someone. It's possible he's the Fawn Lake Killer, but it doesn't feel right. Not anymore."

"You know what they say?"

"That it's always the husband? Yeah, you and Candy need to stop quoting crime shows."

Brad smiled. "Not what I was going to say. I was going to say it's always the quiet ones, but you're right. I'll stop."

"I'm just not sure about him." Freya's voice was level as she poured herself a cup of coffee and took a sip. It burned her lips and her tongue, but she took another. Right now she needed the burst of energy it would give her, needed the jolt from the caffeine, and most importantly needed a moment to think before she said anything else.

"Let me think it through," Brad continued, clearly oblivious to Freya's internal struggle. His voice was quiet as he thought out loud. "He called the police yesterday morning and finally reported the two women missing even though they were supposed to be back the night before. Of course, the only thing he could tell us was that they'd gone camping in the forest and were supposed to already be home. I don't think he has any idea how big Clear Creek Forest is."

"It's more than five hundred acres, but it backs up to Pisgah, remember? And that's a thousand times bigger." Freya took another sip of her coffee.

"It's *that* big? Wow. Well, he was told that forest rangers would be on the lookout, but you saw how far off the beaten path the two of them were. There wasn't much of a chance that anyone was going to accidentally stumble on them, no matter how hard this guy crossed his fingers and wished for it."

"He still could have been involved. Wore some shabby clothes, snuck up after them. Or... Millicent and Jolie knowing him would explain why they didn't put up a fight."

Brad paused. Below them, they could hear the chatter and

movement of the dispatchers. "You know something about this guy that I don't."

"I know Steve's dad, Robert." Even to her own ears, her voice sounded flat. She cleared her throat and took another sip of coffee. It wasn't quite so hot now. "He's... well, let's just say he's not the sharpest tack in the box."

"Has Robert stayed out of trouble since you were in high school?"

"For the most part. He drinks a lot, knocks his woman around from time to time. He's definitely not the type of guy you'd want following you home if you'd gotten drunk at the bar."

"Steve doesn't seem like that." Brad chewed his lower lip for a moment.

"No, he doesn't, but I want to talk to both of them. I think —" Freya said, but whatever else she was going to say died in her throat when Candy appeared in the break-room door. Out of the three of them, she was the only one who looked like she'd gotten a decent night's sleep. In one hand she had a travel mug of coffee; the other clutched a box Freya recognized immediately.

"Esther says hi," Candy said, putting the box on the table and lifting the lid to grab a donut. "Holy cow, that woman can bake, Freya. I hope she never stops sending us treats."

"I'm sure she won't, especially if you keep stroking her ego like that." Freya watched as the two of them helped themselves to donuts. "Candy, here's the deal. I definitely need to talk to Steve Petit again—and Robert too. Have you made headway on Jolie's iPhone?"

Candy shook her head. "No, I can't get in it, and Apple won't unlock it for me, even with a warrant. They said they don't have the ability, so I'm going to reach out to a private company, Cellebrite. And more bad news—there wasn't a single fingerprint on the letter I received, or the wrapping paper on Esther's box. Our guy knows what he's doing."

"I have an idea. I need you to get her phone and go with me to see Lance. We can ask about the tongue while we're there. Brad, wrap up that list of anyone who would want to hurt Jolie and start looking into Millicent's socials. See if anything stands out. Steve sounds good for this, but I don't want to focus too much on him when it's entirely possible someone else killed those women." She paused, thinking.

"Maybe any woman whose husband she was sleeping with," Candy offered. "I stalked her on Instagram after Brad found her. She has a ton of followers, and I recognized some of the names. You'd think you wouldn't be that stupid, to follow the Instagram of the woman you're sleeping with, but apparently not." The eyeroll told Freya exactly what her detective thought about those people's social-media use. "So dumb," she said, repeating the gesture. "I didn't see anything about this camping trip though. It was mostly work stuff."

"Well, we'll just have to get out there and beat the bushes. Find something. Brad has done a lot of work with Jolie's Instagram. The followers are a good idea, but I want us to dig deeper." She turned to Brad. "If you have time to dig into any of those borderline comments on Jolie's posts, like we discussed yesterday, great. But first, I want you to check on the search warrant for Steve's job. We need to know if he was really working Sunday night. I have a feeling he's hiding something."

Brad nodded, and Freya took a donut. The toast she'd had for breakfast wasn't enough.

"We have a long day ahead of us. Let's go."

Brad gave her a mock salute, and Candy muttered that she'd be right back with Jolie's iPhone. Before she returned, however, Freya's phone rang.

"Captain Sinclair," she said. The number was local and looked familiar, but she didn't have it saved.

"Captain Sinclair, this is Cecelia Gardner. I work at the hospital." A slight pause, then when she spoke again, her voice was muffled, as if she were cupping her hand around the receiver. "There's a note here from yesterday about some man trying to break into the morgue. We're supposed to call you if that man comes back. He's here, yanking on the door and yelling. Hurry."

TWENTY

Freya beat Candy to the hospital's front desk, but only barely. A blonde woman stood there, a frown creasing her brow. She held a pen and twisted her fingers around it, only pausing when she looked up and saw Freya and Candy.

Relief washed over her face. "Oh, you made it, good! I'm Cecelia." Her voice was low, and she turned, glancing over her shoulder. "He's back there—or was. I didn't want to approach him in case he freaked out at me."

"Smart. What's he wearing?" Freya looked past Cecelia but didn't see anyone in the hall.

"Umm, jeans. A black hoodie. Black sneakers." Cecelia chewed her lower lip. "I didn't get a good look at his face, but I'm pretty sure it's the same guy. Has to be, right? How many people would be trying to get into the morgue like that?"

Freya rapped her knuckles on the woman's desk and walked around it, listening carefully, looking for any sign of movement. This early in the morning, the hospital was quiet. It wasn't time for the rush of visitors to stream through the front doors, and she was the only one walking down the hall.

Behind her, she heard Candy speaking to Cecelia. "Lance isn't in yet?"

"No, not yet. What if he had been and the door was unlocked? What does he even want down there?" Cecelia's voice trailed off, but Freya didn't turn back around. Whatever she had to say, she could say to Candy. There was no doubt the younger detective could handle it.

Her shoes squeaked softly on the clean floor. Overhead, huge lights made the hall uncomfortably bright. The hospital smelled clean, but the scent was overwhelming. The door to the morgue was only a few feet away, and she moved slower.

Since the door wasn't flush with the wall, it created a small alcove where a person could easily hide. Freya stepped out from the wall so she didn't run smack into Nathan if he were standing there. One hand rested on her taser; the other she held out in front of her a little bit.

She took a deep breath. Stepped out and forward.

Nothing.

Nathan, if it was him, was gone.

Freya exhaled hard, then glanced over her shoulder.

Candy walked towards her, her jaw set. Her eyes flicked at the morgue door, then she looked at Freya. "We'll need to split up."

Freya nodded. "If he went up to another floor, then finding him is going to be a complete nightmare, so we'll have to hope he stayed on the first floor but left this area. I want you going along the hall to the right. Make sure you search every room or at least check every door."

"That leaves the parking garage for you."

"Yep." Freya itched to get a move on. The longer they stood there talking through what they were going to do, the more likely it was that Nathan would get away. "We'll meet back here. Radio if you need help."

"You too." Candy threw the words over her shoulder as she

turned and hurried down the right hall. Freya took a deep breath and spun around, going in the opposite direction.

The hall leading to the parking garage was a lot shorter than the one she'd sent Candy down. It had fewer doors too, but she checked each one. The first was locked. The second opened into a supply closet.

Her heart pounded as she reached the third door. Unlike the others she'd passed, it was open a crack. She hesitated outside it then toed it open, already reaching around to turn on the light.

The light clicked on, and she blinked, stepping into a storage room. Huge metal shelving units lined the walls, each of them groaning with supplies. The shelf closest to her held row after row of Lysol and paper towels. She let her eyes flick over them, seeing but not really paying attention to what was in front of her.

Why had the door been left open?

To her left stood half a dozen cleaning carts. Each of them was freshly restocked with cloths and supplies. She took a step into the room to investigate more when someone spoke.

"You can't be in here." The man sounded angry, and she whipped around, her hand tightening around the grip of her taser. "This isn't a public space."

"Captain Sinclair with the Fawn Lake Police Department," she said, letting go of her taser and touching the badge on her hip. "Your door was open, and I'm looking for someone."

He had the decency to blush. "I had to run to the bathroom. Thought I could leave it unlocked while I did that." A lanyard hung around his neck with a name badge. While he spoke, Freya glanced at it, then back up at him to confirm he was who he said he was.

"Terry Archer," he said, extending a hand. "Who are you looking for?"

"His name is Nathan Caldwell," Freya said, shaking it, then

stepping out of the way. "Have you seen anyone around here this morning who wasn't supposed to be here? He's wearing a black hoodie and jeans."

"Haven't seen anyone like that," Terry said, walking over to one of the carts and pulling it closer to the door. "If you'll excuse me, though, I need to finish packing these carts for the day shift."

"Of course," she said. "Sorry for—"

Someone hit her from behind. Freya took a step forward and reached up, bracing her hands against the wall as she slammed into it. Pain shot up her arms, and she cried out, turning to see who'd knocked into her.

There was a blur of black as Nathan raced past her and out the door.

"Holy crap, are you okay?" Terry was right there, already pulling on her shoulder to try to turn her around. "He must have been hiding behind some of the cleaning supplies. Was that your guy?"

Freya didn't answer. Instead, she yanked her radio from her hip. "Candy, he's this way. Turn back!" She didn't wait for a response, already running out the door as she clipped it back on her belt.

In the hall, she paused, looking down back towards the main lobby. That was the direction Candy would be coming from. No sign of Nathan.

To the parking garage, then.

Her hip screamed at her as she started running, her eyes locked on the door at the end of the hall. A flash of black outside spurred her on, and she pumped her arms, hitting the door at a full run. Instead of opening, it stayed resolutely closed, and Freya screamed, pounding her fists against the glass.

"What happened?" Candy called out as she raced down the hall towards Freya. "Are you okay? Did he hurt you?"

Freya shook her head. "No," she said, putting her shoulder

into the door and shoving as hard as she could. "Not really. But he moved a trash can in front of the door."

The trash can in question was industrial size, black, with a grate across the top to prevent raccoons and opossums from scavenging during the night.

"Help me," Freya grunted, ramming her shoulder back into the door.

Candy did, moving to right behind Freya's back. She grunted as she pushed into the door with her shoulder. "He's freakishly strong, huh?" she asked.

"Drugs," Freya offered. "I'll bet anything it was drugs."

"Probably. On the count of three, ready?"

On three, they pushed together, Freya stepping through the door once it opened enough. The parking garage smelled dirty, like exhaust fumes. She inhaled, trying to catch her breath, then turned to the right.

"You go left!" she called to Candy before breaking into a run, her arms pumping, her head moving as if on a swivel as she searched for any sight of Nathan.

Half an hour later, they met back at the door. Freya had a stitch in her side from running between cars, searching for him. She grabbed her thighs and bent over, sucking huge breaths of air into her lungs.

"He'll be back," Candy sighed. "If he wants to get into the morgue that badly, I don't think one run-in with us will be enough to dissuade him."

"Probably. But at least we have this. Nathan dropped it in his mad dash to get away." Freya straightened up, waving something in the air. Her heart and mind both raced. Nathan had gotten away, but Candy was right. He'd be back.

Candy took the piece of paper from Freya. "That's Jolie."

"Yep." Freya looked at the photo. It was ripped in half, so

whoever had their arm draped around Jolie's shoulders was missing. Jolie was young in the photo, happy. Her hair pulled back in a ponytail, a huge grin on her face. But the girl in the photo grinning at the camera was currently lying in the morgue.

"Why would he have this?"

"That's what I intend to find out as soon as we can catch the guy." She grabbed her radio from her hip. "Central, this is three-zero-one. I need officers dispatched to the hospital to look for a suspicious person." After rattling off Nathan's information, she turned back to Candy. "Please tell me you didn't lose Jolie's phone in all of that."

"I have it right here," Candy said, patting her pocket. "Now tell me: why did I need to bring it to see Lance?"

"Jolie has all her fingers," Freya said, still breathing hard. "You'll want to see this."

TWENTY-ONE

"Heard the police department has a new track program." Lance didn't look up from his clipboard until Freya took his coffee cup and downed what was left in the bottom.

"You should see us run hurdles," she said, putting his cup back down. She gagged. "Gross. You'd think I would have learned my lesson by now about drinking your swill."

"The caffeine will help you run faster." Lance put his clipboard down and sighed. "And it will help me survive whatever this day brings. Did you have an opportunity to chat with the president of my fan club?"

"He's faster than we are," Candy said. She pulled Jolie's phone from her pocket and held it in the air. "But Freya said you could work some magic with this."

"What's that?" Lance took the phone and pressed the main button to turn it on. "Locked." He handed the phone back to Candy and winked at Freya. "Oh, I have a pretty good idea I know what you're thinking. Which woman does that belong to?"

"Jolie. You get the saline ready and I'll make another pot of coffee."

Freya busied herself doing just that while Lance filled a syringe with saline and snapped on a pair of gloves. When he pulled open Jolie's morgue drawer, she and Candy joined him at her side.

"Do you know what we're doing?" he asked Candy. She shook her head, and he grinned, holding up the syringe and depressing the plunger a bit to make some of the saline leak out. "So this phone is locked, and judging by the fact that Freya's staring at me like I'm going to work magic, you two can't get it open."

"No need to get a big head, Lance," Freya said. "If I had saline at home, I'd do this myself."

"It's not rocket science," he agreed. "Jolie's fingerprints will probably be a bit dried out, so I'm simply going to extract some fluid from her body, run a catheter into her wrist, and inject the fluid into her finger to plump it back up. Then it will be easy for you to press it against her phone to unlock it. It's called thanato-practical processing."

"This is awesome," Candy said. "Let's do it."

She and Freya were silent while Lance worked. He took his time, stopping when the ridges in her fingerprint were visible but not overexpanded.

"Alright. Phone." Lance held Jolie's hand in one hand and took the phone from Candy with the other. Carefully he turned it and pressed the finger against the unlock button.

Freya held her breath.

A soft click, then the phone screen lit up.

"You did it!" Candy snatched the phone from him. "Honestly, that seemed like TV magic. *CSI* or something."

"You can't believe everything you see on TV," Lance said, "but it is a pretty cool trick." He covered Jolie back up with the sheet and slid her morgue drawer shut. After he disposed of the syringe and removed his gloves, he poured himself another cup of coffee. "Is that all you two needed?"

"That'll help Candy out," Freya said. "But I want to talk to you about the tongue."

"Oh yes. The tongue." Another pair of gloves and another morgue drawer. Candy stepped out of the way, tapping on Jolie's phone. "I haven't had a lot of time to look at it yet." He glanced at Freya. "Suit up."

She did, snapping on a pair of gloves. When Lance picked up the tongue, she was right there, ready to take it if need be.

"Jolie had a piercing as recently as the weekend," Freya said. "But I didn't see a hole on this. Is it possible it would have closed up that quickly? Maybe she took the piercing out and that's why we don't see any evidence of it?"

"If the piercing was really new then yes, it can close up really quickly. Any idea how long she'd had it?"

"A long time, judging by her photos."

"Then we'd probably be able to see some mark. Some proof of a hole." He handed the tray the tongue sat on to Freya and jerked his chin towards his desk. "Come on. It's microscope time."

She followed him to his desk and waited while Lance set everything up. He took the tray from her and put it under the microscope, the bright light shining right where the piercing would be.

While he looked, she watched Candy. Her detective had pulled a small notebook from her pocket and was busy making scribbles in it. Rather than interrupt her, she turned back to Lance.

"No hole," he finally said, turning off the microscope. "That's my official stance."

Freya's heart sank. "So it's not Jolie's."

"I'd wager not. Sounds to me like you have another victim to hunt down." He pulled off his gloves and tossed them in the trash. "You got any leads?"

"Funny you should ask that. I'm going to head on over to

Millicent's fiancé's house and have a little chat with him. See if he knows more than he's letting on."

"You know what they say about the husband—"

"Not you too." Freya rolled her eyes and glanced at Candy. "What have you found over there, Candy?"

"Well, I already changed her passcode so we don't have to do this again to unlock her phone. Besides that, so far I've been in her social media and it's all the same stuff we've seen already. No secret accounts or anything. I'm looking through her pictures for any with Nathan."

"Nathan dropped a photo of Jolie when we were chasing him," Freya told Lance. "Well, half a photo. Whoever else was in it with her got ripped out."

"The plot thickens." He leaned against the counter.

"Something like that."

"Oh, look at this!" Candy exclaimed, bringing the phone over to Freya. "You can't tell me this isn't weird. Look, right here. Look who was sending her instant messages as recently as two weeks ago."

"Robert Petit." Freya blinked hard at the screen.

"Yep, but that's not the best part. It's what the messages said." Candy flicked the screen to scroll. "He's telling her to back off."

"Back off what?" Freya frowned and glanced at the phone, but Candy was swiping faster now, the words flying by in a blur.

"His son. She was blackmailing Steve."

TWENTY-TWO

Freya barely saw the scenery as she drove to Steve's house. It was her favorite time of day, when everything appeared to be glowing thanks to the sunrise, but she was too focused to enjoy it.

The killer was out of control. Two dead bodies and a tongue that didn't belong to either of them. She had to find them.

It rankled her that Nathan had managed to get away. That last moment when she'd seen him jump out of the parking deck window to land ten feet below on the sidewalk, she'd known she couldn't follow. But, like a gift, the photo he'd had in his pocket had fluttered down to land at her feet.

She wasn't going to look that gift horse in the mouth. So Nathan had half a photo of Jolie and was obsessed with getting into the morgue. Steve hated Jolie, thought she was a terrible influence on his fiancée. And as for Robert?

Brad had mentioned the followers on Jolie's Instagram but, at the time, hadn't recognized Robert. Now that they had access to Jolie's phone though, they knew he'd been in contact with their victim until recently. He also had a violent history.

Freya didn't believe in coincidences.

She pressed down harder on the gas.

Her phone rang, and she almost ignored it but swiped across her screen at the last second. Chief's voice filled her car, flowing from its speakers.

"What's this I hear about you putting a personal detail on Esther?"

She gripped the steering wheel. Counted to three. Only when she was sure she wouldn't blow up at the man did she respond. "She was targeted by the killer, and I need to make sure she's safe."

"You can't take someone off the road to sit at her house."

Even though he couldn't see her, she shrugged. "Fine. Call it an off-duty and take it out of my pay. I'm more than happy to cover the private security to keep her safe."

He sighed, the sound loud. "You're too close to this."

"It's Esther. Of course I'm close to this."

"What I mean is you're going to make a mistake."

"Not happening." She gunned it through a yellow light, ignoring the honking that followed her.

"I'm not going to ask what you did to get honked at," Chief said, "but you need to cut it out, Sinclair. Step back from this."

"Remember how I solved the case of the little girls getting killed?"

Chief didn't respond.

"I proved myself to you. I can handle this, Chief." Her heart pounded, blood rushing to her head. Both of her palms were sweaty, and she let go of the steering wheel, wiped them on her pants, then gripped it again. "As soon as I find this guy I'll get rid of the detail on Esther, but having someone keep her safe isn't optional. I need to know she's okay."

"We have no reason to suspect the killer is going to target her."

"Except he did, didn't he? He sent her a tongue, so I don't know what you'd call that if not *targeting*."

"He's trying his hardest to get under your skin, and you're letting him. You need to hand the reins over to someone else, Sinclair. I mean it."

"Not going to happen." Her finger hovered over the red *end call* button. Sure, Chief would know right away she'd hung up on him, and yeah, he'd be pissed, but at least she'd be able to concentrate. "I'm onto something, Chief. Trust me."

Another heavy sigh, like she was some errant child and he could barely stand to put up with her any longer. "Sinclair," he said, dragging her name out like it was a warning.

"Trust me." Her self-control failed, and she hit the little red button. Blessed silence filled her Jeep, and she sighed, trying to push the conversation from her mind. Everything at work was personal. When an officer or detective loved the people in town like she did, every slight against them was personal, was something to be handled, was something they couldn't ignore.

And now this killer had dragged Esther into it.

Freya would do anything to end this.

Her mind raced as she drove, and she approached the guard house quickly, barely tapping the brakes before the arm was raised. After waving at the attendant, she pressed down harder on the gas.

Barely slowing down, she pulled into Steve's driveway. It was packed with cars, and she paused for just a moment. There might be a crowd there. But it didn't matter. People were already beginning to gossip about the man who might have killed the woman he loved. She'd seen it online, heard it whispered about by some of the officers.

Steve had to know this visit was coming. And even if it took him by surprise, Robert shouldn't be shocked.

Making a fist, she eschewed the doorbell and banged on the door, then stepped back, her arms crossed on her chest. Candy had taken the phone back to the department to keep digging through it, and Freya was alone. She felt the need to look as intimidating as possible, and she rolled her shoulders back. There was a moment of silence, then another, then the door swung open and a small bent woman with gray hair tilted her face to the side to look up at her.

"I need to speak to Steve."

"Steve's not here." The woman's eyes flicked to the badge on Freya's hip, then back up to her face. "I can tell him you came by perhaps?"

"It's imperative I speak to him. Now. Where is he?" She leaned to the side, glancing past the woman. If she could see past her, see Steve watching her from inside the house, then she'd be able to call him out. Make him come talk to her.

Because it was very likely he was in there, wasn't it? Watching her. He'd probably spent the day gloating about the tongue, gloating about what he'd done to not only Millicent but also two other women.

Worse than that? He could be hiding another body this very minute. She did have a tongue to deal with after all.

Anger washed over her.

"He's at the funeral home with his father, picking out Millicent's casket." The woman blinked, her eyes wet with tears. "My grandson didn't do anything—you need to know that. He wouldn't. He loved Millie; we all did. Whoever hurt her and that other woman, you need to find them, but you won't be able to if you keep thinking Steve's the murderer."

Freya heard her words but let them roll off her back as she spun away from the door and hurried down the porch stairs. There was only one funeral home in town—Blue Ridge Funeral Home. If this woman was telling the truth, that's where Steve was.

And Robert as well. *Could they have been working together?*

In her car, she paused, the key already in the ignition, her hand ready to turn it. What about Steve's grandmother? Even the elderly will lie to save the people they love. Was it possible that both Robert and Steve were in the house, trying to figure out their next move? There was a chance, but the only way she was going to be able to get into the house to see for herself would be to come back with a warrant. Fat chance of getting that quickly enough. Still, she dialed Candy as she backed out of the driveway.

"I want a warrant to get into Steve Petit's house. And Robert's. I'm on my way to the funeral home, and I need you to start working on it."

"Of course, but what do you want me to put on the warrants?" Candy sounded confused—warrants had to be for something specific. "What are you looking for?"

"We've been too easy on both of them. Steve's at the funeral home with his father right now, and I'm on my way there. I want a search warrant for the knife used to kill Jolie."

Candy exhaled hard. "Okay. I'll get started on it."

"Send an officer to meet me there, would you? I'm bringing them both in." Freya hung up. It was a jerk move, but the only thing that mattered right now was getting to the funeral home and talking to Steve. He was with Robert, and the old man might be whispering in his ear, telling him how to hide evidence of what they'd done.

She pressed down harder on the gas.

Less than ten minutes later, she screeched into the funeral home parking lot on two wheels. It was just beginning to mist, the light rain coating her windshield as she parked and settling on her shoulders when she stepped out. Large concrete steps led up to the main building, and on them stood Steve and Robert.

Freya could barely keep her temper in check as she stormed across the parking lot. She was halfway up the stairs before the two men turned to her, their expressions darkening with rage.

"Detective," Steve said, stepping a little in front of his father. "Is there something I can help you with?"

"You can come clean with me about what really happened this weekend, Petit." Barely sparing Robert a glance, she focused on Steve. Robert was involved, but Steve was the weak link. He was the one who had just lost his fiancée and had his daddy trying to protect him from Jolie. If one of them were going to slip up, it would be him. She still had to question Robert, but one thing at a time. Keeping her voice soft, she continued. "It's one thing to kill Millicent and Jolie because you didn't want to marry your fiancée, or you were angry at her best friend, but it's another entirely to escalate. Why didn't you report Millicent missing Sunday night? Why wait until Monday morning?"

He was already shaking his head before she stopped speaking. "I was busy. Lost track of time."

"Who's your alibi?"

"Work, remember?"

"Right. *Work*. The law firm that so conveniently won't speak to us about what you were doing Sunday night. Tell me, what *were* you doing at work on a Sunday evening?"

"It doesn't matter."

Freya barked out a laugh. "Oh, I think it does! You're coming with me. We're going to the station so you can answer some questions."

A car pulled in behind her, and she glanced over her shoulder. Good. Another officer. Splitting up Robert and Steve was the best idea for right now.

"I'm planning Millie's funeral." Steve's jaw was tight. He looked ready to fight. Honestly, Freya wouldn't have minded throwing a few punches if it meant it would get rid of the sick feeling growing in her stomach that she might have made a mistake by giving Steve the benefit of the doubt.

"Your grandmother can take over planning, I'm sure. The

station. Now." Without thinking about what she was doing, she reached to her hip for her handcuffs. Her fingers rested on the cool metal. "Listen, Petit, I will happily put you in handcuffs and drag you to the station if that's what it takes. Or you can ride with me, act like you're happy to come answer some questions. Your choice. Either way, this is happening now."

"You can't take him." Robert stepped forward. His eyes flashed as he stared at Freya. When he exhaled, there was the faint scent of rum. Time hadn't been kind to Robert. He needed to shave, and he really needed to hit the gym. Next to his clean-cut son, he looked a mess. Honestly, next to Steve, anyone would look a mess.

Diamond's words about how nice Jolie's client looked echoed in her head. Steve fit the description perfectly. Robert? Not so much.

"I can do whatever I want, Robert, and you're coming too. I want both of you in interview rooms to discuss exactly what happened to Jolie. History does tend to repeat itself. Where were you Sunday night?"

Robert sucked in a breath. He glanced at Steve, who was staring at his father like he couldn't wait to hear the answer either.

"Dad?"

"I was at the bar. Anyone can vouch for me." Robert glared at Freya.

"Yeah? Is that where you first met Jolie? Or did you find her on social media and reach out to her there?"

He blinked, then his face hardened. "I didn't kill those women, and neither did my boy. You're looking at the wrong guys."

"Maybe so," Freya said, grabbing Steve by the elbow and pulling him with her down the steps. "But nobody would be surprised if I was right, Robert, least of all me." She glanced at the officer standing to her right. "Bring him with you."

Freya and Steve rode to the police station in silence. She was seething, her teeth grinding together so hard her jaw hurt. She had to focus on making each turn, on keeping the car between the lines, on being sure that she stopped at every stop sign and red light.

She managed a nod at Kathy when they walked into the police department. She led Steve up the stairs and straight to an interview room where they wouldn't be disturbed. Chief was coming down the hall, carrying a cup of coffee, and he raised his eyebrows at the sight of them.

"I'll send in Ellinger," he said, then disappeared.

Freya didn't want a partner there with her, didn't think it was necessary. Still, maybe it was a good idea. Maybe having Candy there would keep her focused and make sure she didn't do anything stupid.

TWENTY-THREE

The interview room at the police department wasn't designed with comfort in mind, but it was nicer than perps deserved. The chairs were padded, supportive. Books and movies made out like all the chairs in interview rooms had one leg shorter just to mess with suspects, but that wasn't true. The floor was tile, in case someone threw up or spat to make a point, the lights over-head bright enough to ensure the interviewing detective didn't miss anything on the suspect's face.

Soft classical music from someone's office filled the hall, but with the door closed, the room was silent. Freya stared at Steve, who sat across from her, his hands folded on the table between them, his gaze unblinking. Candy was on her way, if Chief was to be believed, and even though she was itching to get started, she wasn't about to tick off her superior even more by jumping the gun and starting the interview solo.

Besides, there wasn't anything like some silent time in the interview room together to make a suspect start questioning whether they'd been completely honest about everything. Steve reached up and wiped his hand across his brow. Freya grinned.

A soft knock at the door took her attention for a moment.

Candy walked in, her face pale. Putting an open folder down in front of Freya, she sat wordlessly, her hands in her lap.

"That's a warrant for us to search your house, looking specifically for the murder weapon used to kill Jolie," Freya said finally, turning her gaze to the man across from her. "The judge was more than happy to sign it, considering everything we're up against."

"You won't find anything there that will prove I hurt either of them." Steve spoke through gritted teeth. "The more time you waste looking at me as the suspect, the easier it will be for the real killer to escape. You need to see that."

"What I see is a man sitting across from me with anger running through his veins." Freya flipped the folder closed. She couldn't wait to get inside Steve's house; couldn't wait to search for the murder weapon. Millicent's DNA would be all over the place, but all she needed was the knife.

It would have Jolie's DNA on it. If Steve hadn't dumped it —which was a possibility—Freya would find it. Then she'd end this and lock him up.

Nobody could stand being blackmailed for very long. There was no doubt in Freya's mind that Steve might have snapped, that Jolie could have pushed him too far.

"You don't have an alibi for Sunday night. You were also closest to Millicent, and one of the last people to see her alive." Spreading her hands in the air as if to prove she wasn't hiding anything, Freya shrugged. "Our hands are tied."

"*I wasn't on the mountain Sunday.*" Steve leaned forward. New beads of sweat had popped out along his hairline but he didn't wipe them away. "I promise you."

"We don't deal in promises." Candy's voice was firm.

Freya was surprised. It was always interesting to watch someone newer at the job handle a suspect. Candy's jaw was tight, and Freya could see the tension in her forehead. She wasn't the only one who thought Steve might have killed the two women then.

"We deal in facts, so unless your job is suddenly going to confirm your alibi that you were working Sunday night, I'd suggest you go ahead and hold out your wrists so we can cuff you and keep you safely out of the way while we search your house."

Steve's mouth fell open, and he looked between the two detectives. Finally, there was fear in his eyes. Freya smiled to herself.

She loved to see it.

Steve wore an analog watch, and the ticking sound of the second hand was loud in the silence. Freya started to count. She'd let herself get to twenty and then call it. Candy could go with her to search the house, and they'd let Brad know what was going on.

Ten.

Steve shifted in his seat. His face was pale, and he reached up, looping his finger in the collar of his shirt and tugging on it, like he couldn't breathe.

Twelve.

When Freya glanced at Candy, she hadn't moved. Her eyes were still locked on Steve like she was daring him to try something stupid. Her gun was on her hip closest to Freya, her hand resting on her thigh right by it.

Eighteen.

"I wasn't alone." The admission burst from Steve like he had been trying to hold it back and no longer could. A dam had broken in his mind and now the words spilled out. "I had company. An alibi. I wasn't alone. I... I was with someone."

Freya didn't give the man time to think about what he had just said. "Who?"

"Listen, I promised her I wouldn't drag her into this, that

her name wouldn't be mentioned. You have no idea how upsetting this has been for her."

"Upsetting because you two were having an affair and then Millicent ends up dead? Yeah, I can see how that would be real upsetting." Leaning forward, Freya planted her hands on the table.

"Did you kill your fiancée because you were in love with someone else and couldn't man up and break it off?" Candy's voice had an edge to it. If looks could kill, Steve would be dead.

"It's not like that." Steve dropped his head into his hands and let out a low moan. He sounded like an animal in a cage that has finally accepted there isn't any way out. "She's not... Millie didn't know about her, but it wasn't anything like that. You have to believe me: I wouldn't ever hurt Millie. I wasn't ready for her to know the truth yet, but I was going to tell her."

"Who in the world are you so willing to protect?" Freya's mind raced as she tried to get ahead of what Steve was going to say. "This woman must be really important to you if you're willing to put your neck on the line for her."

Steve hung his head, and Freya knew the man had been lying from day one. He was just like his father, willing to use other people to get what he wanted, and now he'd been caught. Having a mistress made him look bad enough. Refusing to tell the two of them who it was made things even worse.

"Can you keep it out of the papers?"

When Steve finally raised his face to look at them, all Freya saw was the shell of a man, absolutely broken. His mouth was pressed in a thin line, his eyes weary. His well-dressed exterior didn't match what was going on inside.

"I can't promise anything until we know who you were with," Freya said. "But if there's a good reason to keep it quiet, and it doesn't interfere with our investigation, then we'll do our best to protect whoever it is."

Candy inhaled hard. "We know about your daughter," she said.

Steve's mouth dropped open.

Candy continued, not looking away from him. "We read messages that referenced her. She's who you were with, isn't she? You're not having an affair; you're hiding a child."

"Yes." He paused. "I was with my daughter. Millie didn't know about her. Most people don't. I'm older, right? And I have a child. I was going to tell Millie before the wedding obviously, but I just never had a chance."

Freya exhaled hard then turned to look at Candy, who arched her eyebrow and nodded.

"You need to tell us everything," Freya said.

Steve's shoulders sagged. "She's fifteen and argues with her mother almost every night. I just... She'd called, telling me that she'd gotten in another fight with her mom, begging me to let her come over. What was I supposed to do—not be there for my daughter when she needed me?" He shook his head ruefully. "Not a chance. She's everything to me."

Freya exhaled and closed her eyes, leaning back in her chair as she tried her best to wrap her mind around this new information. Next to her, Candy was also silent.

"She's fifteen?" Freya finally asked. "So how old were you when you had her?"

"Nineteen." Steve lifted his chin as he spoke, daring the two of them to comment on how young he'd been when he became a father.

"We're going to need to talk to her." Steve nodded but wouldn't look at her. "We'll have to make sure she can corroborate what you're saying and will need some proof. Timestamps of texts, pictures—"

"Here." Steve pulled his phone from his pocket, swiped it on, and handed it over. "You can look at the pictures I took of the two of us. We were goofing off. Check the date and times on them. I wasn't on that mountain doing anything to Millie and Jolie. I was with my daughter. I lost track of time and then thought I should come clean with Millie anyway, that it might be the day to do that. We waited at the house, but Millie didn't show up... I called her, but it went to voicemail. Jolie... she could have easily convinced Millie to camp one more night, and I thought Millie would be home by the morning. And she wasn't, so I called you guys."

"What's her name?" Candy asked. Freya was busy flipping through pictures on the phone, and she grabbed a pen and paper from the table. "I'll need her name, phone number, and address."

Steve rattled off the information then sighed again, taking the phone back from Freya when she handed it over. "But now do you see that I didn't do it? I wouldn't kill Millie. I hid Charlotte from her, but I wasn't going to forever. You have to believe me."

She did believe him. Steve wasn't a great guy, not by a long shot. Hiding a child from his fiancée was a jerk move, but that didn't mean he was a murderer.

"Tell me everything about the blackmail. You and your dad got pretty heated about it, especially in his DMs to her," Freya said.

The change in topic surprised Steve. He straightened back up, his brows crashing together. "You seem to know everything."

"I know a lot of things," Freya said. "And I'm about to walk into the interview room next door and talk to your dad, so you better clear some things up for me before I do that."

He was already shaking his head. "It's so stupid," he said, rubbing his temples. "Jolie... she saw me out with Charlotte and asked if Millie knew. I told her the truth; asked her to keep quiet."

"Did she tell Millicent?" Candy asked.

Steve shook his head. "No, but then she started texting me.

Asking for money. I sent her some, which was stupid, but I didn't feel like I had a choice. She stopped for a bit but then kept reaching out. Kept pushing."

"So your dad got involved," Freya said.

"I didn't know he did, I swear!" Steve sounded panicked. "All I know is that she just... stopped. Said she was moving, then never texted again. The camping trip was supposed to be the last time I ever had to deal with her in our lives."

"How much did she take you for?"

Steve groaned. "Just over ten grand."

"Ouch. That's why you hated her so much. It's why you didn't want her anywhere near Millicent, isn't it?" Freya leaned back in her chair, exhaling hard. "You didn't want Millicent to know."

"I was going to tell her about Charlotte, I promise." Steve scrubbed a hand down his face. "I screwed up by not being honest with her from the beginning, but I promise you, I was going to come clean."

She shook her head. It had looked like a simple, although grotesque, murder. Now, though, there were so many moving pieces it was becoming more and more convoluted.

"What are you going to do with me? I can't sit in here. I need to plan Millie's funeral." His eyes were wide, his cheeks red. "Please. I didn't do anything to Millie. I loved her."

"You're going to sit here while we figure things out. I'm going to go talk to your dad now, so if there's anything else you want to tell me before I do that, now's the time."

Steve didn't speak. He stared at her, panic written across his face. "Are you arresting me?"

"We're holding you," she corrected.

"Have Brad get in touch with Charlotte," she said to Candy, standing up and stretching. "We've got another interview."

TWENTY-FOUR

Before walking into the interview room, Freya took a deep breath. Held it. Exhaled slowly.

She wasn't afraid of Robert Petit. Hadn't been, not even when she'd seen him attack that girl up in the woods and had intervened. Hated him? Sure. Loathed him? Definitely.

But been afraid of him? Never, and she wasn't about to start now.

Candy lightly touched her on the shoulder. "Hey, you okay? You ready to do this?"

"I'm more than ready." Freya gave her detective a small smile, double-checked that the camera clipped to the front of her shirt was recording, and entered the room.

Robert didn't respond to their presence. He stared at the table between them, a frown furrowing his brow. It wasn't until both Candy and Freya had sat down with him that he gave his head a little shake as if to clear away his thoughts and looked up at them.

"Why am I here?" In addition to smelling like a bar, his voice was of someone who had smoked a pack a day for most of his life. Each word sounded like it passed through gravel before leaving his lips. "Can't you see our family is grieving? What right do you have to bring me here? I should ask for a lawyer."

"And you're well within your right to do that." It was the last thing Freya wanted, but she still waited, giving him time to make good on his threat. When he didn't, she continued. "Steve's alibi is looking pretty good for Sunday night. But yours is... what? The bar?"

Robert nodded.

"And you paid with a credit card?"

"Cash." There was a smudge on the table, and he rubbed at it before looking back up at her.

"That's convenient. Listen, Robert, I'm a busy woman, so why don't we get right to it? You knew Jolie."

Robert blinked but didn't deny it.

"Not only that, but you were involved in trying to stop Jolie from blackmailing Steve any more than she already had." Freya spoke slowly, giving every word plenty of weight. "Do you want to know what I think happened?"

"Entertain me."

"I think you found out Jolie was blackmailing Steve. You may or may not have liked Millicent—I haven't sussed that out yet—but you love your son, and you probably love Charlotte too, don't you?"

He nodded. Freya didn't mention that Charlotte wasn't much younger than the woman Robert had attempted to rape when they were younger. No doubt he'd already thought about that.

"So you're probably willing to do anything for the two of them, am I right? Steve's not going to get his hands dirty, but you've already been in jail before. What's one more stint?"

"I didn't hurt Jolie." Robert leaned forward, his eyes locked on Freya. It was as if Candy didn't exist. "I wouldn't."

"Ahh, but you would. Let's not pretend you've always been

a saint, Robert." Freya turned to Candy. "Feel like reading us a little story, Detective Ellinger?"

Candy responded by unlocking Jolie's iPhone. A few taps later and she glanced up at Freya. When Freya nodded, she started reading.

"'I don't care if you're dead, you'll leave my son and grand-daughter alone.'"

"Ouch," Freya said. "That doesn't sound great for you, Robert. What else, Candy?"

Candy nodded. Flicked the screen to scroll. "In response to her asking for more money, you said, 'Watch out—greedy snitches end up dead.'"

Freya tapped the table to get Robert's attention. "Care to explain those?"

"I was upset." He spread his hands on the table. They were large, his fingers thick and strong. Freya glanced at them, then back up at the man. "You don't know what it's like."

"What what's like? Why don't you explain it to us, Robert?"

"To know that someone is trying to hurt your family." He glared at her. "And to know that your child is so good he'll never take care of things on his own. It's not Steve's fault that Jolie's insane."

Freya narrowed her eyes. "Ooh, I really don't like it when men call women insane. Try again."

"Fine. She was *off her rocker*. She thought she could milk our family for all we're worth, but I wasn't about to let that happen. Steve made a mistake giving her any money to begin with. No way was I going to let him continue with that."

Freya leaned back in her chair and watched him. She'd dealt with a lot of liars in her career. A lot of killers. A lot of rapists. No way did she think Robert was telling her the entire truth. There was something more there, something he was keeping hidden.

And she had every intention of finding out what it was.

"Fine. Say you didn't kill Jolie, which I don't really believe for a second. Then who did?"

Robert scoffed. "I'm surprised you want me to do your job for you."

"I'm just asking you to look at it from a criminal's perspective," she said, and his face hardened. "You've never been on this side of the interrogation table before, but you have been on that side a few times. Use your brain, Robert."

"Probably one of the guys she was screwing for money."

"A John? Okay, let's consider that. Then why kill Millicent?"

He threw up his hands. "I have no clue! They probably had a better motive than I would have. Steve loves her. Why would I want to make my son suffer?"

"Because you didn't really like her." Freya watched him, looking for any sign she was on the right path. "Because you thought Charlotte's mother was a better fit for him."

He rolled his eyes. "I didn't hurt her. I wouldn't."

"Fine. What bar were you at Sunday night?"

"Drunken Eddie's."

Freya winced. Did they have security cameras there? She wasn't entirely sure.

"Detective Ellinger is going to call over there. See if they have you on camera. If not, you better pray someone remembers you."

"Fine. Do it. I was drinking Jägerbombs all night long with Larry Fish. Find him and he can vouch for me." Robert leaned back in his chair, satisfaction written all over his face.

But Freya wasn't finished. "I hardly think Larry Fish qualifies as a reliable witness, especially if he was going head-to-head with you with your Jägerbombs."

She glanced at Candy. "Please go call Drunken Eddie's. Send someone to Larry's house and to the bar to find him. And put out a BOLO."

Candy leaned close to Freya. When she spoke, her voice was barely a whisper. "You know as well as I do that Chief won't want you in here by yourself. Not with him."

"Oh, Robert and I go way back, so don't worry about us. Besides, we're almost done. Thank you, Candy." She stared at the man across the table from her.

Candy stood, moving slowly, then left the room. The door closed with a click.

Silence fell between the two of them.

"Your detective thinks you need a babysitter," Robert finally said. He grinned at her, his tongue probing a spot where he was missing a tooth.

"You and your son are close," Freya said, ignoring the jab.

"So what of it? Not all parents are killers, Captain."

"Oh, but some could be if there isn't anyone there to stop them."

Robert chuckled, shaking his head. "Just say it. You think I killed Jolie and Millicent because of what I did when we were younger. Newsflash, Captain, people grow. They change. I'm not that guy anymore."

"We'll see about that." She stood, doing her best to keep her temper under control. Losing it while she was alone with Robert would be terrible.

"You arresting me?"

"Not yet. I'm waiting until Candy can verify your alibi. Or not."

"Wonderful. And Steve?"

"Don't worry about Steve. Hey, do you know Michelle Hawsey?"

Robert blinked. "Who?"

"Michelle Hawsey, the victim of the Fawn Lake Killer. Name ring a bell?"

"Should it?" Robert shifted in his seat. He was beginning to look uncomfortable. "Wait. You think the cases are connected, don't you? That's why you're asking."

"Just covering my bases."

"No way. I didn't kill her. I didn't kill anyone. You think Jolie was so innocent, was so sweet? Don't forget she was blackmailing my son. That should tell you a lot about who she really was."

Freya ignored him. "Hey, quick question. Steve has a really nice house. Your wife just got that new car. And there's the blackmail money to consider. Where, exactly, did the Petit family come into that much cash?"

"Luck." Robert grinned at her.

"I don't believe in it." Freya should leave. She knew she should. If Chief found out she was in there with Robert, all alone... he'd lose it. She was on thin ice, especially since he'd already warned her she was too close to this case. But how could she walk away now? The messages with Jolie didn't look good for Robert. Freya could arrest him, but the messages alone weren't enough to convict, so she'd have to hurry to find something else.

Robert shrugged. "Where my money comes from is none of your business, Captain."

"Don't pull that with me. Millicent was a nurse, and there's no way she made that much money. Besides, she'd notice Steve draining their accounts to pay Jolie. That tells me he had a separate account, or you were funding his blackmail payments. My money is on the former, because who's going to hire an ex-con like you? Nobody offering a nice 401(k) match. So Steve is getting money somehow. Or thinks he'll have it somehow. It would also explain that nice new car your wife is driving."

She tilted her head, considering Robert. The man hadn't given much away, but the way he swallowed, how his cheeks were suddenly paler than a moment ago... she was on the right track.

"Was it gambling or a huge insurance policy on Millicent that you were counting on getting even before she died?" Freya asked. "You can tell me now, or I can find out myself."

Robert didn't respond.

"Cool, I'll find out myself. Nice chatting with you."

"It's gambling." The words flew out of Robert in a rush. "Gambling, okay? Are you happy? I hit it big, bought Jayne a car. I promise you, nobody in my family hurt Millicent. We wouldn't."

Freya eyeballed him, waiting for anything else he might say. When he didn't speak up again, she cleared her throat. "You're free to go. For now."

Freya left the interrogation room, nodding once to the officer stationed outside the door. But before she could say a thing to him, someone cleared their throat.

Chief. And he looked ticked.

TWENTY-FIVE

Freya took a deep breath, then leaned forward, lightly resting her hands on the podium in front of her. It was made of wood, and old, and had probably been used in countless press releases. She forced a smile to her face, but that didn't mean she liked what she was doing. Chief stood behind her, off to the side, looking for all the world like he was there to support her, but she knew the truth.

It wasn't so much support as it was keeping her on a leash. She'd gone off book before in an interview and now had earned herself a babysitter in the form of a balding police chief with anger issues.

It certainly didn't help that Chief had caught her interviewing Robert on her own. His face was still red from their encounter, his hands still clenched in fists.

"Okay, you're on." The skinny guy holding a TV camera on his shoulder pointed at Freya, and she swallowed hard.

"Good afternoon, residents of Fawn Lake." Her voice was clear. Powerful. It didn't shake, and if people didn't know how worried she was, she doubted they'd be able to tell. Thank goodness she had control over that one thing.

"I'm Captain Sinclair with the Fawn Lake Police Department. As many of you know, two women were killed camping in Clear Creek Forest over the weekend. They have been identified and their families notified. Unfortunately, the killer is still at large."

A man Freya had seen before stepped forward, a microphone clutched in his hand. He pushed it closer to her, but she ignored him. The press loved events like this, loved anything that they could use to drive numbers. *Leeches.* But at least she could count on them getting the word out about what was going on.

"We ask residents respect the families' privacy at this time. They're dealing with enough as it is, and the last thing they need is people showing up at their homes or places of working looking for information about the case. While we don't think there's an immediate danger to the residents of Fawn Lake, we do recommend that you make sure you're aware of your surroundings."

Someone in the crowd coughed.

Freya shifted on her feet and continued. "If you're going to be out in the woods, especially after dark, go in larger groups. Don't approach strangers on the trail until we find the killer and have them in custody. Leave information about your hiking or camping plans with friends, and check in both before you leave and after you return. This will allow family members or friends to monitor your whereabouts and alert us as quickly as possible if you go missing."

Dark. This was dark. Who would want to be out in the woods right now with someone who killed women and cut out their tongues, Freya didn't know.

"Have there only been the two victims?" That man with the microphone.

Freya wasn't done talking, and she blinked hard, getting her thoughts back on track.

"The two women in the woods. Are there more victims?"

"As of right now, we don't know about any other victims." It wasn't a lie, not really. They had a tongue, but without a body, it didn't mean much. "We just want to encourage residents to be careful."

"Do you have any idea who killed them?" Not the man this time, a younger guy, his face red with nerves.

"We're working a few leads, and that's something we need help with. Nathan Caldwell is wanted for questioning regarding the murders." Without turning around, Freya knew the man's picture was now on the screen behind her. "We do not know what, if any, role Mr. Caldwell played in the murders, but we would like to ask him a few questions. If you know where he is, it's best to call the police, not approach him on your own."

"So you think he's dangerous?" The first man again.

"Operating with an abundance of caution is always recommended in cases like this. The last thing we want is for anyone to presume they can handle what should be police business and end up putting themselves in a dangerous situation." Did it matter that it sounded like she was reading from a script? Not really, not as long as she was able to get through to people.

"Did someone see him up there with the women?" That same man, more of a thorn in her side than a reporter.

Freya bit back a sharp retort. "Like I said, we're looking to talk to Mr. Caldwell about any information he might have regarding the murders. That doesn't mean he's a suspect, and it certainly doesn't mean anyone saw him near the crime scene."

When the man prepared to respond, she looked down at him. "I'd appreciate it if you'd stop putting words in my mouth."

His mouth snapped shut. Chief shuffled his feet like he was going to step forward and take the microphone from her, but she wasn't finished.

"If anyone has any information regarding the murders of

Jolie Marin and Millicent Woodward, or any information regarding Mr. Caldwell's whereabouts, please give me a call or stop by the police department. We have officers and detectives working around the clock to get justice for the two women, and we aren't going to stop until we've done just that."

She turned away to leave the stage and let Chief have his moment in the sun, but what was shouted at her next stopped her dead in her tracks.

"Do you have time to talk about your parents?"

Freya closed her eyes; forced a deep breath. This is how it always went—anytime the press had unfettered access to her, they asked her questions about her parents. You know what? Enough. She normally ignored them, chalking the questions up to morbid curiosity, but she hadn't fought to have a wonderful career just to have people hang her parents' crimes over her head every chance they could.

She spun around. Now Chief really was stepping forward, probably to stop her, but she gripped the podium, her knuckles turning white, and searched the crowd for whoever had spoken.

There. Off to the side. Dressed in jeans and a black ball cap, the man looked young, like he was still in college. High school maybe. Too young to have seen her parents' crimes splashed all over the news, so he must now be living vicariously.

"What do you want to know?" Even without speaking into the microphone, her voice was loud enough to be heard through the entire room.

The crowd murmured. Chief grabbed her arm, but she shook him off.

"No, you know what?" She kept her voice lower so only he could hear her. "This has followed me long enough. I need to clear the air on it, or this is all people are ever going to talk about."

She cleared her throat and turned back to the man. Boy. "What do you want to know?" she repeated.

"Did you know what was happening when you were a kid?" His voice trembled, and Freya shook her head, disgusted.

"Did I know that my parents were serial killers and murdering people left and right?" Her voice was tight and rose as she spoke. "Did I know that my dad would bring his victims back to the basement, the one room in the house he'd sound-proofed so nobody would ever know what he was doing? Did I know about my mom helping him cut the bodies up before scattering them along the river?"

She was leaning forward, her breath coming in little gasps. Her eyes were locked on the boy, and she saw how his cheeks flushed, how he looked down and away from her, almost ashamed, then right back up at her. His chin jutted out. She couldn't see his eyes but knew the defiance she'd see there if she could.

"No, I didn't know any of that. Next question." Freya glared out at the crowd. Some people's mouths had dropped open. Others looked down at their feet. At least two had their phones out, surely capturing video that would end up on YouTube or TikTok before the day was over.

Silence. Nobody moved. Nobody spoke. Chief leaned over, grabbing the microphone and jerking it at an angle. "We're not taking any further questions. Anyone with information needs to contact our department." His hand closed like a vise on her elbow, and he jerked her back.

Freya stumbled after him, away from the podium, away from the watching crowd. They'd barely made it into the hall, the door clicking softly shut after them, when Chief wheeled on her, his eyes wide, his mouth tight.

"What was that?" he demanded. "This was supposed to be about the murders."

"That was me ending this," she said, flapping her arm in the air. "This... speculation. Gossip. Do you have any idea how hard it is to do your job with the specters of your parents hanging over your head? It's almost impossible. It's exhausting. I can't do it any longer."

"You made a fool of yourself."

Her temper flared. Getting into an argument with Chief wasn't a good idea, but this had been a long time coming. "My parents made a fool of me. My parents are the ones that made me out to be an idiot, to be someone who doesn't know what's going on under her own roof. All I did was clear the air. The fact is, I can't stand in front of a group of people without them dying to know everything about my past. Unless I tell them, unless I come clean, they're just going to keep wondering and questioning what I'm doing, and doubting if I'm good enough for the job. So excuse me for trying to handle it."

"You want people to know what happened with your parents? Write a book. But don't make my department out to be a bunch of idiots."

"Write a book, right." Freya hissed the words at him. How thick were the doors here? Was it possible there were reporters listening, their greedy ears pressed up against the wood, drooling with every word they heard? Maybe. But it was too late to stop now. "I'm sure a tell-all wouldn't have any negative impact on the department."

"Whatever you do, you can do it on your own time. You're suspended."

Her mouth dropped open. Her hands clenched into fists. "I'm what?"

"Suspended." Chief grinned, then shook his head. "You're a liability right now, Sinclair. Interviewing Robert by yourself? Come on—that was stupid, and you know it. Everyone in town knows you attacked him when you were younger."

"He was going to rape someone!"

Chief didn't act like he'd heard what she'd said. "And putting personal detail on Esther? We don't do that. We don't have the manpower to babysit anyone who might be scared. I'm pulling the detail."

She opened her mouth to speak, but Chief held up a hand. "No, don't argue with me. You may not want to admit it to yourself, but it's true. You're distracted. You can't separate your feelings from the case. I can't have that. Not if it's going to lead you to making stupid decisions like you did today. Go home. Straight home. Don't dally around town in your Jeep. Start your book. You can even make sure you have a chapter about this little interaction. Maybe dedicate it to me. Now give me your gun and badge."

"You can't do this," she said, already snapping the badge off her duty belt.

He laughed. "I can do whatever I want. It's my department, and you're a loose cannon right now." Her badge disappeared into his pocket, and he snapped his fingers for her to hurry up. "Gun, Sinclair."

Freya slowly pulled her gun and turned it, offering it to him by the grip. He snatched it from her then turned and stomped off, leaving her with a sick feeling in her stomach.

No. This couldn't be happening. There was no way he could actually take her off the case, not when he knew how personal it was, not when she was the only one who really understood the killer. A wave of dizziness washed over her, and she reached out, bracing her hand on the wall and taking deep breaths through her nose.

In, two, three, four. Out, two, three, four.

Her vision cleared, the fuzzy black around the edges disappearing. Freya stood, then ran through a mental list of what she had to do.

Disappear from the police department.

Go to Food Mart and pay off Roy's tab.

Not fall into a bottle.

Most importantly: figure out how to work the case without anyone knowing.

TWENTY-SIX

The park bench he sat on was hard, and the slats cut into his back as he reclined against it. Still, even though it wasn't nearly as comfortable as a seat at the coffee shop a few blocks down, the bench gave him the perfect vantage point to keep an eye on the bakery. He'd been sitting right here when he'd come up with his plan to bring Esther into his little game, and sitting here when he'd seen her leave the bakery, her face white, his present clutched tight in her hand as she'd hurried down the street to the police station.

He'd been at the press release. Of course he had—there wasn't any way he was going to miss it. It had been mostly reporters, but there was always room at the back of the room for residents to watch.

Afterwards, he'd just walked across the street. Sat down. He could keep an eye on Esther from here and look out for Freya.

He giggled, the sound high and girlish, and he clapped a hand over his mouth. A young woman glanced at him as she walked by, her purse clutched tight against her body. Unable to stop himself, he wiggled his fingers at her, then grinned as she looked in the other direction and hurried on.

He didn't care. They could look askance at him like this all they wanted.

He pulled out a pad of paper from his pocket, flipped open the cover, and ran his finger down the front page. Jolie's name was right on top, scratched out with a black felt marker, the ink bleeding to the edges of the paper. It soaked through a few pages in the notebook, but he didn't care.

Freya thought she was so great, going on TV and calming people down, telling the residents of Fawn Lake that they had nothing to fear.

And then she'd completely lost control.

The thought made him giggle again. It was a terrible habit, one his mother had cuffed him upside the head for time and time again when he was younger, but he couldn't help it. He was excited. He was ready to ratchet this game up a notch.

He thought for a minute then uncapped his black felt marker. Wrote a new name at the bottom of the list.

Freya Sinclair.

TWENTY-SEVEN

Candy called again, but Freya tapped the red button to hang up on her. That was the third time she'd called since the press conference, but Freya couldn't speak to her.

Not yet.

It felt strange not wearing her duty belt as she pulled up to the Amos Hotel, but she pushed that feeling from her mind. She still had the badge in her wallet—Chief hadn't thought about taking that one when he'd taken the one off her hip—and some business cards.

People would talk to her.

The parking lot was empty compared to the night before. A few cars sat here and there, some of them on half-deflated tires, making them look like permanent fixtures. Freya parked next to one and killed her engine, then locked her Jeep and hurried inside, anger at the killer spurring her on.

The girl behind the counter looked way too young to be out of school. Her long blonde hair in a ponytail, she wore a black tank top and choker necklace and snapped her gum, speaking without looking up from her phone. "Do you need a room?"

"I need information." Freya rested her hand on the counter

between them, thought better of it, and wiped her hand on her pants. "Are you Lorna?"

When the girl looked up, nodding, she held out her phone. "Do you recognize any of these men?" Steve's photo was first, followed by Robert's. She waited a moment then swiped her thumb across the screen, bringing up Nathan's photo.

The girl wrinkled her nose. She had on dark eyeshadow and loads of mascara. Her lashes fluttered as she glanced at the phone. "Swipe back to the first guy."

Freya's heart thudded in her chest as she did what the girl requested.

"I think... No, you know what? I don't know them." The girl leaned back, chomping down hard on her gum. "I thought I did, but I must have been mistaken."

Freya groaned. "You really want to play it this way?"

The girl shrugged.

"Shouldn't you be in school? What are you, sixteen?"

"Nineteen," the girl shot back. "But my boss said I look young."

"And I bet he loves that about you." Freya jerked her wallet from her pocket and pulled out a twenty. "Here. Now, which one of the men do you recognize?"

In a wink, the money was snatched from her hand. It disappeared into the girl's cleavage. "None of them."

"None of them?" Freya gripped the edge of the counter. "Are you serious right now? What, you just thought you needed an extra twenty bucks?"

"Hey, I thought I knew them, but they all look the same, you know? Johns? But that first one looks too clean-cut to be showing up around here." She shrugged, one bare shoulder rising before she curled in on herself a little. "That's not the type of guy we get around here very often, you know?"

"Okay, so you're totally sure you've never seen this guy before?" The photo of Robert was zoomed out a little and Freya flicked her fingers across it, making it so the girl could get a good look at him. "Take your time."

She leaned forward, chewing her lower lip. After a moment, she shook her head. "I'd remember him." A moment later, her expression darkened. "What are you, the police?"

"Not really."

"What are you looking for him for? Is it drugs? I bet it's drugs."

Freya arched an eyebrow at her. "Why do you think that?"

Another shrug. "Clean-cut guys always do drugs. Now the other two, they might have come here before, but they look like all the other guys who come through that door."

"How so?"

The girl sighed. A bit of hair had fallen free around her face and she twisted it absently, still looking at Freya as she did. "The guys who come here aren't the best guys—you know that, right? You have to know that." She pinned Freya in place with a stare. "Those second and third guys, they could totally come here. They look the part."

"Look the part. You mean bad. Mean."

"Mean, yeah." The girl nodded eagerly. "But they don't stand out enough for me to know who they are, sorry."

Freya exhaled, turned off her screen, and slipped her phone back into her pocket. "It's fine. I'd hoped this was going to be easier than it is." She paused, thinking, then the words slipped from her lips before she could stop them. "You don't go into the rooms with the Johns, do you?"

Lorna had a hard exterior, like any person who had been exposed to too much, too young. Lost innocence wasn't something that could be recovered, no matter how hard a person tried. What she had seen working here, what she might have taken part in, it was enough to break Freya's heart.

"Into the rooms? No way. I wouldn't. I sit here and let people in, but I'd never go back there with someone." She wrinkled her nose in disgust. "You don't have to worry about that."

"Good." Freya pulled a business card from her pocket and handed it to Lorna. For a moment, the girl didn't reach for it, but then she took it, turning it over in her hands. "I want you to call me when you decide this isn't the place you want to work."

She scoffed out a laugh. "You're going to give me a badge and a gun?"

"No, but I'll help you find somewhere to work that isn't here. Somewhere you'll be safer, where you won't have to worry about what kind of things go on down the hall." Freya stared at her. "Will you do it?"

A pause, then she responded. "Maybe."

"Well, Lorna, I hope you'll call me." Freya rapped her knuckles on the counter. "Be safe."

With that, she turned and left the seedy hotel. It smelled rank in there. Freya hurried to her car and cranked the key, the engine sputtering to life.

She'd been so confident that Steve was the killer. Steve was bold—she would give him that. And plenty of men cheated on the women they claimed to love. But this was one step farther. Meeting Jolie at the hotel, though, that would make sense. Not picking her up off the sidewalk where anyone could see, but making plans to meet her here where nobody would know who he was. It was despicable, but it could work.

Except for the fact Lorna was convinced she'd never seen Steve there, and maybe she was right. Candy was checking out his alibi, and if—

Candy. That's why she'd been calling. Not to check in with her after the most humiliating press conference ever but to talk about what Brad might have found out about Charlotte, Steve's daughter—or what she'd found out about Robert.

"Crap." She started her Jeep and called Candy. "Please pick up, please pick up."

The phone rang once, twice, three times, and Freya was just starting to sweat when Candy's voice filled the car. "You okay? I tried to reach you."

"I'm fine. I had some things to do. Did Brad talk to Charlotte?"

"He found her. Mom is debating letting him speak to her, and since she's fifteen, he doesn't have much of a choice. Brad said that from the way they were shooting daggers at each other, he'd wager Steve was over there recently. We'll know more later, but we just have to wait this one out right now."

"Well, I just left the Amos Hotel and the girl who works the front desk kinda confirmed what we're thinking. Steve hated Jolie, but the girl said he wasn't the type of guy to ever darken their door. Now Nathan and Robert, on the other hand..."

"Right. Those are the men of the hour. Why don't you come by the office and we can figure out how we're going to hunt Nathan down? I haven't heard from Brad on that yet, so I doubt he's getting anywhere. We can put our heads together. As for Drunken Eddie's, no cameras, just like you thought. I put out a BOLO on Larry Fish, but who knows what dark corner he's crawled into to drink himself into oblivion."

Freya chewed her lower lip and pulled to a stop before turning onto the road. "Good work, Candy. But as far as coming in... I can't."

"What do you mean? Are you okay?"

"Chief suspended me."

"What? Are you serious right now?" Candy's voice grew louder and louder. "Why would he do that? Doesn't he know we're close to cracking this thing? We need you here, Freya— you have to be here."

"I know." She rubbed her temples, explaining to Candy about losing her temper.

"So what are you going to do?"

A car pulled up behind her to leave the parking lot, and

Freya slowly turned out onto the road to get out of their way. Apparently, she wasn't going fast enough, because it crossed the double yellow line to get around her.

She reached for her siren, then put her hand back on the steering wheel with a sigh. "I want to keep working the case."

"Sure, but if Chief finds out, he might do more than just suspend you."

She didn't respond.

"Freya? I don't mean to piss you off, but I don't want you to get in more trouble."

"Right. I know. Thanks."

"I mean, I'd tell you to team up with me and look for Nathan, but you can't be involved with bringing him in. And you can't question him." Candy's voice was high and tight. "What was Chief thinking? Why did he think this was a good idea?"

"It doesn't matter. I know you can handle it." Freya cleared her throat. Tears stung her eyes, but she refused to let them fall. "Just keep me in the loop as much as you can, okay? But if I show my face at the office..."

"Right, I know." Candy sighed, sounding miserable. "What are you going to do?"

"Whatever I can from home without Chief knowing I'm still working." Freya put as much fake cheerfulness into her voice as possible. "I'll talk to you later." She forced herself to hang up. Pressed down harder on the gas.

She may be suspended and certainly couldn't get caught driving around town working the case, but sitting around waiting wasn't an option either.

TWENTY-EIGHT

The backroads and alleys of Fawn Lake were dark and dangerous, a far cry from the glittering Main Street that most residents and tourists saw. It wasn't just the dumpsters in dire need of being emptied, their trash overflowing, sticky liquids leaking out from the bottom to pool on the ground. It wasn't just the line cooks being line cooks, standing behind restaurants, sucking down cigarettes, using language that would give a priest a heart attack.

It was the men roaming, looking, their hands and eyes always on the move. They stuck to the shadows as much as possible, driven there by police and public opinion, but sometimes they stuck their necks out, ventured out into the light, caused problems that brought the force of the entire police department down on their heads.

Freya drove down one such alley. As long as she stayed far away from Chief and the rest of the on-call officers, she could check a few things out on the way home. At least, she hoped so.

At the far end of the alley was a man, leaning against the wall, his foot propped up behind him, a cigarette glowing in his finger.

It could be Nathan.

A jolt of excitement burst through her, and she rolled down her window, leaning out to get a better look. The man turned to stare at her, one eye glossy and white, the other intently fixed on her.

Not Nathan.

"Do you know this man?" She held out her phone, keeping her fingers tightly wrapped around it so he couldn't take it.

He glanced at it. Glanced at her. Shook his head.

Frustration coursed through her, but she wasn't done. She'd work her way up and down every alley branching off Main Street then head home. She glanced up at the sky, noting the way the sun was already starting to sink.

After an hour of pulling over asking people if they knew Nathan, Freya was exhausted. The emotion of what had happened at the press conference washed over her. Parked behind the defunct bowling alley, she leaned her head on her steering wheel.

How many times had she been tempted to call Candy or Brad? The fact that Brad hadn't reached out to her made it obvious to her that Candy had clued him in. That or he'd seen the press conference himself.

Her ears burned.

When her phone rang, she didn't move, letting it click over to voicemail. It was only when she'd sat up and wiped away her tears that she checked it.

Esther.

A minute later, she had the phone ringing.

"Darling, I wanted to check in on you." Esther's voice was calm, soothing. She spoke to Freya like Freya was a feral cat. It had always worked on her as a teenager, helping her calm down, and even now Freya felt her shoulders relax.

"I'm hanging in there."

"Come to dinner—you owe me."

"Esther, I have to work." She squeezed her eyes shut. Maybe Esther wouldn't pick up on the lie.

But the sigh over the phone told her Esther knew the truth. "Freya, I know everything that happens in this town. And I don't blame you for how you responded. Two officers came in here talking, so I heard you're off the case for a while."

"Off the force is more like it." The words were bitter in her mouth.

"So come to dinner. Let me feed you." A pause, then: "If you've been off work for the afternoon, where have you been? You know what, don't tell me. I know what you've been doing, but if Chief comes to ask me anything, I want to be able to tell him the truth, that I don't know anything."

"You're the best."

"I know. Come to dinner. It's getting dark out already, and I want to go home. I just haven't felt the same since that horrid tongue."

Guilt washed over her. "Okay, yes. I'll do that. Just let me make one more stop, okay? I have one thing I keep forgetting to do, and I need to take care of it. Then I'll be over."

She hung up and made the drive to Food Mart in record time.

Once inside, the first thing she did was go to the front desk and pay off Roy Waters' tab. That done, she grabbed a roast chicken, some baked potatoes, a key lime pie and checked out, keeping her head down, not wanting to look at anyone.

Esther opened the door before she could knock. She had on an apron, flour down the front of it, and took the groceries from Freya. "You need to rest," she said, locking the door behind her. She slid the deadbolt at the top then peeked through the curtains covering the front windows. "And so does that poor boy out there." She paused. "Oh, wait. Looks like he's gone home.

That's good. I was going to take him some dinner, but he must have gotten hungry and already left."

He hadn't just gone home—Chief had made good on his promise to leave Esther here without anyone keeping an eye on her. Freya swallowed hard, trying not to let the worry that something might happen to Esther eat at her.

"Esther." Freya stopped on her way to the kitchen. "You're not supposed to leave the house—you know that."

She scoffed. "What, you think I'm going to let someone starve out there while they're watching my house?" She shook her head. "Not a chance. Now, what brings you here?"

All Freya could do at first was stare at her. Esther was the type of person who couldn't walk by someone homeless without stopping to give them some change or food.

When she was younger, Esther was always making extra food and taking it to people who needed it. Then, as Freya grew up, she came to realize that it was the same kindness that led her to feed the hungry that had encouraged her to open her home to Freya when she had nowhere else to go.

"You invited me to dinner."

"Oh, Freya." She reached out and patted her shoulder. "I was joking. Just trying to keep you on your toes." She glanced down at the bag of groceries in her arms. "I hope you didn't stop by the store just for me."

While Esther spoke, she led Freya into the kitchen, gestured for her to sit at the counter, then made them each a plate.

"I didn't want you to have to cook something from scratch," she offered, and Esther cupped her cheek in response.

They ate in silence. At the end of the meal, she hugged Esther. The woman was thin, and she squeezed her tight. Exhaustion crept up on her, and she finally shook her head, forcing herself to take a step back.

"Lock me out. No more trips outside right now, okay? I want you in this house, Esther. Safe."

"I am safe." Esther smiled at Freya, then cupped her cheek. "You're the one I'm worried about, darling." She paused, and Freya was about to turn away when something on the kitchen table caught her eye.

Pulling away from Esther, she grabbed the envelope. It was simple, thin, no flourishes on it, but the sight of it made her stomach twist. The letter was to her, in care of Esther, with Esther's address.

From Smithfield Correctional.

"When did this come?" she asked. Her voice was tight.

"Today." Esther paused, then took the letter from Freya. She dropped it back on the table. "It slipped my mind, darling." Another pause. "Do you want to read what they have to say?"

Freya shook her head. "My parents send me letters, too." She paused, not wanting to know the answer to her question but having to ask it. "Do they write you a lot?"

"This is the first one. They must really want to talk to you," Esther said, but Freya was already shaking her head again.

"They lost all rights to talk to me when they killed those people. When they shot me." She paused, her fingers drumming out a beat on her thigh, then pulled her keys from her pocket.

Recently it felt like just existing was putting Esther in danger and that thought made Freya feel sick.

How dare they?

She picked the letter back up and shoved it in her pocket. Not to read but to put with the others. Away from Esther.

"I'll call you, okay? Stay in the house." Freya managed a smile.

She started towards her car then changed her mind and beelined to the house two doors down. Before she could ring the bell, Marla threw the door open, smiling up at her through gap teeth.

"Freya's here!" She bellowed the words, gave her a curtsy, then disappeared down the hall.

Freya couldn't help but grin. Even though she hadn't seen Paul or his daughter in over a week, the little girl always seemed to know what to do to raise her spirits.

"Freya, hey." Paul leaned on the doorframe. His hair was wet, and he smelled woodsy, like nice body wash. "You doing okay?"

"Not at all," Freya admitted. "But I don't want to talk about it. I wanted to ask if you'd keep an eye on Esther for me while I work this case. Do you mind?"

"Not at all." He ran his hand through his hair. "Do you want to come in? I promise, you can just sit and drink tea without saying a word."

That made her smile. "Thanks, but I just want to go home. Shower. Pass out."

"I get it."

She sighed. "You saw the press conference, didn't you?"

"I did, but that doesn't change what I think about you. Let me know if I can do anything else for you, okay?"

"Will do, thanks." She threw him a tight smile, then hurried to her car.

Driving home, she went slower. Exhaustion was making it difficult for her to think straight, and she kept both hands firmly on the wheel, not letting herself look away from the double lines in the middle of the road.

At home, she tossed the letter in the drawer with the others and collapsed on the sofa without turning on the news. The last thing she wanted was to see her photo splashed across the screen. Well, that or think about the letter from her parents.

For just a moment, she considered opening it, but the day was already terrible. No reason to make it even worse reading their excuses for what they'd done. Freya was sure that was all it was, them trying to explain away their actions, trying to get her to see their point of view.

As if she ever could.

TWENTY-NINE
WEDNESDAY

A barrage of text messages, one after another, was what finally woke her up. Groaning, Freya rolled over, flinging her arm out to the bedside table where she always kept her phone charging at night.

It wasn't there.

She forced herself to sit up, her head pounding. Her tongue stuck to the roof of her mouth, and her eyes felt like they had sand in them. Moving slowly, she rubbed the sleep away and swung her legs to the side to get out of bed.

It was only then that she realized she'd passed out on the sofa, not in bed.

Still dressed in her clothes from the previous day, she stood, groaning as her hip screamed at her. Her mouth was dry, her curls matted to the side of her head. And was that... drool? Disgusting.

She felt disgusting.

Her phone lit up yet again, and this time she saw it sitting on the coffee table. Lunging forward, she grabbed it, then sank back into the soft cushions. The sofa had to have been at least ten years old when she'd picked it up from Goodwill over the summer, but she never felt that she had time to go shopping for a new one.

"Okay, who has their panties in a twist?" she muttered, swiping on her phone. It lit up, shining right in her eyes, and she groaned, blinking hard for a moment. "Candy. What in the world?"

Her string of texts started an hour ago.

Talked to Steve's baby momma again last night. She threw a fit about Brad trying to talk to her daughter. But she agreed to talk to me.

You'll find this interesting—guess where Steve spent the night on Sunday after hanging out with Charlotte? Spoiler: it wasn't alone in the bed he shared with Millicent.

He definitely has an alibi, but no wonder he didn't want to tell us the truth. Sleeping with your baby momma who isn't your fiancée? Not a good look.

Are you around? We need to regroup. I know what Chief said, but he can shove it. You have to work this case.

Freya?

Freya, where are you?

Freya, I swear I'll drive out to your house right now if you don't answer me.

The last text was the one that finally lit a fire under her. Clearing her throat, she tapped the call button, turned down the volume, and held the phone up to her ear.

Candy picked up immediately. "Come on, I was beginning

to think you were dead. You know you can't just disappear in the middle of a murder investigation. People will start to get worried."

"Good morning to you too. You do know that if Chief found out you were looping me in on the case, you'd be suspended with me, right?" Freya knew she sounded terrible and cleared her voice again. "Just texting me is enough to set him off."

"Yeah, right. What's he going to do, suspend all the detectives? I think not. Can you imagine how quickly everyone in town would turn on him? He's hotheaded, but he's not stupid. Besides, Freya, we need you."

She scrubbed a hand down her face. "So, Charlotte is a solid alibi for her dad?"

"Only up until about nine p.m., when he finally figured out Millie wasn't coming home and took Charlotte back to her house. But then dear old mom invited him to stay for a nightcap after he dropped Charlotte off. One thing led to another, and now it makes sense why he didn't want to share his alibi, but he has one until early Monday morning." She paused. "It also makes sense why he didn't call to report Millicent missing for as long as he did. Didn't want people to know he'd hooked up with his ex instead of waiting at home for Millicent. There's going to be drama, but it's not our problem. We need to regroup and decide what we're going to do next."

"Yeah, I know." She forced herself to stand, then walked out of the living room and into the kitchen. Huge windows spanned the entire wall looking out over a small yard that ended abruptly in thick woods. Once a week in the summer she'd take the weed eater out and hack the grass back a little, but aside from that, Freya didn't have a lot of patience for yard work. Besides, it wasn't like she had neighbors to complain if things started to look too overgrown.

But she'd noticed the yard was out of control over a week

ago and had meant to tackle the problem this week before life turned into a hot mess.

Freya paced while she talked. It was preferable to sitting still. She walked over to the large windows and leaned against them, looking out into her yard and letting Candy's words roll off her back.

"We need you. Ignore Chief and come on in already." Candy paused. "That was way too forward, wasn't it? I'm sorry. I just really want to get this solved, and you're the one to do it, no matter what he says. People are worried, Freya; they're—"

"Candy, I need you here." Freya's voice was tight. She gripped the phone so hard her fingers started to cramp, but she was physically unable to make herself loosen them. What she saw out her kitchen window was so terrible she couldn't tear her eyes away, no matter how badly she wanted to.

"Freya, we need to—"

"*Now*, Candy. I need you here now."

"What's going on? "

Freya didn't respond. She couldn't.

"Okay, I'm on my way." There was a click, then Freya dropped the phone from her ear.

As much as she hated to admit it, she had probably just found the woman whose tongue had been sent to Esther.

THIRTY

Light slanted in through the kitchen windows, illuminating the specks of dust floating in the air. It made the room look like something out of a fairytale or like the inside of a snow globe.

Freya's phone was back in her pocket so she wouldn't have to worry about accidentally setting it down and not being able to find it when she needed to make another call. She reached down, patting her pocket to remind herself that it was still there, the entire time still staring through the window. She needed to move, but right now she seemed physically unable to do anything but look out at the body spread-eagled on the over-grown grass outside.

In her yard.

She walked to the kitchen door, unlocked it, pulled it open. At the last minute, she remembered to pull on the muck boots she kept by the door and grab a pair of gloves from the counter, then she carefully shut the door behind her. As she got closer to the woman, her fears were confirmed. She was dead alright, and had been for a while. Flies circled the body as she approached, the braver ones refusing to leave their posts at the corners of her mouth and eyes.

"Get," Freya said, waving them away and crouching next to the body to get a better look. Her stomach turned. No matter how many dead bodies she saw, it was always difficult.

"Who are you?" she asked the lifeless form. The woman was pale, with blonde hair that looked like it would be soft if it weren't stuck to the side of her neck. Her throat had been slit, the edges of the wound ragged. Freya didn't have to open her mouth to know her tongue was gone. Still, she snapped on a glove and carefully pulled down the woman's chin.

No tongue. Just blood, the smell of it rancid and thick.

A flash of silver caught her eye, and she paused, then lightly touched the woman's neck. The necklace was mostly covered with blood. If the sun hadn't hit it just right, she probably wouldn't have seen it at all.

Carefully, she looped a finger under the chain. The drying blood stuck it to the woman's skin, and she tugged it gently, working it carefully away from the neck until she held a locket in her hand.

A swipe of her gloved finger across the front of the heart wiped away the blood and revealed initials.

V.O.

Sighing, she stood, then pulled the phone from her pocket with her other hand. Candy was already on her way and would probably bring officers with her, but she needed Lance to come too. She spoke quickly once he picked up, making sure not to leave out any details, walking around the body as she did so she could get a better look. Any evidence left on it would quickly degrade if it was left out in the open like this.

Freya went back inside, cracked the front door open in anticipation of Candy's arrival, and grabbed her work camera. She was in the process of snapping pictures of the crime scene when she heard her pull up. Candy beeped her horn in the driveway, and Freya straightened, her hand pressing on her hip. Sleeping on the sofa last night hadn't done it any favors.

"Backyard," she called, her voice carrying in the silent morning. "Come in the front and go through the kitchen."

"Okay!"

There was a pause, then she heard the front door slam. A moment later, the kitchen door swung open, and Freya turned to see Candy's mouth fall slack.

"Who is that?"

"That's what I'd love to know too." Freya exhaled, wiping sweat from her forehead. "I'd just woken up, was talking to you, looked in the yard, and there she was. She is wearing a locket with some familiar initials. V.O."

"No way." Candy walked past her and crouched by the body. "Do you have any idea who this is? She could be the owner of the scarf."

"Not yet, but she's missing a tongue. Maybe it's the one Esther received."

Her hip really hurt. Rubbing it harder, she walked over to see what Candy was looking at. She had moved down to the victim's feet and was looking at her shoes. "What? Did you find something?"

"Nope, just looking. These shoes are super muddy. Do you have mud like this around here?"

"I noticed that. And no. I'm surrounded by the woods, but there isn't a lot of mud. So obviously she was dumped here after she was killed, then lovingly arranged for me to find." Freya kneeled too. "Look. I didn't want to move her, but you can see that she has mud down her back as well. Like she fell in it."

Candy nodded. "Or was pushed and slipped."

The sound of more car doors slamming filled the air, and Candy stood, wiping her hands on her pants. "I'll go let them in. You sounded a little panicked on the phone, so I figured you'd want backup. Or I'd want backup. Either way, you've already taken a lot of pictures, right? So they can get her moved quickly? Have you talked to Chief?"

"Nope." Freya didn't have any desire to talk to him anytime soon. She could just imagine what the man would say and how upset he'd be that she was both suspended and at the epicenter of the case.

Candy nodded. "He knows though. I made the call for backup, and you know as well as I do how much he enjoys sitting by his radio and listening to everything that's going on."

"Sure. I also know he's going to be pretty pissed about this." Freya watched as Candy walked to the house and kicked off her shoes before going inside, then turned back to the woman's body.

She had to find something. Every perp made a mistake.

"Hello there..." she said, her eyes landing on something white. There was a corner of something sticking out from under her body. She plucked it out with her gloved fingers. "Annaliese Nowland." She frowned. Not the V.O. woman then.

The woman staring back at her from the driver's license looked happy, full of life. She was smiling, even though the DMV workers always told people to keep their face neutral. The expression on her face was that of someone who had just told a joke and was happy about how well it had been received.

"Candy," she called, when she heard the kitchen door open and close again, "we've got an ID. I don't think she's the owner of the locket, if we're right that V.O. is someone's initials. Let's find out everything we can about this woman. We need to go to her house, figure out if she has any ties to Jolie."

"You don't need to go anywhere." Anger rippled through Chief's voice.

Freya spun around to look at him, still holding the ID.

"How is this getting so out of control? I suspended you! What are you doing with a body right now?"

"We have a serial killer on our hands. What, you think I opted to wake up to a dead woman in my yard this morning?" Freya planted her hands on her hips. "Hate to break it to you,

Chief, but my real plan was reading the news, drinking coffee, and enjoying my forced break."

"I'm not apologizing for suspending you."

"I'm not asking you to, but this?" She gestured around her. "This isn't my fault."

"It might be." Chief glared at her, then changed tactics. "Why isn't Steve Petit in jail?"

"He has a rock-solid alibi." Freya looked past Chief for a moment to see Candy leading some uniformed officers out into her backyard. "He didn't have the opportunity to kill Jolie and Millicent. We're chasing down a few leads, including Robert Petit. Now Robert? He has motive and a past history of violence." She paused. "But he claims to have an alibi for the night Millicent and Jolie were murdered, we just have to find the guy. Candy sent an officer out to look for him and will put a BOLO out for him if they can't track him down. I'm thinking someone else is involved."

Nathan could have had the opportunity. The Fawn Lake Killer could have.

"Dedicate someone to checking his motive so we can arrest him if we need to." Chief spat the words and looked down at the woman's body. "Name?"

"Annaliese Nowland. Lived over on Blue Hutch Lane. I'd head there now, but, you know. Suspended."

He glared at her. "I'm taking care of this. It's out of control."

"Out of control?" Freya inhaled sharply. Even though she knew the smart move would be to slow down, take a deep breath, and organize her thoughts before speaking again, it was impossible for her to do that. Nothing angered her more than when Chief came into a discussion about a case and tried to play the big-dick game. Sure, he was at the top of the food chain in the police department, but it had been a long time since he'd worked a case himself.

"Out. Of. Control. I'm going to turn it over to the SBI."

Freya stepped closer to the Chief. "You do that, you lose the confidence of every single person in Fawn Lake. If you were Sheriff, you'd never get re-elected again. You'd be out of work and you'd have to pray for a job cleaning toilets in the department."

"But I'm not Sheriff," he scoffed. "I'm Chief. Which means I'm not elected, and I don't care if people don't like that I called the SBI. They'll like that the case was solved, and they can stop worrying about getting their throats cut just walking in the woods."

Candy walked up, standing right next to Chief, her eyes wide.

"Turning this over to the SBI is a huge mistake." Freya fought to keep her voice calm and level. Yelling at the man who signed her paycheck wasn't ever a good idea, but especially not now. "They'll come in here and handle the case, sure, but nobody will trust you to solve anything ever again. Just because you don't have to worry about re-election doesn't mean you don't have to worry."

"Are you threatening me?" Chief straightened his back, forcing himself even taller as he tried to intimidate her.

"I wouldn't dream of it," Freya lied. "All I'm saying is that the city manager is not going be happy if you call in the feds. Fawn Lake relies on tourism—you know that. Tourists can overlook a serial killer—some weirdos will come here specifically because there *was* a serial killer—but the city manager will not appreciate the SBI crawling all over this town. That's when people decide to stop coming."

Chief's face was red, his hands clenched into tight fists. Every breath he took was shallow, slow, measured.

"Freya's right."

Candy speaking up surprised both of them. Chief turned his angry gaze on the younger detective, and Freya winced.

"About what happens when the SBI gets involved, I mean. I

watch a ton of true-crime documentaries and read cold cases. Towns get a bad reputation when the SBI shows up. You call them, tourism here is as dead as these women. We have a great lead now—we know who this latest victim is. I wouldn't be surprised if there's a link to Jolie and Millicent. We can figure out who murdered her. But we need our captain back to do that."

Chief breathed heavily, but Freya didn't look at him. She couldn't look away from Candy, whose face was pale.

Chief turned back to Freya. Candy's face tightened. Was she frustrated that he was ignoring her or annoyed because she thought her little speech hadn't worked?

"Fix it." Chief stabbed a stubby finger at her chest. "Fix it now. We need to make sure people feel safe here, and we also have to make sure we keep getting the tourists. We can't have this turning into one of Ellinger's crime documentaries."

Freya focused on Candy and took deep, intentional breaths to slow her heart. Her palms were sweaty, her stomach tied in knots. Chief said he didn't want this to turn into something worthy of a crime documentary: That statement only under-scored just how out of touch he was.

It already had.

THIRTY-ONE

"Cute place," Candy remarked, leaning forward to get a better look at Annaliese's apartment. "I didn't know what to expect."

"Me either." Freya killed the engine and pulled the keys from the ignition. It felt good to have her badge and gun back. After popping by the department to pick them up, get a warrant, and let dispatch know she was back at work, she and her detective had hurried across town.

The small apartment building they were parked in front of looked like something out of a storybook. It had two units, one on the ground floor and one on the floor above, a brick walkway to the lobby, and perfectly manicured landscaping. The ground floor units each had a small garden and their own entrance. There was only one car parked out front, but it appeared to be in okay condition.

Unlike some other apartment complexes in town, this looked like a decent place for a single woman to live. Freya left the warrant—which allowed them to enter the apartment looking for anything related to Annaliese's death—on the dash, got out of her Jeep, and stared at the door to Annaliese's unit. "It's open," she commented, pulling her gun.

Candy fell into step behind her, pulling her gun out as well. "Do you want me to call for backup, just in case?"

"No, we're fine. They're busy taking care of the crime scene. We can handle this." Her heart thundered in her ears as she stepped closer to the door, which squeaked as she toed it open. Inside, the apartment was dark.

Moving slowly, she pushed the door the rest of the way open then stood in the doorway, waiting for her eyes to adjust to the light. The weak sun cast a dim glow through the trees in front of the apartment and into the building, allowing her to see a bit farther inside.

Nothing moved. She spun to the right, into a small room. It was filled with boxes and coats, everything ripped apart like someone looking for something hadn't cared what the room looked like when they left.

"Clear to the right," she murmured, keeping her voice low so Candy could hear her but hopefully nobody else, if they were in the apartment, could. "Head to the left—see what's in this main room."

Annaliese had an upstairs neighbor. If there had been a struggle recently—which would explain how messy the apartment was—chances were good they'd have heard it. She made a mental note to talk to them before they left.

As Candy walked away from her, Freya turned in the other direction. The small room she entered was a galley kitchen, with one way in and one way out. Just like the rest of the apartment she'd seen so far, the kitchen was messy, but there wasn't any sign of a person anywhere.

"Clear." Candy's voice was strong and carried easily to her. "There's a room here with the door closed."

"I'm coming." Hurrying now, Freya met up with Candy, following right behind her as she kicked open the door to the bedroom. She stepped past her, her gun still out in front of her.

The bed was made but strewn with clothes. It looked like

half of Annaliese's wardrobe had been pulled out and thrown onto the bed. The closet was a mess, with hangers at every angle, a huge pile of shoes and clothing on the floor. Cheap costume jewelry was scattered around the room, and something crunched under her boot as she walked.

At the bathroom, Candy kicked open the door. Freya watched as she carefully entered it, turning in a circle. She heard the sound of a shower curtain ripping back. "Nothing in here. I'm going to turn on the light, if that's okay?"

"Do it. I'm going to call dispatch, let them know the apartment was open when we got here."

She walked back to the living room, then headed outside and looped around the building before reaching the single car parked outside. Grabbing her radio, she called dispatch.

"Central, this is three-zero-one. We're at Annaliese Nowland's residence on Blue Hutch Lane. It was open when we arrived. I need you to look up the following plate." Freya rattled off the plate and waited.

"It comes back to a Doug King, seventy-eight, also lives on Blue Hutch Lane. Do you need me to look for any warrants?" The dispatcher sounded oddly chipper, considering everything that was going on today.

"No need. But I need you to look up Annaliese Nowland, find out if she has a vehicle registered to her, and put out a BOLO on it. We need to find it." Freya stalked back to Annaliese's apartment. Her car wasn't here, which meant she hadn't been killed at her apartment, the murderer had come back and moved the car after the fact, or had used it to transport the body. She wouldn't know for sure until she could piece together everything that had happened right before she died.

The stairs to the second-floor apartment were to her right, and she jogged up them, not pausing on the landing before knocking on the door. After a moment, an elderly man opened the door, his back bent, a wool sweater hanging loose on his frame.

"Can I help you?"

"Mr. King?" Freya asked. When the man nodded, she continued. "I'm Captain Sinclair with the Fawn Lake Police Department. I'm looking for Annaliese; have you heard anything from her recently?"

"Annaliese? The girl downstairs?" Mr. King gave a small nod. "Not since Sunday? Monday? The days run together. I was trying to nap, and it sounded like a herd of elephants downstairs."

"She didn't say anything to you?"

"No. What's this about?"

"Just checking. Did you hear anyone else in the apartment with her?"

"Just her. Probably talking on the phone, since we never heard anyone else moving around. She was crying, carrying on. I watched her throw some things in the back of her vehicle and tear out of here. Is she okay?"

"You're sure she was alone?" Her heart beat faster.

"Quite sure. I thought about asking her if she was okay, but it would have been a stupid question. Upset women don't like being asked if they're okay."

"What kind of car did she drive?"

He paused, thinking. "A Corolla."

"Thank you so much for your help," she said, then gave him a smile before hurrying back down the stairs to Annaliese's apartment.

"That's not her car," she announced to Candy, walking into the living room. "And her upstairs neighbor said he heard her down here Sunday or Monday afternoon talking like she was on the phone. And crying. Then he watched her throw some stuff into her car and tear out of here."

Candy nodded but didn't look at Freya. She was walking around, a frown on her face.

Freya frowned. "What? I've seen that expression on your face before."

"This place is a mess," Candy remarked, looking up at her while gesturing at a pile of books on the floor that had been kicked over into a landslide. "Does anyone really live like this? She was in her twenties, right? Isn't there a point when people stop living like absolute slobs?"

Freya thought back to how messy her place could get when she was in a funk or tied up with problems at work. "Well, sometimes it creeps up on you. When you're stressed, over-whelmed, when you just can't seem to focus."

"When you're running from your problems—" Candy began.

Freya stared at her, cutting her off. "When you're running from your problems. That's it. Mr. King said Annaliese was really upset and that she threw a bunch of stuff in her car before leaving. That doesn't sound like a planned vacation or a trip to the store. It sounds like someone who's freaking out." She turned and hurried into the bathroom. "What do you take with you when you need to make a run for it?"

"Um, clothes?" Candy was hurrying after her. "Yeah, clothes, your toiletries."

Freya bent, opening the bathroom vanity. "Her toiletries are gone." Turning, she yanked back the shower curtain. "No body wash, shampoo, conditioner."

"Okay. Makeup. Hair stuff. A hairdryer, if you have time to pack it."

Freya shook her head. "All of that stuff is gone too."

"You'd need underclothes," Candy said, leaving the bath-room and practically running into the bedroom. "Bras, under-wear. Besides the obvious jeans and tops, she'd have to have underthings or she'd be going to a mall really soon to pick up the necessities."

Candy stood in the middle of the bedroom and turned in a slow circle. "There are tons of clothes here, and I don't want to dig through them without knowing for sure that she wasn't killed here and that we're not looking for evidence of her killer, but I don't see a single bra. Most women have a few of them. You'd think there would be at least one of them visible in this mess."

"You'd think so," Freya said. "It looks more and more like she had to make a run for it. She grabbed what she thought she'd need and headed out. Got in her car, drove away... but then met up with our killer. Mr. King said she was alone when she left, so she must have run into him later." She closed her eyes, visualizing the scene.

"Maybe she knew him," she continued, leading the way back into the living room. "It's entirely possible that she knew this guy and wasn't afraid when she ran into him. Maybe he flagged her down. Or maybe they had planned to meet up."

"Maybe she had car trouble." Candy shrugged when Freya gave her a skeptical look. "Happens more often than you'd think. Murphy's Law, for sure. You're in a hurry to get out of Dodge and what happens? A flat tire. Maybe she needed help and he pulled up. She didn't have to know him if that was the case; she might have just been happy for the help."

"Only he didn't help her. He killed her. He might have thought that he could use her to make a point, or maybe he chose her." Freya walked over to the window and pulled the blind slats apart a bit to peek out. "Thick woods around here."

"Thick woods everywhere in Fawn Lake."

"Perfect for watching someone." She turned back to Candy. "But that's just speculation. We're getting ahead of ourselves. Let's list the things we do know. She was here, probably recently, since nobody has reported her door open or come by to check on her. She left, taking with her a lot of the things someone would usually need if they were going on the run. Her car isn't here, so it's probably still where she died or was abducted. We need to find it quickly and then hope there's going to be some evidence there that can lead us to our killer. I already called in a BOLO for it. Any information in here on where she works?"

"I'll look for a paystub," Candy said. "What are you going to do?"

"Dig through her Facebook." She cringed. She hated Facebook, hated the concept of feeling compelled to update friends, family, and sometimes complete strangers on what was going on in your life. It wasn't natural, at least not to her, but it seemed like she was one of the only people in the entire world who felt that way.

It only took a few taps on her phone to sign in to the fake account she'd made. Carla Moore wasn't a real person, but hopefully the account could be helpful. A quick search brought up Annaliese's profile.

The woman looked happy in her profile picture. She held a small dog, cuddling it close to her head. "Did you see any sign of a dog?" Freya called.

"None."

Maybe it belonged to a friend. Annaliese didn't update her page very often, and the most recent post Freya found was from a month ago. She'd been hiking with friends and had posted a shot from the top of the mountains. But what else was there?

As patiently as possible, she scrolled through her photos, looking for something that would jump out at her. Annaliese wasn't one of those people who posted selfies every single day, but she had been tagged in a number of shots, and these were the ones Freya was most interested in.

You could easily curate your profile if you worked hard enough on it, but it could be tricky to keep other people from tagging you. Annaliese had been tagged in a number of pictures. High school ones, it looked like. Someone uploading photos, perhaps to preserve memories from years gone by.

Swiping through the pictures, she found herself going faster and faster, then stopped. Excitement thrummed through her as she swiped back then tapped the picture and used two fingers to enlarge it.

Four girls, all grinning, their arms looped around each other, staring at the camera. They were dressed in hoodies and jeans and snuggled together on a bleacher like they'd been at a football game. Annaliese was easy to pick out in the photo, even without looking at her tag. Freya had her face seared into her mind.

But Annaliese wasn't the one Freya was staring at. Next to her, her head resting affectionately on Annaliese's shoulder, her hair in a high ponytail, was Jolie Marin. She'd deleted her tag, but Freya immediately recognized her.

"Candy..." She kept looking at the photo.

"What's up? You'll never guess what I just found." She held up a piece of paper, waving in the air. "Paystub." Finally, she looked at Freya; clocked the expression on her face. "What's wrong?"

"Annaliese and Jolie knew each other," she said, turning the phone so she could see the picture. "This is from high school. Look how close they are, how they're snuggled up together. You can't tell me the two of them weren't good friends; didn't hang out."

"Holy cow." Candy took the phone from her and tapped on the screen to make the tags pop up. "So who are these other girls? Mary Frost and Courtney Moore? And if Jolie and Annaliese both had something with the initials V.O. on it, where's that girl?"

"I don't know, but two of the girls in this photo are dead. We need to find Mary and Courtney. Now."

THIRTY-TWO

Freya drove, the windows down, cold air blowing in, her foot heavy on the gas pedal. Even though she knew she should probably slow down, knew that driving this fast was dangerous, there wasn't any way she was easing up on the gas. They needed to get to Mary Frost's house, needed to make sure that she was okay, needed to keep her from getting killed like two of her high school friends.

Candy was in the passenger seat, her fingers flying over her phone as she tapped on the screen, enlarging a photo to get a better look before flipping past it to move on to the next one. From time to time she muttered under her breath, and it was this that finally caused Freya to look over at her while they were stopped at a red light.

"Please tell me you've found something good." They'd called dispatch and gotten Mary's address, but she had no landline so there wasn't any way to reach out to her to warn her of what was coming except by doing it in person. She lived all the way across town, in one of the nice, newer neighborhoods, and Freya had to hope that the neighbors there were so nosy nobody would try anything stupid in broad daylight.

"So, Courtney lives out of town, which we already knew, but only one town over, in Taylors. It's not like she moved halfway across the country. She's still local. Going to see Mary first is the smart move since she's here in Fawn Lake."

Freya's phone rang. Candy stabbed the screen in front of them to answer, but it was Freya who spoke first.

"Brad. What do you have for me?"

"Lance has the body back at the morgue. I just left him there and am going to lead a search around your property to see if there's anything else we missed."

"Great. Do you have any good news for me?"

"Good news?" He chuckled. "How about someone shipped Lance a box?"

Freya's heart sank. "Please tell me there wasn't a tongue in there."

"Sounds like the killer is cutting out the middleman and helping us out by delivering his trophies straight to the morgue." He sighed. "Lance wanted me to call you because he jumped right into work mode. No piercing hole on the tongue."

"So it wasn't Jolie's."

"Safe assumption. I'll call you when I have more."

He hung up, and Freya turned to Candy.

"Call the PD in Taylors; tell them we think Courtney's in danger and we worry she may be dead. They need to perform a health and welfare check immediately. Two women out of the four in that picture are dead and I want to know why. The only way we're going to get any answers is to get to Courtney or Mary before the murderer does, and with another tongue... it may be too late for someone."

Candy nodded and tapped her phone again before pressing it up to her ear. She chewed on her lower lip before speaking, and Freya only half-listened as she let her detective's words wash over her.

Just a few more turns and they'd be at the Frost house. Just a few more minutes and they'd know if Mary was still alive. She pressed down harder on the gas, blowing through a stop sign when she saw she was going to be the only one there and taking a turn on two wheels as she sped into Mary's neighborhood.

A polite sign reminding her to slow down because there were children playing caused her to take her foot off the gas a little. Then her GPS beeped at her, and she slowed even more, turning up the driveway of one of the largest homes she'd ever seen.

"Crap. Courtney's been reported missing." Candy hung up, leaning forward to get a better look at the house. "She didn't show up for work, and her coworkers haven't been able to get in touch with her. I told the officer I spoke to that she was likely in danger."

They hopped out of the car, slamming their doors behind them. The sounds were loud in the silence of the neighborhood.

"Let's hope Mary is here." Freya got out, leading the way to the house, Candy close on her heels. She would have loved to spend some time walking around the property, familiarizing herself with the layout, looking to see if anything appeared out of place, but she didn't have time for that right now.

She pressed the doorbell and stepped back as Candy walked along the wide front porch, trying to peer in the large windows. Even from where she stood, Freya could see heavy drapes in all of them. They were thick, hung to prevent people from being able to do precisely what Candy was attempting. Candy cupped her hands around her face and pressed her nose up against the glass.

"Anything?" Freya asked.

Candy stepped back; shook her head. "There's a light on, but I don't see any movement. Can't see much of anything, thanks to these curtains."

"Yeah, well, that's the idea." Freya pressed the doorbell again, then rested her hand lightly on her gun. She hoped she wouldn't need it, but fear tickled the back of her neck. The house was still, so still, but there was an energy to it. It felt like it was breathing.

Someone was inside.

Just as Freya was about to slam her fist on the door to try to get anyone's attention, they heard the door being unlocked. Two deadbolts slid back, and the door swung open just a hair.

"Can I help you?" It was a woman's voice, and Freya stepped to the side. The sight of the hand curled around the door made her think this woman couldn't possibly be Mary. The woman they were looking for should be in her twenties, and there were age spots on this woman's hand that made her look much older.

"We're looking for Mary Frost," she said, pulling her badge from where it was clipped on her belt and holding it out to show her. "I'm Captain Sinclair with the Fawn Lake PD, and this is Detective Ellinger."

The door swung open a bit more, giving Freya her first real look at the woman in the house. She was older, just like Freya had thought, with a slight stoop and hair that was graying slightly. Her hair looked wispy but had been pulled back and fixed into a tight bun on the back of her head. Her skin was pale except for the age spots, and she was dressed all in black with a half apron tied around her waist and a rag in her free hand.

"Mrs. Frost is not here. She left this morning, and I don't expect to see her back until afternoon." The woman sounded like a recording, as if she knew exactly what she was supposed to say when asked. She began to shut the door.

"Where did she go?" Freya's foot flew out, and she blocked the door, shifting her weight forward so there wouldn't be a chance the woman could push her out of the way. "We need to find her. Now."

A pause. The woman didn't answer at first. She eyeballed

Freya and then turned her head to look at Candy. "Mrs. Frost doesn't like to be bothered during the day."

"Ma'am, do you read the news?" Freya's patience was thinner than it had been in a while.

A slight nod.

"Then you know about the dead women. Now, I know it's easy to lock yourself in a huge house like this and pretend like terrible things aren't happening in the real world, but we have reason to think that Mary might be in danger. We want to find her, make sure that she's okay. And we need your help to do that. We're worried about her safety."

"Oh dear." The woman exhaled and hung her head. After a moment, she looked back up at the two of them. "Okay. Yes. She's getting her hair and nails done right now at Francine's Salon and then was going to go dress shopping before her charity dinner."

Freya felt a muscle in her jaw twitch. Some people were so out of touch with how everyone else lived that it was almost laughable. "Where's this dinner being held?"

"At the country club—where else?"

"Where else indeed? Thank you for your time—you've been very helpful. Do you have her cell number? That would allow us to contact her, in case we can't find her."

She was already shaking her head before she finished speaking. "No, I'm not allowed to give it out. She'd be really upset with me. It happened once before when I didn't know not to give it out and she was really angry." The woman sounded like a little kid who'd gotten in trouble.

Freya took a deep breath and removed her foot from where she had it blocking the door. "Alright. Thank you again for your help."

She spun on her heel, Candy right next to her.

"I already have the salon plugged into my phone," Candy said, getting into the passenger's seat. "I don't know it. I know that might come as a surprise to you, given how fancy and on top of the latest fashions I am."

Freya snorted and shook her head. "Are you totally sure about that? I'm pretty sure I've seen you shopping in the outlet mall up towards Asheville."

Candy laughed. "Busted. It's true, Freya—I dress way down at work so nobody finds out that I'm a secret fashionista."

"I knew it." Freya glanced at her phone to see where to turn next and then pulled out into traffic. "Hey, what's our ETA?"

"If the app's to be believed, we'll be at the salon in ten minutes. Hopefully Mary's still there, or we're going to have to try to track her down at the country club before our murderer does." She paused then turned to her. "You really think she's the key?"

"I think it's possible she's the last one alive, and I hope she'll realize that if she wants to stay that way, she needs to talk to us."

"Or she'll die?"

"Well, that sounds like a threat." She waited impatiently at a stop sign. "But yeah, I think if she refuses, then she's going to die. How to phrase it without it sounding like we're going to be the ones to kill her though..." She shrugged.

"She'll see reason, I'm sure of it. Two of her closest high school friends are confirmed dead, a third is missing. Do you believe in coincidences?"

Freya shook her head. "Nope. Jolie and Annaliese died in the same way. We have two tongues, and we don't think either belong to Jolie. Without DNA testing we won't know for sure if one belongs to Annaliese, but that still leaves us with an extra tongue."

"Courtney." Candy's voice was hard.

"That's what I'm worried about. We don't have time to go to Taylors right now to search for her, so we have to hope the officers there turn something up."

"Freya, I hate to say it, but why would the Fawn Lake Killer be targeting these women? On the surface, the murders all look similar. But once you start digging into them, the threads tying them together fall apart. And the fact that our current victims were friends in the past... I don't know, it makes me wonder."

Freya smacked the steering wheel. "I know. I can't wrap my mind around that. Michelle's death was terrible, but it was a crime of opportunity. And she wasn't missing her tongue. There wasn't anything with V.O. at her crime scene."

"But the initials match at both our crime scenes. So there has to be something there. And I know you've been thinking it's the original killer, but what if it is a copycat?"

Freya didn't respond. Instead, she pressed down harder on the gas. "I'm afraid of that," she finally said. "It all fit so perfectly that it was the Fawn Lake Killer, but I could have been wrong."

Silence fell between the two of them. Freya's hand was sweaty on the wheel, and she gripped it tighter, not wanting to think about what she'd just admitted to Candy.

Candy cleared her throat. "These women. Do you think they did something? It's one thing to target random women because you're a killer but another entirely to take out a high school friend group."

Freya didn't answer at first. "I think if the girls were involved in something bad then there's no way Mary doesn't know why they're being targeted. We need to find out who V.O. is. There are too many missing pieces to assume anything for sure."

"Oh, I'd wager Mary knows. We just have to get her to tell us." Candy drummed her fingers on her knee. "V.O. wasn't in that photo."

"Nope. So we have to hope Mary will have information for us." Freya took another turn, then hammered the gas. Just a few more minutes and they'd find her. Hopefully then all of this would make sense.

THIRTY-THREE

Freya had never been in Francine's Salon, but it was exactly what she pictured. All white walls, tons of greenery, classical music. The staff wore all white, the clients looked perfectly coiffed and made-up, and everyone stared when she and Candy walked in the front door.

"We're looking for Mary Frost," Freya said to the woman at the front desk. The woman had long nails and thick hair she tossed over her shoulder.

"I can't give out the names of our clients."

"You're not a doctor's office; you do nails and hair." She tapped her badge. "Where is Mary Frost?"

The woman took a step back, then pointed to the right. "There. She's letting her nails dry in that massage chair."

"You've been so helpful," Freya said, rapping her knuckles on the counter before she and Candy walked over to Mary Frost. The salon chair she sat in was white and puffy, the massage motor barely audible.

"Mrs. Frost?" Freya lightly touched her on the shoulder. She was so still she could be sleeping.

The woman didn't move.

"Mrs. Frost, we need to talk to you." She tapped her on the shoulder and was about to grab her and give her a little shake when the woman's eyes flew open.

"What?" she snapped, pulling an earbud from her ear and opening her eyes. Immediately she held up one freshly manicured hand to help block out the light while glaring at Freya and Candy.

"Mary Frost?" Even Freya could hear the relief in her voice. "We need to talk to you."

"Is there a problem?" Mary sat up, taking her time. "What's going on? Did something happen to Brian?"

"Not that we know of. I'm Captain Sinclair, and this is Detective Ellinger. Is there somewhere private the three of us can talk?"

"Not right now." Mary settled back in her seat, throwing them each a dark gaze. "If there isn't an emergency, then I don't see why the two of you bothered me. I'm very busy, as you can see. There's a fundraiser dinner I'm heading to later today and I have to make sure that I look my best."

"Mrs. Frost," Candy said, "you're not listening to us. It's imperative we talk to you. Now."

"*I'm busy.*" Her voice was full of ice. "Can't you see that I'm busy and you're bothering me? Am I going to have to get the owner to ask you two to leave?"

"Well, we can talk right here if you don't want to go to a private room." Freya raised her voice. "I don't care if we cause a scene."

"I'll call the police—"

"We *are* the police, Mrs. Frost, and we're here because at least two of your high school friends have been murdered and we'd like to talk to you about it," Freya said.

The room went completely silent. Glancing around, Freya wasn't at all surprised to find that everyone else had stopped doing whatever they were up to and were openly gawking at her.

Mary squinted at them. "What was your name? Saltzman? Saintclair? It doesn't matter. I'll call your superior. This is harassment."

"No, this is us making sure you don't end up dead like your friends," said Freya.

"You can't possibly think I had anything to do with it," Mary hissed. "I didn't kill anyone, and if that's what you're insinuating—"

"We're concerned you might be next." Candy cleared her throat. "We need to talk to you, see why the killer is targeting your high school friend group."

Mary didn't respond, but her hand fluttered up to her neck, tracing a line there.

"You saw in the news Jolie had her throat cut, didn't you?" Freya raised an eyebrow. Someone had turned the music down so they could hear what was going on. "Sounds like a terrible way to go, doesn't it?"

"This is police harassment." She dropped her hand from her throat, her face growing red. "Whatever you two are trying to do, I don't want any part of it."

"Well, if you don't want to help us make sure you don't end up next on the killer's list, then we'll have to ask you to come down to the station for questioning. How about you join us outside? Our car is waiting." Candy jerked her thumb over her shoulder.

Mary's mouth fell open. "You're arresting me?"

"You're not cooperating with our investigation." Candy shrugged as she spoke. "If you don't cooperate, then we have to do whatever it takes to get information from you. I'm sure you understand."

"Fine. I'll cooperate." Mary grabbed her purse, slung it over her arm, and stood up. "But I have a charity dinner I have to attend. This can't take long."

Freya took her by the elbow. Not that Mary looked like the usual suspect who made a run for it, especially not on those heels, but she didn't want to risk it. "This will take as long as it needs to, Mrs. Frost."

Candy stepped in front of them, holding the door open, then closed it carefully before the three of them walked over to a picnic table under an oak tree.

It was only when they were all sitting, Freya and Candy on one side, Mary on the other, that she spoke. "Should I call a lawyer?"

"Do you think you need one?" Freya cocked her head and stared at her. Was the woman simply rude and used to getting her way all the time? Or did she know something?

"What was your name again?"

"Captain Sinclair. If you want a lawyer here, Mrs. Frost, you're welcome to give one a call. We're not going to stop you."

A car pulled up in the space closest to them, the driver staring at the three of them through the windshield. Mary turned her head and lifted her hand to block the woman's view. "No, I'll answer your questions without one present."

"Great." Freya tapped on her phone then handed it across the table to her. "Tell me about this photo."

"That's me and three of my friends. Courtney, Jolie, and Annaliese. But I think you already know that or you wouldn't be here talking to me." She chewed her lower lip but stopped when Freya noticed.

"Two of them are dead and the third's missing."

Mary's face twitched, fear there and gone in a second. "Who's dead? I saw Jolie's death on the news, but I didn't know anyone else had died."

"Annaliese," Candy said. The younger woman was eyeballing her, obviously trying to figure out how much Mary knew and what she was thinking. "Courtney's been reported as missing. We don't want to assume anything, but we're worried for her safety."

Mary took a deep breath and planted her hands on the picnic table.

"You look pale, Mrs. Frost. Have you heard from Jolie or Annaliese recently?" Freya asked.

No response.

"Why would someone be targeting the four of you?" Freya tapped the table to get Mary's attention. The woman's eyes flicked up before she looked back down. "Mrs. Frost, I hope you can understand, it's more than a little worrisome to us, all that's going on, and we think there must be something connecting the four of you. What is it?"

"I don't know." Mary took a deep breath and rolled her shoulders back before staring directly at Freya. "Why do you think I should know? High school was years ago." She forced a laugh.

Freya stilled. Mary had all but confirmed that something had happened in high school.

"Some people have very long memories," offered Candy. "Mrs. Frost, if someone is killing the women in your high school circle of friends, then I'm sure you must know why. If you tell us, we can help you. If you don't, then you'll be on your own... and you'd better hope that whoever killed Jolie and Annaliese doesn't know where you live."

No response. Mary was flushed and couldn't look Candy or Freya in the eyes. She picked at a stop on the picnic table with one long nail.

"Do you know someone with the initials V.O.?" asked Freya.

Mary froze. She stopped picking at the table. Slowly, she looked up at Freya.

And shook her head.

"You sure? There wasn't another friend in your group with those initials?"

"No."

Freya arched an eyebrow. Mary had started picking at the picnic table again, and she reached out; stilled her hand. "We want to help you, but in order for us to do that, you have to help us first."

Mary swallowed hard and shook her head. "I don't know that I can help you. I think you're on your own." She stood up, bracing her hand on the picnic table for balance. Carefully she stepped back over the bench she'd been sitting on. "Am I under arrest?"

"No, ma'am." Freya stared at her. "We'll let you know if we need to talk to you again."

"Good. This was a farce, and I have things to do." Mary turned back to the salon, but what Candy asked stopped her in her tracks.

"Hey, Mrs. Frost, do you happen to have any tattoos?" asked Candy.

"I hardly think that matters." She didn't turn back to look at the two of them.

"Oh, I think it matters a lot." Freya stood, taking her time. They didn't have any reason to hold Mary, no way to keep her from walking away from them. Sure, she was in danger, but that obviously didn't seem to matter much to the woman. She was free to walk away from them at any time. "It must be hidden somewhere you can keep it covered up."

"We're done here," Mary said, then glanced at the two of them over her shoulder. Her mouth was pulled tight into a line, her cheeks bright red. "I can't talk about this any longer. Please leave me alone."

Freya and Candy watched her go. Mary hit the salon door at a half-run.

"Well, she was just delightful," Candy said sarcastically.

"Here we are, trying to keep her alive, and she cares more about what she looks like than the fact that someone might be looking for her."

Freya shrugged. "She's absolutely terrified, Candy. She knows a lot more than she's letting on. Let's find out what it is."

THIRTY-FOUR

His car was hot with his windows rolled up, but they were tinted, and that was the best way to keep anyone from seeing what he was doing.

Watching. He was watching.

He'd watched as the two detectives hurried into the salon. Watched as Freya frog-marched Mary out. Watched as they sat at the picnic table.

How funny that he'd sat at that same picnic table just last week watching the woman get her hair done.

How fun to see Mary with Freya. The next time they were together it would be because Mary was dying.

The thrill made his heart beat faster.

Oh! Mary was up. Her gaze cut across the parking lot, and he froze, but her eyes slid over his car. She hurried back to the salon, leaving the two detectives at the table.

They sat there a moment longer, then rushed to Freya's Jeep.

Fascinating. They were so close to figuring it all out, but they didn't have a chance.

He was too far ahead.

THIRTY-FIVE

"Mary Morgan Frost," Candy read from her cell phone as Freya drove them back to the office. "We'll get more information on her when we look her up through The Last One, but right now there are a few things I can tell you thanks to her prevalent social-media use."

"Of course she's a social-media fan. Hit me."

"She and her husband, Brian, were high school sweethearts and just celebrated their anniversary. He's in finance, which explains the expensive look thing she has going on. And from her 'about me' section, it doesn't look like she's ever held down a job."

"Okay, so she's a trophy wife?"

"Mmhmm. She's big on working for charities. More than one person has written on her Facebook thanking her for all the hard work she's done for their charity. Breast cancer research, helping with animal adoption events, making sure businesses are ADA compliant, you name it, she's doing it."

"Really?" Freya frowned and tapped her brakes at a red light. "It probably sounds terrible to say, but that's not the impression I got from her during our little meeting."

"She wasn't super personable, was she? But you mentioned you thought she was scared. That still feel right to you?"

"It does." Freya pulled through the green light and gassed it. The sooner they got to the police department, the sooner they could do more research on Mary. "It just feels like the person we met and who other people think she is are totally different. That could be fear."

"Because you think she knows more than she's letting on."

"I do, yeah. You saw her, almost completely unable to make eye contact with me while we were talking. If that's not the sign of someone hiding something, I'll go back through Basic Law Enforcement Training."

"I'd miss you," Candy said dryly, then swiped at her screen then tapped a few times.

"Is she friends with anyone with the initials V.O.?" Freya asked.

"Nope. I just checked. She is friends with Jolie, Annaliese, and Courtney though. So it seems like they kept in touch."

Freya pulled into the police department parking lot and killed the engine. "That's good, but it's still not enough. I want to know everything about this woman." She paused, considering. "Let me see a picture of her and her husband."

"Here you go. The happy couple. He looks about like you'd expect a finance guy to look like."

"That's a fake tan," Freya said, taking the phone from Candy and enlarging the picture. "And nobody has teeth that white. But look at this, look at how he has his arm around her."

"Tight," Candy said, and Freya nodded.

"Really tight." She swiped. "And here. And here. Man, he's a little protective, isn't he?"

"You want me to look into Brian as well, don't you?" Candy asked, and Freya grinned.

"You got it."

"Ooh, then you'll love this little tidbit," Candy said. "Mary and Brian both graduated from Fawn Lake High School, but according to her Facebook, she also went to another high school. Care to guess which one?"

"Don't leave me hanging."

"Taylors High School."

Freya froze. "Wait, what? Taylors? That's where Courtney lives."

"And it's where Mary is from. Hang on." She tapped a few times. "And Brian. They're both from Taylors."

"And then they both ended up graduating from Fawn Lake High School? No way is that a coincidence. What about Jolie, Annaliese, and Courtney? Where did they go to high school? I'm going to go out on a limb and say it was Taylors."

Candy tapped. Nodded. "You're a good guesser."

Freya glanced at her watch. The police in Taylors could look for Courtney themselves. She had to figure out what had happened to Jolie and Annaliese.

"Hey, you never told me where Annaliese worked," Freya said.

Candy frowned. "You're right. The day got away from me. She worked at Over Easy."

"No, she didn't." Freya frowned, trying to remember. "We'd recognize her, right? I'm certain I've never seen her before, so how would that be?"

"We only know the waitstaff, but there's a whole host of people who work in restaurants," Candy told her. "I know you've never experienced the joy of waiting tables, but I did it all through high school. Annaliese could have been working in the back as a dishwasher or she could have been helping run the place."

"That could explain why we didn't recognize her. Okay, let's go with that for now, at least until we figure out exactly what her position was. I want to talk something out with you again."

"What's that?"

"I think you may be right about the Fawn Lake Killer. The bite on Jolie's ear was the same. You received a letter that perfectly matched the one I received when I was working the case. The similarities are too intense to believe it's two totally separate perps." She paused, gathering her thoughts. "The only explanation if it's not the same guy is that it's a copycat."

Candy nodded. "But those details weren't released to the public, so it had to be someone intimately involved in the case to know them."

Freya nodded. "Right, but we're forgetting one important thing—perps love to share what they've done. There's no reason why it couldn't be a protégé. Maybe the Fawn Lake Killer has gotten too old to be out chasing women through the woods."

"Or maybe this killer just wanted to mess with you. He knew the Fawn Lake Killer, and he's playing with you. Making the murders so similar you'd immediately leap to it being the original killer is a real mind game. The question is why. Why would someone want to mess with you so badly? Why would a copycat killer want to pretend to be someone else instead of forging their own path? Or how would they know so many details that very few people do?"

Freya's stomach twisted. The thought that it wasn't the same guy, that she'd been barking up the wrong tree? It was enough to make her sick. Shaking her head, she pushed that worry away. Now wasn't the time to beat herself up. She needed to act. Handle things.

"Right. Nathan is an option. He had that photo of Jolie with him, and that bothers me. What I wouldn't give to find him right now and bring him in for questioning."

"Okay, but what about Steve or Robert Petit? They fit the bill, if it weren't for their alibis. Steve couldn't have killed Jolie and Millicent, and Larry Fish came through for Robert." She caught the way Freya raised an eyebrow and nodded. "Yeah, an officer found him and talked to him. I got that text while we were talking to Mary. We need to look elsewhere."

"That's what I don't like. We have plenty of things to do." Freya nodded while she spoke, the words coming faster and faster. "First thing when we get back, talk to Brad and give him information on Mary. He's going to be in charge of keeping her under surveillance, of making sure there's an officer on her at all times. We also need to talk to someone at Over Easy, see if they knew anything about Annaliese maybe having problems with someone and try to narrow down when she disappeared. We need to find out who V.O. is. Look into the Frosts. It really seems like that group of friends is being targeted, but why? Nathan's still in the wind, and we need to talk to him, and—"

Freya's phone rang, and she reached out; tapped the screen to answer it. "Esther, hi. Is everything okay?"

"Fine, Freya, fine. I didn't know if you had time to come by tonight."

She closed her eyes for a moment, then shook her head. "Esther, I wish I could, but I think we're going to have to choose a rain date. Is something going on?"

"No, no. Don't worry about me." The woman laughed, the sound light and airy. "Just wanted to see you, that's all. Call me sometime, darling."

She hung up before Freya could respond. Candy reached out, touched her on the arm.

"Hey, you okay? I know Esther was sent a tongue, but you told her to stay in the house, right? Nothing will happen to her."

Freya nodded. "Right. She's fine. Totally fine."

"Just worried about you," Candy said, and Freya nodded.

"Sure, she does that." She glanced at the time. "When does Over Easy close?"

"Late," Candy said. "Eight maybe? You headed there now?"

"After we check in with Brad. I want to make sure all three of us know what we're doing first."

As if on cue, their phones both vibrated. Candy grabbed hers and opened up the text. "Speak of the devil," she said. "Brad just sent a picture of a car on the side of the road."

"Annaliese's? Let's move."

THIRTY-SIX

"We're back from seeing Mary Frost," Freya said to Brad's back. The detective was standing in her door and whipped around at the sound of her voice. "You have good news for us, don't you?"

"We found Annaliese's Corolla," he said, handing her a photo. "The back was packed with suitcases, and there was a bank bag from Over Easy on the front seat. She got stuck in some mud on a backroad and couldn't get herself out."

"Explains the mud on her shoes and body," Candy said. "If she got stuck and got out, it also gives the killer a prime opportunity to attack her. Backroads tend to be less traveled, so chances are good nobody was going to drive by, and she couldn't leave since her car was stuck."

"Good point," Freya said. "And it sounds like she probably wasn't waiting tables, if she had a bank bag with her."

"Just like we thought," Candy agreed. "So she got out, walked for help, and ended up running into the killer?" She made a face. "That doesn't really seem to fit his MO."

Freya spoke up. "No, I'd bet anything he was following her. It was probably just his lucky day that her car got stuck and he was right there to swoop in."

"Do you think she knew him?" asked Brad, and Freya nodded.

"More and more it seems like it's not the Fawn Lake Killer." The words stuck in her throat, and she swallowed hard. "Candy and I have been talking it through, and I think we need to pivot in regards to the motive. Jolie and Annaliese were friends in high school. And Mary definitely seemed worried when we talked to her, which tells me she knows more than she's letting on. The idea that they knew each other and might know the killer makes sense to me." She tapped her chin. "Brad, did anyone search the car? Take fingerprints?"

"Yep. I have a team working on that now, but let me tell you, it was a mess. I'm talking fast-food wrappers on the floor, empty cups, dirty laundry. The suitcases in the backseat tracks with your theory of her skipping town. It's going to be like finding a needle in a haystack to dig up anything worthwhile."

"We're closing in on this guy," Freya said. "I feel like we were one step behind him, but now we know about Mary, so we have that going for us. I want you in charge of following Mary Frost. Hate to tell you this, but she won't be happy you're there. Keep an eye on her from a distance and pull officers as needed to watch her. You don't have to be the only one, especially since I want her covered twenty-four-seven."

Candy sighed. "You'd think she'd be grateful we're trying to save her, but you'd be wrong."

"You got it. Anything else?" Brad seemed eager to get going.

Freya sighed. "I'm pretty sure it's fear making her act like she is, but Candy's right, she's not got a great attitude. Rich people tend to think money will protect them, and now she gets to find out for the first time that it doesn't. She's rich, but that doesn't matter to a killer."

"Got it. Scared and rich aren't a good combination," Brad said.

"Not really," Freya replied. "By the way, did you ever find

anything on Nathan Caldwell? The man is a ghost, and I really would love to chat with him."

"Yeah, right. Nothing from the hospital, no reports on him even existing. I put out a BOLO on him, and it's like he up and disappeared."

"Of course he did." Freya paused, thinking. "Okay, Candy, research," she said, pointing at her. "Not Nathan, because he'll show up when he does, but the Frosts. Something's going on there." When Candy nodded, she turned to Brad. "You, Mary Frost duty."

"And you?" Candy was already walking towards her office. "What are you doing?"

"I'm going to where they found Annaliese's car. I also want to reach out to Lance, see if he has anything he can give me about the tongue someone sent him. And I really want to know why Mary transferred here in high school." Her head hurt.

"Okay. Sounds good." Brad gave her a grin. "We're close to ending this, guys. We have to be."

"We have to be," Freya agreed. "Keep in touch—let me know how things are going out there."

The three of them scattered. Freya had barely turned on her car when her phone rang. She stabbed the green button to answer the call.

"Lance, my favorite person to hear from when it's all falling apart. Got anything good?"

"Remember Jolie's tattoo and how we couldn't make out all of the numbers?" Lance's voice was deep, a sound that settled heavily in Freya's bones. "I'll give you one guess who has a matching one."

"Annaliese." Her mind raced. She'd been right—there was something to the tattoo. "I need that date, Lance."

"I'd love to tell you that, I really would. It's on her ankle, but it looks like she tried to cut it off."

"She tried… to cut it off?" Her stomach lurched. "How do you cut off a tattoo?"

"I'll show you if you swing by. It's illegible, I'm so sorry. If I hadn't already seen the one on Jolie, I'm not sure I'd have recognized it as a date."

Freya sighed. "Bad news for me. But I found a photo tying the two women together. I just wish we knew what the date was on their tattoos. It could make this whole thing a lot easier." She paused. "Is it another stick and poke like Jolie's?"

"Sure is. And I guess you figured Annaliese was missing her tongue."

"I peeked."

He chuckled. "I figured. And Brad told you about my mail?"

Freya's stomach lurched. "I'm really sorry about that. I don't know why you're being targeted." She paused. "Are you okay?"

"I'm fine. You think a tongue is really going to bother me? Maybe if they'd sent a different body part. Not sure if you've spoken to Brad yet, but there's no piercing hole in it , so we can rule out that it belonged to Jolie."

Her stomach twisted. "I'm worried I might know who it belongs to. Okay, you handle what you're doing, and I'll do what I do best. Talk to you."

Freya hung up. She drummed the steering wheel, barely aware that she had slowed to a stop in the middle of the road. It wasn't until the car behind her honked that she snapped out of her thoughts.

"Sorry," she called, holding her hand above her head. "I'm sorry. I swear I'm not an idiot." She shook her head to clear it, then jerked the wheel and mashed down on the gas to pull into a bank parking lot.

On one hand, she could get involved in the search of Annaliese's car. It was under control though—she was sure of it. It would be fine. Patrol was good, thorough. Besides, if the car was as much a mess as Brad was saying, what good would she even be?

What she really wanted to do was dig into the date both Jolie and Annaliese had tattooed on them. It wasn't uncommon for close friends to get tattoos to commemorate events or friendship, but why a date? And why a stick and poke?

Normally people got tattoos at reputable salons. Unless, of course, they were too young to get them. Or they didn't want anyone else to know what the tattoo was. If only she knew the date, she'd be able to tell if it was something important or just a whimsical friendship tattoo.

And if it was important, it might help her make strides in the case.

Over Easy was right across the street, and Freya hopped out of her Jeep and hurried to it. The bell on the door tinkled as she walked in, the smell of pasta greeted her, and it felt almost normal to be walking into the buzz of human conversation.

"Captain Sinclair, hi." Penny appeared, an oversized laminated menu in her hands. "Just one?"

"I just need to talk to someone about Annaliese Nowland," Freya said. "You work with her, right? How well do you know her?"

"Yeah, I work with her. Kinda. She's in more of a manager position, so it's not like the two of us catch up in between waiting on tables, but I know who she is." Penny fanned herself with the menu. "She didn't show up for work this morning, so I got called in early, to handle the books and make sure the cash drawer was ready to go, which is not something I ever have to do. No idea why she missed; she didn't pick up her phone when we tried calling her. It's frustrating, if I'm being honest. I was really looking forward to sleeping in." She paused, eyeballing Freya. "Why?"

Freya chewed her lip, unwilling to give the woman any information she didn't have to. "Just following up on something.

How did she seem last time you saw her? And when did you last see her?"

"Oh, Annaliese is always in a hurry, always looking over her shoulder. I like calling her a rabbit because of the way she jumps at loud sounds." Penny frowned. "As for when I last saw her... over the weekend. Why? Will you tell me what's going on?"

"First, tell me about her tattoo."

"Tattoo?" Penny shook her head. "I don't think she has one. Let me think. But remember, it's not like the two of us hung out a lot outside of work, but no... no tattoos. Not that I know of anyway."

Freya changed tactics. "When did you move to Fawn Lake?"

"Oof, lemme think. Six years, give or take. Why? What in the world are you asking me about that for? Before you ask, I didn't know Annaliese when I first moved here. I met her working here."

"Thanks for your help," Freya said. "I'll get out of your hair, but you've been great."

"Have I? That feels like a lie." Penny laughed and shook her head.

"You never know how something random you say will end up being useful," Freya said. "So I appreciate your time. Enjoy the rest of your day, Penny." With that, she turned and left Over Easy, hurrying back across the street to her Jeep.

Before finding the connection between Annaliese and Jolie, she would have told Penny to stay safe, but there wasn't any reason to. Penny wasn't the one in danger. Mary was. Courtney was, if she was still alive.

And while she had clues and hints that should point her to the murderer, she felt just as lost as she had the day before. He was sneaky, that much was obvious.

The killer was good.

She had to be better. The four women were the key. Two were dead, one was missing, and the fourth... well, the fourth had her own host of problems.

Her phone rang. "Candy. Everything okay?"

When Candy responded, her voice was high and tight. "I just talked to Taylors PD. They found Courtney's body."

THIRTY-SEVEN

Even though she wanted to come, Candy stayed behind to research Mary and Brian Frost. There was just too much work for Freya's team to do for anyone to buddy up, although having more eyes on the scene wasn't ever a bad thing.

Freya pushed her Jeep as hard as she dared, not wanting to speed excessively but driven by the need to get to Taylors as quickly as possible. The sooner she got there, the sooner they could wrap all this up.

An hour later, she parked her Jeep in a small gravel parking lot. Throwing on a high-res jacket with POLICE written across the back, she locked her Jeep and walked over to a crowd of officers.

Beyond them, caution tape was strung around the scene, the bright yellow of the plastic still highly visible even though dusk was falling. On the other side of the caution tape sat an investigation kit. Two evidence bags were next to it in the grass.

Freya barely glanced at them before speaking.

"Who's in charge here?" she asked, grabbing her badge and flashing it at the first man, who turned to look at her. He had a high forehead and thick black hair pushed back from his face.

His jaw was tight, and it barely relaxed after taking in her badge.

"Captain Lopez," he said, shaking her hand. "Marco. You must be the Fawn Lake captain who Detective Ellinger told me would be coming to the scene."

"Call me Freya," she said, smiling at him. "And thanks for giving us a call to come out and check out the scene. I appreciate it." Not all departments were willing to work freely with others. The fact that there was a serial killer working their way through a group of women had probably been instrumental in inspiring the inter-department collaboration.

"I appreciate you coming out. I'd warn you that the scene isn't pretty, but I have a pretty good feeling that it isn't going to bother you, so come on." He lifted the tape for the two of them, and Freya ducked under it, following him over to where a single detective snapped photos of the crime scene.

"Freya, this is Holly Kline, one of my detectives. She was the first on the scene." The woman's brown hair was pulled back in a tight bun, her face free of makeup. No-nonsense. Freya liked it.

"Hey," Freya said, shaking her hand, "what can you tell me?"

Holly juggled the camera and gestured at the body. "First off, we have a positive ID. Her driver's license was tucked right under her body. It's like the perp wanted us to know who she was."

"He's been doing that," Freya said.

"Considerate. As you can see, her throat was slit. After you guys called us to do a health and welfare check and it came out that she hadn't shown up for work, we put out a BOLO on her car. Got a hit and found her here in the park."

"Please tell me nobody else has seen her."

Courtney's throat was cut, the slash gaping. Even though night was falling, flies buzzed around her, crawling on her cut flesh, feeding. They lifted in a cloud when Freya snapped on a pair of rubber gloves and bent down, carefully opening the woman's mouth.

"No, just us." A pause. "What are you doing?"

"Our two victims had their tongues cut out. Looks like Courtney did too." Freya sighed and stood, her eyes flicking over the scene. "Do you have the pictures you need? Can I move the body?"

"Sure. What are you looking for?" Holly asked, stepping closer. "I can help."

"If you two have this under control," Marco said, "I have some things to do. Send an officer to her house, notify next of kin. You two good?"

"We're great," Freya said. She kneeled by Courtney, carefully picking up her wrist and pushing back her sleeve. "I'm looking for a tattoo."

"Got it." Holly dropped to her knees on the other side of Courtney.

The two women worked in silence, looking on Courtney's wrists, then her ankles, for a tattoo. Even though that was where Jolie and Annaliese had their tattoos, they didn't get lucky until Freya teased up the bottom of Courtney's shirt.

There. Peeping out from the top of her pants, just inside her right hipbone, a tattoo. It was a coverup, a heart tattooed over... something. She couldn't quite make out what was under the heart, but something was there.

She was sure of it.

Her heart beat faster. "Found it," she said. "Grab your camera, will you?"

Holly did, hurrying back to kneel by Freya. As Freya tugged Courtney's clothes out of the way, Holly snapped pictures. "Got 'em," she said, and Freya pulled Courtney's shirt back in place before standing.

"Could you read the date? Under the heart. It's a coverup—

there are numbers under it, but I can't tell what they are," Freya said. She stepped closer to Holly and looked at the woman's camera screen. Holly enlarged the photo as much as possible without making it grainy.

"It looks like it could be a date," Holly said, "but that coverup doesn't give a lot away."

"The original one is stick and poke," Freya said. "The other two victims have matching ones, but it's impossible to tell what the numbers are on either of them. I hoped this one would be better."

"Looks like Courtney wanted to keep it a secret." Holly flicked to the next photo and zoomed in, but the result was the same.

While the heart wasn't the best coverup Freya had ever seen, it was good enough to do its job. Whatever date was underneath was mostly obscured.

"I see a two," Holly offered. "In the middle, like it's the day. Twenty-something? But I can't quite tell what the other numbers are. Courtney wanted this hidden."

Freya snapped off her gloves and tossed them into a small biohazard bag Holly must have set up. "There's something important about that date—I know there is. Why would all of them have matching tattoos if not?" She ran her hands through her hair and closed her eyes, trying to slow her thoughts.

She was tired after not stopping all day. Her brain wasn't working the way she needed it to for her to wrap her mind around what was happening. By now, darkness had fallen, cicadas and crickets singing. Bright lights shone on the crime scene, small moths battering themselves against them. The lights cast an unearthly glow on Courtney's body.

Her thoughts just kept swirling, making it difficult for her to focus. The Fawn Lake Killer. The photo of the four girls in high school. Matching tattoos. V.O.

V.O.

She whirled around to face Holly. "Have you found anything here that seems out of place for a crime scene?"

Holly blinked at her, obviously a little off-guard from Freya's sudden change in demeanor. "Yes, actually. I was going to mention it, then we got distracted with the tattoo. Here." She walked around Freya to the investigation kit, bent, and picked up the two evidence bags Freya had noticed earlier. "This is her driver's license, so nothing exciting there. But this... it's strange, that's all."

She handed the evidence bag to Freya and continued speaking. "Sure, a kid could have dropped it. It is a public park after all, but it was right next to the body. And when I say that, I mean it was leaning up against her. Makes me think the killer staged it. I can show you some photos I took so you can see its exact location."

Freya heard her but didn't respond. Her heart hammered in her chest. The teddy bear in the evidence bag was dirty, old. Its eyes were scratched, its purple fur mostly gray, but she wasn't looking for signs of how old it was.

She turned it over, her breath coming in little gasps. Holly kept talking, but Freya couldn't focus on her words.

There. On the back. Written in black marker, the letters so old they were almost faded away.

V.O.

THIRTY-EIGHT

THURSDAY

Freya knew Fawn Lake High School like the back of her hand, which is why she bypassed the visitor's lot, the farthest from the building, and zoomed over to the teachers' parking lot. There was always an empty space or five in here thanks to the national teacher shortage, and she chose one as close to the building as possible.

What the high school lacked in teachers and funding, it made up for in landscaping. The horticulture teacher at the high school was obsessed with propagation, and Freya walked past huge garden beds on the way to the front office.

She grabbed the door and yanked, but it was locked. Frustrated, she mashed the call button to the right of the door then cupped her hands around her eyes to peer through the glass. She was early, she knew that. Her watch read 6:23, which was way too early for students to be at the school. Even though she'd known she should probably wait a little longer to head over to the school, she hadn't been able to stop herself.

Not when she was so close to finding answers.

Someone had to be in the office. Once again she pressed the button. This time a tinny voice responded.

"Fawn Lake High School will open soon. If there's an emergency—"

"This is Captain Sinclair. I need to speak to someone in records."

A pause, then a beep, and Freya yanked open the door. She understood the reason behind the increased security—anyone in the United States would—but anything that slowed her down right now frustrated her.

A wide hall with tan tile flooring stretched out in front of her. Ahead, it teed, splitting into left and right wings of the school. Freya turned to the right before reaching the tee and was greeted by a teacher leaving the office. He carried a mug of coffee and held the door for her. She thanked him before stepping inside the front office.

While the rest of the high school generally smelled a little like body odor, this part of the school was an oasis. A diffuser hidden in the room made the entire place smell like lavender, and there were ferns hanging in the window. To her left sat a squashy chair, and there was a coffee maker brewing to her right.

"An early-morning visit from the police department?" The woman sitting behind the desk in front of her rose and stretched out a hand. "Please tell me nothing bad is going on."

Freya shook the woman's hand. "I'm Captain Sinclair. Thanks for buzzing me in; I won't take up too much of your time."

"Not a problem. I'm Teresa Webb. Tell me what you're looking for, Captain. Maybe you want to pick up a few classes during the week? We could use the teachers."

"I'd rather not." Freya forced a smile as she sat down. "I'm actually looking for information on a student who may have gone here. Do you think you can look it up for me?"

"Do you have a warrant?"

Freya blinked at her. "Do I need one?"

"For personal information, yes." Teresa sat back down and took a sip of her coffee before inclining the mug to Freya. "Want some?"

"No thanks. How about this: I'm not looking for any personal information at this time. I just need verification that they were a student here."

Teresa frowned. "That's not much better, but you seem stressed. That tells me something's going on." She chewed her lower lip. "I'll tell you what you need to know. But only if they were a student here, nothing more."

"Perfect, thanks. I don't know their name, just the initials. V.O."

Teresa raised an eyebrow. "You want me to look someone up by their initials?"

Freya nodded. "And tell me if they went to school here. That's it, I promise. I'm trying to find this person and running into dead end after dead end."

A pause, then Teresa gave a curt nod. "Okay, give me a minute." She wiggled her mouse to wake up her computer then started typing furiously. "No V.O."

"Are you completely sure?" Freya leaned forward, but the computer was turned so she couldn't see the screen. "I think it might be a woman, so maybe we can search for various V names."

"No need to do that. I entered V in the first name field and O in the last name field. No records are popping up. Whoever your mystery student is, Captain, they didn't go to school here."

Freya sat back in the chair. Her stomach felt tight, and she was tired of running down dead ends. How many times was she going to feel like slamming her head against the wall on this case?

"Okay, thank you." She stood, her mind already racing. "I appreciate your help."

"Could she have been homeschooled?" Teresa asked.

"I don't think so," Freya said slowly. "But she may have gone to another school in Taylors. I'll have to reach out to them, see if they'll help me. I have this photo of girls I think may have been her friends, and I hoped you'd have a name for me."

It was a small lie, but she was desperate. For the girls to have items belonging to V.O., there had to have been a connection. Were they friends? It was possible, but it was also possible they weren't.

"Do you have the photo?" Teresa perked back up.

"Sure, hang on." Freya pulled her phone out and tapped at it to bring up the photo she'd found on Facebook. When it was on the screen, she handed the phone to Teresa.

"Taylors, you say? Oh, I remember this game." Teresa handed the phone right back. "Yep, we played against East Rock High School in Taylors. See the lanyards the girls are all wearing? They're not ours; they're from Taylors, who just so happens to be our biggest rival, which tells me the girls all went there. Everyone remembers that game."

Freya paused. "This game?" she asked, tapping the phone. "Why in the world would you remember this particular game?"

Teresa's eyes grew wide. "East Rock and Fawn Lake are huge rivals," she said, speaking slowly like she was afraid of losing Freya. "That was the big football game between them. Before the murder."

"What?"

Teresa nodded. "Yeah, I remember it, and I know it's that night because look at the scoreboard," she said, gesturing for Freya to show her the photo again. "They wiped the floor with us. Zero to seventy. There was practically a riot in the stands. This picture must have been taken right after the game ended but before everything fell apart."

Freya leaned back in her chair and exhaled. "I'm going to need you to start at the beginning and tell me everything about that night."

"Okay, but I don't have much time." Teresa took a sip of her coffee. "Like I said, we were destroyed by East Rock. After it, a lot of Taylors kids had parties of course. But later that night a girl went missing. They found her in the quarry."

"How do I not know any of this?" Freya asked, but then it hit her. She'd been dealing with her own issues when this had happened. "When was this?"

"October twenty-sixth was the date of the game," Teresa said. "I'm sorry, you'd have to look up the exact year, but it was about five years ago."

Holly was right; she had seen a two in Courtney's tattoo.

Everything started to click into place. The four girls in the photo had been at the game the night another girl had died.

That little pressing thought at the back of her mind that the four girls might have been involved in something terrible? It was no longer a little thought. Her brain now screamed at her.

"Do you remember the girl's name? The one who died?"

"Oh, geez." Teresa tapped her chin and stared up at the ceiling. "You know, I'm sorry, but I don't."

"Victoria? Violet? Veronica? Valentina?" Freya was grasping at straws, but the connection was there, she was sure of it.

Teresa shook her head. "I'm sorry, I really don't."

"Thank you, Teresa. This has been so helpful." Freya stood. Adrenaline pumped through her veins, making her feel like she could run a marathon. "I've got to go." She didn't want to stay and talk, not when she finally had another lead. She hit the front school doors at a jog, then ran out to her Jeep.

Once on the road, she glanced at the time. The day was moving quickly now that she felt like she had things to do. She wanted to call Candy and Brad and fill them in, but her mind kept racing. She had to find out more about the girl who'd died.

. . .

Back in her office, she fired up her computer and printer. Her fingers trembled with excitement as she typed in the search bar: *Fawn Lake quarry accident.*

The page went blank. "Come on," Freya muttered, checking the internet connection. "Of all the days for this to happen."

A knock on her door made her look up. Brad leaned in, a cup of coffee in one hand, a folder in the other. His mouth was tight. "Candy wanted me to keep an eye out for you," he said, then saw her finger on the trackpad. "Internet's been wonky since I got in by the way."

Freya glanced down at her computer. The page was slowly loading. She could read the first result and slid her cursor over it.

Taylors Student Found Dead in Quarry.

"What's going on with Candy?" she asked as she clicked.

In one smooth motion, he tossed the folder on her desk.

Freya grabbed it and flipped it open. "Talk to me, Brad. I'm about twenty seconds from putting all the pieces of this together." She glanced at the screen, which was currently blank. "Or twenty minutes, with my luck."

"That's her research on Brian and Mary Frost. High school sweethearts, philanthropists, voted most popular in high school. But more than that, he's an alcoholic who her friends say will do anything to keep his wife submissive, pretty, and quiet."

Freya frowned. "Break it down for me even more."

"Candy talked to some of Mary's old friends. Good old Brian here looks great on paper but has always been rough behind closed doors. He's been that way since he was the star quarterback of the East Rock Mountain Lions."

"He's an abuser?"

"Never officially charged."

Freya closed her eyes. "How far back do these allegations go?"

"As far back as you can imagine, but his juvenile record is sealed." Brad sighed. "I have a personal detail on Mary twenty-four-seven. What are the chances we're keeping her safe from her own husband?"

"I want you looking into it more. If he's abusive, there's going to be a paper trail, even if she lies about her injuries. Call the hospital, find out how many times she's shown up there claiming that she tripped or fell down the stairs. Abuse is one thing, but making the leap to murder?" Freya closed her eyes to think.

Before she could say anything else, her phone rang, and she answered it.

"Candy, good work on the Frosts. Right now I have to—"

"Freya, listen. I have Nathan Caldwell, and he's refusing to talk to anyone except for that detective he saw give the news conference. Right now. Hurry out here before he changes his mind. He's erratic and is determined to see you. Trust me, the sooner you get out here, the better for everyone involved."

Freya groaned, wiggling her finger on the trackpad to try to make the article load faster. No dice. "Text me the address. I'm headed to my Jeep now."

THIRTY-NINE

It took ten minutes for Freya to get from the police department to the empty grassy lot behind the library where Candy sat on the ground with Nathan Caldwell. She approached them slowly, looking around for any sign that something was amiss. It was still early, and while there were some cars in the library parking lot, Candy and Nathan were alone.

"Here she is," Candy said, inviting Freya to sit with the flourish of her hand. "I told her you'd come, Nathan."

She sat, never taking her eyes off the man sitting across from her. He was handsome in a dangerous way, with hair that needed a trim and dark eyes that darted around the two of them without landing on either of them. While Candy sat with her hands resting in her lap, his were cuffed behind him.

"Handcuffs?" Freya asked, turning to look at Candy. It was then she noticed the grass stains on her detective's knees, the bit of sweat on her forehead, how her hair had fallen across her face.

"He's a runner," Candy said in explanation. "Cardio first thing in the morning isn't really my thing. I don't care to repeat it."

Freya nodded; turned to the man sitting in front of her. "Hi, Nathan. I'm Freya. I heard you want to talk to me."

His head was moved as if on a slow swivel as he turned to look at her. "I saw your press release." His eyes locked on her. While she'd been hoping a moment ago that he would stop looking around them and make eye contact, she regretted it now. A furrow appeared on his brow.

"You and most of Fawn Lake," Freya joked. "I think we can both agree it wasn't my finest hour. But I don't think you wanted me to come here to talk about myself, did you? I want to talk about you."

"I'm not that interesting." He chewed the inside of his cheek, the muscles in his jaw working and bunching, but if he noticed the way Freya kept glancing at his mouth, he didn't give any indication. "You're the interesting one."

"I'm flattered." She paused, then pulled out her phone. Next to her, Candy sat silently, watching. She hadn't moved since Freya sat down. "Why are you trying to get into the morgue, Nathan?"

He stopped chewing. Tilted his head. Stared right at her. "I wanted to see her."

"Jolie? Why?"

Nathan didn't respond. His eyes flicked to Candy, then he looked back at Freya.

"We found the picture of her you dropped. You must know her, huh?"

Nothing.

She changed tactics. "Do you mind taking a look at this photo? Tell me if you know the girls in it."

She turned the phone to him so he could see the high school picture. It was the only one she had of all four women together, and she didn't feel like showing him multiple pictures he had to scan through. His attention span was too short for her to take a long time talking to him.

"Maybe." He glanced down at it. "Wait, yes."

"Who do you know?"

In response, he rolled his shoulders forward.

Freya got the hint but wasn't about to bite. "I think we'll leave the cuffs on, Nathan. Use your words."

Nathan stared at her, his brow furrowing even deeper. He leaned forward, rising up onto his knees.

She braced herself.

He cleared his throat. "I recognize them all. Especially Jolie. She's on the news."

"She is," Freya said. "She's dead now; it's really sad. Did you ever see her when she was still alive?"

"Yes. Maybe." He shrugged. "Hard to remember. Why?"

"Because we're looking for the man who killed her." Freya spoke slowly, watching for a reaction.

There wasn't much of one.

"That's why you were on the news," he said, and Freya nodded. "You talked about your parents."

"I did, but that's not why I'm here."

"I want to know more." He sounded eager.

"Were you at the press conference, Nathan?" Freya closed her eyes for a moment, trying to remember the boy in the ball cap who had been asking her personal questions. She hadn't gotten a good look at him. Could it have been Nathan?"

"I was. You answered my question then. Will you answer more now? Did you really not know what your parents were doing?" He smiled, showing most of his teeth.

Freya leaned back to put some space between the two of them and caught Candy's eye. Her detective shook her head, the movement small, but she ignored her.

Nathan had to have some information for her. He was playing this game because he wanted something.

Even though they were sitting in an open field, the air felt tight. Thin. She forced herself to smile at the man. He was locked on her now, his mouth hanging partly open. "You answered my question, and it's only fair if I answer yours. Right? Question for question?"

He nodded.

"Good. That's fair. And no. I didn't know what they were doing. I was young and not at all paying attention to what they were up to. Your turn now. Jolie was hooking. Did you ever hire her?"

Nathan smiled. "No. I knew her in high school, and I tried to hire her, but she said she was already booked for the night." A slight pause. "Do you still talk to your parents?"

Candy sucked in a breath, but Freya didn't look at her.

"No, I don't. Is that why you killed her? You felt snubbed?"

"I didn't kill her." His breath was rank and washed over Freya in little puffs of air. "Why can't I go see her?"

Freya paused. "Because it's off-limits, Nathan. And you look guilty as can be trying to break into the morgue to be near her—you have to see that. Then you pulled that little stunt where you ran from us, so things don't look good for you. And then you did it again this morning. Honestly, makes me wonder if you had more to do with her death than you're letting on right now."

"I knew her in high school. I loved her."

"You dated her?" She got no response, but he didn't ask her a question either, so she continued. "Where were you Sunday night?"

He paused. "Home."

"Which is where?"

Nathan jerked his chin to the side so quickly his neck popped. He grinned at her. "Home is wherever I want it to be."

"So you don't have an alibi? If you have one, you really need to give it to me, Nathan." Nothing. "Okay, do you know Annaliese?" Freya tapped her phone, enlarged the photo, and centered Annaliese's photo before showing it to Nathan.

"We went to high school together. Now she works at the diner."

He licked his lips. They were cracked and dry. At first glance, she'd thought him attractive—someone who wouldn't have any trouble taking a woman home from the bar. Close up though, all the issues he had were starting to show. He was falling apart.

"Your turn." He grinned, then shot a look at Candy. "You can't play." When she shook her head, he turned back to Freya. "Do you dream about them?"

"Who?"

"Your parents."

She shrugged. Easy question. "Sometimes. Did you kill Jolie, Courtney, and Annaliese?"

He barked out a laugh. "Do you think I did?"

"That's not how the game goes. If you did, I'd love to talk more. Play more of the game. If not..." She shrugged. "We're done here."

"I could lie, tell you I did it just to make you talk to me." He frowned, leaning even closer to Freya. "You didn't think of that, did you? Thought you were so smart, but you couldn't even think of that."

"You didn't do it. You're trying to get into the morgue because you were obsessed with Jolie in high school, and I bet she wouldn't give you the time of day. Now she's gone and she can't ignore you, is that right? But you can't get into the morgue to see her so you just keep hanging around." Freya shook her head. "And you're desperate to talk to me because you just want to know all the terrible details of my parents. That's why you were at the press conference, and it's why you wanted to talk to me today. Why? What is it about my parents that fascinates you so?"

Nathan moved so quickly neither Freya nor Candy could predict what he was about to do. He was already on his knees and launching himself forward, his shoulders hitting Freya's, his bulk pressing her to the ground.

"Everyone knows who your parents are!" He screamed the words, his mouth by her ear. "Everyone! And Jolie doesn't even know who I am!"

Panic coursed through Freya, and she bucked back at him, grabbing his shoulders to push him off of her. His hips ground into her, pinning her in place. She adjusted her grip, digging her nails into the soft skin of his neck, twisting down and to the side to get him to release.

"Get off her!"

Candy's voice cut through Freya's fear. One moment Nathan was still on her, the next he was off, jerking side to side as Candy yanked him back by the handcuffs.

He screamed, the sound brutal. It cut off when he fell to the ground.

"Stay down!" Candy stood over him, her taser out, her eyes locked on the man.

Freya exhaled, closing her eyes for a moment. She gave herself to the count of five then stood, pressing her hands flat onto the ground for leverage.

"I'm not my parents," she said. She cleared her throat. Got closer to him and bent down, her face right by his. "You need to understand that. You, and the rest of the town. My parents hurt a lot of people, and the sooner you understand that I was one of them, the better off we'll all be. Trust me, I wish people didn't know who they are. And as for Jolie, she's dead." Freya swallowed hard. "She'll never think about you again."

Nothing. No response. Freya stood and jerked her chin to the side to get Candy to move away from him.

Her detective did, backing away, so she could keep her eyes on the man.

Nathan never moved. His head was turned, his cheek pressed into the ground.

"I want a psych eval on this guy," Freya said. "He's the type to slip through the system. Almost looks like things are working smoothly upstairs, but when you lift off the roof, you find out it's just a bunch of rats running around. He needs help."

"He needs a jail cell," Candy scoffed. "He attacked you, Freya."

"He attacked me because he needs help. He needs meds. We get him off the street and it will be a win for all of us. Take him to the jail and see about getting him committed for an eval, okay? I'm happy not to press charges if he'll agree to seeing a doctor."

"Nope." Candy shook her head. "What if his hands had been free? Do you see how strong this guy is, Freya? He could have killed you if he wanted to and I wasn't here to stop him. He's obsessed with Jolie and is transferring the anger he feels about her not knowing who he was to you. Yes, he needs help, but he also needs to be arrested for what he did."

"He's not the killer though." Freya reached out and touched her friend on the arm. Candy hadn't looked away from Nathan. She kept her eyes locked on him; his were locked on the ground.

"Sure, but that doesn't mean he's good." Candy exhaled hard and finally looked at Freya. "I can book him, see about getting him help, but I'll charge him to keep him off the streets for as long as possible. At least until he's no longer a threat."

"Do that. This case? I'm about to crack it open. There was a murder, Candy. After a big football game, the same game where that picture of the four girls was taken."

"You think the girls were involved in the murder?" Candy brushed some hair out of her face. "That they're being punished?"

"I think so. Jolie, Annaliese, Courtney, Mary... they did something. Or they know something."

She turned to the man standing by Candy. "Hey, Nathan," she called. He jerked like someone had startled him and stared at her, his gaze absent. "You're going to take a little ride with Detective Ellinger, okay? Try to be good."

Nathan nodded. Stood.

"I'm close," she said to Candy as she led him to her Jeep. "I'm going to find out what happened, what the four girls did. That will lead us to the killer."

FORTY

This was interesting.

An officer keeping an eye on Mary. Far enough away from her the entire time, of course, so she didn't realize anyone was even following her. Heck, she hadn't noticed them and they'd been on her tail for a lot longer than just an afternoon.

The salon. The country club. Her house. The bar. Mary didn't have much variety in her routine. It made it even easier to follow her.

He found it interesting that Freya had sent someone to look after Mary but hadn't done it herself. Either she thought she was really on to something, really closing the net around him, or she didn't care for the woman.

To be honest, he didn't care for her either. She'd grown up from the small-town girl next door into the type of woman he hated. Rich. Powerful. Rude.

But why wasn't Freya the one watching her?

His fingers twitched by his leg, and he forced himself to still them. No use pulling a knife now, not in the middle of the day, not in the middle of the country club parking lot. Annaliese had been during the day, but that was different. It was on a back-road. Courtney was all alone at the park. It wasn't the same.

He was eager but not stupid.

And as for Jolie? Well, he did his best work at night. She never saw him coming.

Mary, though, he wanted her to see him coming. He wanted her to look at him and know just how badly she'd screwed everything up. That there wasn't any way out. That she couldn't hide, couldn't run, couldn't escape. She had to face what she had done.

She'd been guilty since she decided to lie. And guilty people didn't deserve forgiveness.

He'd just have to do it later, without that officer hanging around.

Freya's lackey.

He'd have plenty of time with Mary because he knew how to draw her out.

Tonight.

FORTY-ONE

Freya was typing away furiously on her laptop when Candy entered her office. The first news article she'd found had led her to another, then another, and she felt like she was going down a rabbit hole.

"Get Nathan taken care of?" Freya glanced up at Candy but kept her hands on her keyboard.

"Sure did. He identified a suspect in Jolie and Millicent's murder."

Freya froze. Her mouth fell open, and she stared at Candy. "What? Who? You've got to be kidding me."

"Brad Pitt," Candy groaned. "Even if he did know who killed the women, he's unreliable at best. No way could we listen to him, but he agreed to a psych consult, so hopefully he can get some help. Please tell me you have good news," she said, right as the printer behind Freya started to whirr.

Freya held up a finger, then turned and grabbed the sheets of paper as the printer spit them out and shoved them across her desk at her.

They were still warm. She tapped them on her desk to line up the edges before reading the headline out loud. "'Local

Student Valerie Odem Found Dead in Quarry.' I didn't know anything about it, so I dug into it."

"V.O."

"Exactly. What do you know about it?"

"I'm fuzzy on the details because the murder didn't happen in town and I was keeping my head down, trying to impress Chief," Candy replied. "It's one of the area's cold cases; happened in the quarry on the edge of town. The victim was from a town or two over. Our police didn't work the case. Keep reading."

Candy pulled out a chair across from Freya and sat down, leaning forward, her elbows on the edge of the desk.

"Let me give you the short version," Freya said. "Valerie went missing after a huge football game. Her mother was terrified for her safety and called police when she didn't make it home. Police reached out to her friends from school, but nobody knew where she was. Search and rescue teams combed the area around the family's home, looking for any sign of her, but they came up empty."

"Because they didn't think to check the quarry."

"It finally came out that she'd snuck out to meet friends and had made her little brother, Mikey, promise not to tell anyone where she was going. When the officers reached the quarry, they flooded it with flashlights to see what they were walking into. Nothing could have prepared them for what they found. They left out the really gruesome details, but we can read between the lines."

"Let me guess? Raped and murdered?"

Freya nodded. "The entire quarry was shut down while an investigation was underway, but nobody was ever charged. Her friends at school were questioned. Had they seen anyone paying extra attention to Valerie? Had she ever talked about anyone who made her nervous? Had she often gone to the quarry alone? No answers."

"Her friends. Let me guess, they're not named in the article, but they're probably Jolie, Annaliese, Courtney, and Mary. So the scarf, the locket, the teddy bear we found at their crime scenes... those were all hers?"

"The initials match. The killer, whoever they are, had access to Valerie's belongings."

"Family member. Boyfriend." Candy drummed her fingers on Freya's desk. "Her parents would have access to them of course."

"A family member," Freya mused. "I was leaning towards boyfriend. I was about to make a phone call to find out if the four girls were friends with Valerie. I'll ask about a boyfriend." She glanced once more at the phone number for East Rock High School and typed it into her phone, putting it on speaker as soon as it began to ring.

"East Rock High School. This is Collette."

"Hi, Collette. This is Captain Sinclair with the Fawn Lake Police Department. Do you have a moment to help me?"

A pause. "I'm actually just covering the phones. If you give me your number, I can have Leona—she's the secretary—call you back."

"I bet you can help me and I'll be out of your hair in no time. Were you working at the school when Valerie Odem was killed?"

Silence. Freya and Candy looked at each other. Freya's palms grew clammy, and she put the phone down on her desk then wiped her hands on her pants. The last thing she wanted to have to do was get a warrant and drive to Taylors.

There just wasn't time.

"I was."

"Wonderful. Can you tell me about Valerie's friends? News articles reference them."

"Oh, it's terrible, isn't it?" Collette's voice dropped. "I saw about three of them being killed."

Bingo.

"So Jolie Marin, Annaliese Nowland, Courtney Moore, and Mary Frost were Valerie's friends?"

If Collette heard the doubt in Freya's words, she didn't act like it. "You know how high school girls are," she said, talking faster but still keeping her voice low. "Everyone knew the popular girls liked to haze potential friends, and those four girls were popular. They just had to make it to the quarry, bring back a rock to prove they were there, and then they'd be in the popular group. Only poor Valerie didn't make it home, did she?"

"She didn't."

"It was such a shame. So horrible. And their senior year too. The poor Odem family, I don't think they ever recovered from the trauma. And the girls? How do you stay friends after that?"

"I have no idea. What about a boyfriend? Did Valerie have someone she was serious about?"

"Not that I remember. You know high school kids, always dating for a while and moving on to the next person. Is there anything else you needed? I have a huge to-do list."

"That's it. Thank you so much for your help," Freya said, but Collette had already hung up. She arched an eyebrow at Candy.

"So, the girls in that photo," Candy said, tapping her finger on Freya's desk. "They're definitely involved—they sent Valerie to the quarry to haze her, then she ended up dead. Could they have been part of it or was it just a terrible accident? She was raped, so maybe there was a guy working with them..."

"Maybe. But they were never arrested, which means the police couldn't prove anything. Explains why they grew up and moved away though, doesn't it?"

"Nobody wants to spend time in a town that hates them," Candy agreed. "So this girl ends up dead and now the girls she used to hang out with in school are dying? That can't be a coincidence."

"If they didn't kill her, what did they do? Why is the killer obsessed with taking out this friend group?"

"You know as well as I do that groupthink is dangerous. Look at how many sororities and fraternities get in trouble every year for hazing new members. These four girls? They were close. The popular kids. Popular kids are powerful and tend to believe they can get away with whatever they want. Someone blames the girls for what happened to Valerie, and they want to make them pay."

"I agree. Why cut their throats though? Why cut out their tongues? It's way more brutal than it has to be. Just killing someone is one thing, but this person is going above and beyond." She was thinking out loud and stood up, coming out from behind her desk to pace.

"Cutting the throats is easy. It's fast. Quiet. Easier than strangling someone, that's for sure. Even if you're not really strong, you can cut someone's throat if you have the right knife. Everyone thinks you need to cut the trachea, but all you have to do is hit the jugular and let someone bleed out."

Freya stopped pacing; looked at Candy. "The girls never came clean about what happened that night. There's got to be more there."

"There's no guarantee, but maybe. Mary changed schools halfway through her senior year, didn't she? Chances are good the girls knew what happened."

Freya wracked her brain. "You found information on Mary and Brian. That he's a piece of crap behind closed doors."

"Yeah, she's been covering for him for years," Candy said. "*Lying* for him."

Freya stopped pacing. "That's it. The tongues. The killer thinks the girls were liars. That's why he cut out their tongues."

Candy nodded. She began drumming her fingers on Freya's

desk, thinking it through. "They lied about their alibis, lied about what they were doing that night when she died. As for who raped her..." She shrugged.

"Okay, they were liars, so the killer cut out the tongues to punish them, so they couldn't keep lying," Freya continued. "It makes sense, but it still doesn't explain the connection to the Fawn Lake murderer. The killer still knows things about the Fawn Lake Killer he shouldn't."

The idea sickened her. It was bad enough to consider there was a killer who had never been caught and who, now that the case had gotten even colder, might never be. But to think that same man, the one who tormented her just by existing and the fact that he wasn't in jail might have a protégé ?

It was almost too much.

Candy cleared her throat. "Tell me about Valerie's family." She grabbed Freya's computer and spun it around to work on it.

"A brother, Mikey. No other siblings. I'm not finding much on her parents. We need to find her brother. And the parents, if they're still around."

"Dead. The parents are anyway." Candy typed quickly.

"Dead. Crap. Of course they're dead," Freya groaned.

"I can't find her brother on social media, but I don't see an obit either, so I'm assuming he's still alive." Candy's fingers were flying again. "That's weird, right? Not to have an online presence?"

"Very weird, especially for that age group. He's in his twenties: most people at that point in their lives like to alert the world every time they inhale or exhale. I'll call dispatch."

Freya pulled her radio from her belt. "Dispatch, this is three-zero-one. I need you to run a name for me, tell me if it comes back to any addresses."

"Three-zero-one, go ahead."

"Mikey Odem. He's in his twenties. That's all the information I have."

"One minute please."

While Freya waited, she leaned over Candy's shoulder to get a better look at what the detective was working on. She had multiple tabs open and clicked through them to show her what she saw.

"Look. Facebook. Instagram. X. TikTok. LinkedIn. Nothing." Pausing, Candy tapped her finger against her chin as she thought. "Even just a simple Google search doesn't bring up any hits. This guy is a ghost. He doesn't exist."

"Oh, he exists alright. And... I know there are some people who aren't on social media, but doesn't it strike you as odd that he hasn't left any sort of online trail at all? Most people have at least one account somewhere they set up and then either forgot about or abandoned."

"Three-zero-one, I have something for you."

"Dispatch, go ahead." Freya closed her eyes for a moment, hoping this would be it. When she opened them again, she saw the same hopeful expression on Candy's face.

"Looks like we have one Michael Odem in the area, twenty-one years old. His license was renewed at the beginning of the year. Address listed as 116 Fifth Avenue East. No vehicles registered to his name."

"I'll head there now."

"Ten-four. Since you're in a hurry, I'll email you a copy of his driver's license."

"Thanks." Freya slipped her radio back into its holder on her belt and pulled her keys from her pocket.

"I'll drive." Candy stood, grabbing the keys from her. "No offense, boss, but you have a lead foot, and I don't want to get into an accident."

"You got it." She watched as Candy locked her computer then followed her from her office. Suddenly she stopped and groaned. Rubbing her temples, she finally spoke. "There's one thing you need to know though, Candy."

"Yeah, what's that?" Candy barely looked at her over her shoulder while she spoke, she was so focused on getting to the stairs and out to the parking lot. Freya understood the drive in her. Normally, she'd want to hurry out there to find the killer too.

"116 Fifth Avenue East."

Candy stopped, her hand on the door to the stairs. "What about it? I feel like you know something major and you're keeping it from me. Just spit it out, Freya."

"That entire block was demolished this past spring to make way for the new parking deck that's going in over there. The city paid a pretty penny to the landlord to buy the row of apartments. The guy took the money and moved somewhere south, somewhere warm."

"Florida?"

"Mexico, I think. Not important. Point is the apartments are gone. Unless our guy is squatting in the corner of a parking deck, there's no way that's his current address."

FORTY-TWO

Candy sighed, her head resting on her arms on Freya's desk. When Freya didn't immediately respond, she sighed again.

"You're being dramatic," Freya told her, even though she was feeling the pressure too.

"Ech. I'm just frustrated with this apartment owner for selling the apartments. At this Mikey guy for moving and not updating his license. Oh, and the fact that he might be a serial killer. That's a little annoying too."

While Candy sighed, Freya opened up her laptop. Angling it towards herself, she opened the email dispatch had sent with Mikey's driver's license. A moment later, the picture of a young man with dark hair popped up on her screen.

Her stomach lurched. *No way.*

"I know this guy," Freya said, leaning forward to get a better look at the computer screen. "I've met him."

"You know Mikey?" Candy twisted in her seat to take in the screen.

"No, I know Trent." Freya closed her eyes for a moment, conjuring up a mental image of the man she'd met at the Amos Hotel. Dark circles under his eyes. Thinning hair.

Michael, the man on her computer, looked healthy. Robust. He had color in his cheeks.

"Take a look at this guy," she said, turning the computer screen so Candy could see. "Does he look okay to you?"

"He looks fine. Why?" She dropped her phone into the cup holder and turned the screen a bit more to get a better look.

The DMV photographer had gotten Trent's shoulders into the shot. Candy was right. The man was wearing a tight T-shirt, and it was easy to see just how strong he was.

"Because I met him, I swear I did. But he was... just thin and exhausted. He looked ill when at the Amos Hotel." Freya pointed to the screen. "Look. Michael Trent Odem."

"Mikey," said Candy.

"Trent. I met him as Trent."

They were silent as they looked at the screen.

"So, he's changed a lot from this picture but is still strong enough to kill these women. That photo could be years old. Just because you renew your license doesn't mean you update your photo." Freya let the words hang in the air between them for a moment while she tried to decide how plausible that sounded. "It takes a lot of strength to bash someone's head in like he did Millicent."

"Or adrenaline," Candy pointed out. "You know as well as I do that perps can sometimes do insane things when their adrenaline kicks in. Like mothers who lift cars off their kids when there's an accident. Science can't explain it, but it happens."

"So maybe Millicent took him by surprise. We know Jolie was his target if we're basing our belief on the picture we found on Facebook. Millicent was there, he didn't think that would be the case, he Hulked out, and that was the end of her?"

Candy nodded. "Okay, so you said the guy is thinner now. Could be he lost his job and couldn't afford as much food. Or he was drugged out. Drugs will tear someone up. Or sick even. Chances are good he'd try to clean up a little bit before attacking the women so he could blend in a bit more, like we've thought before."

"That makes complete sense, and it's why I don't think it's drugs. Users don't think things through that far, and this man, if he's the killer, has been one step ahead of us the entire time. But it could be that he lost his job. When I spoke to Gary at the Amos Hotel he mentioned Trent quit working there about a week ago. This guy knows how to bait us. The letter in your mailbox, the tongue delivered to Esther, then another to Lance... I don't know why he zeroed in on the two of us, but it's clear he's been making a point."

"Great. Okay..." Candy exhaled hard and then dug in her pocket for some gum. She held a stick out to Freya, shrugging when her captain shook her head and popped it in her mouth instead. "Okay, so this Mikey-slash-Trent guy wants to hurt these four women because they were involved in his sister's death way back in high school."

"Right. Only that's so obvious, right? It would be much too easy for people to point the finger at him for what he's doing, so he's shaking it up. I don't think he's the original Fawn Lake Killer; he'd have been too young to be murdering and raping back then. But I do think he knows the guy and is trying to throw us off. And it worked."

"But why? What's the point of that? He's obviously bold and completely unafraid of getting caught. I mean, seriously, coming into your backyard to stage Annaliese's body is a step too far. I can't think of any other perp we've ever dealt with who would have the guts to do that. So why would he be modeling himself after someone else when he's clearly unafraid of... anything, it seems like? Why not just kill and keep your true identify hidden?"

Freya took a deep breath and let it out slowly. "Because he wants to torment me," she finally said. "I've always operated with the belief that you shouldn't ever take anything that a perp does personally, but for some reason, somewhere along the way, I did something that this guy didn't like."

"Or he's just insane. Insane people target others for no reason all the time," Candy pointed out.

Freya inclined her head. "That's true, but we have to look at this from all possible angles. I made him mad. He's acting out. No matter what the link is, I doubt we'll figure it out before we find him. We have to hunt this guy down and stop him from hurting Mary. Only then will we be able to learn his real motivation for dragging the two of us into it."

Candy was silent for a moment, then blinked hard, coming back to the present. "Wait. What?"

"You got a letter, but I don't think there was any real reason why he targeted you. I think he only did it because you and I are working together. I don't think that you're in danger."

"Neither do I." Candy smiled at her, but it didn't reach her eyes. The sight of the worry etched across her face made Freya's stomach twist.

"Candy, I'm serious. The Fawn Lake Killer was messing with me. I don't know why, and I won't unless I get the opportunity to ask him. Honestly, I think that's what you're facing. This is a game to him. Remember that. We're all doing everything we can to catch him, to stop him, but he's just having fun."

Candy nodded. "You're right, and I know you are. I just want to catch this guy and make sure he doesn't hurt anyone else. Is that too much to ask?"

"Not at all." The two of them fell silent for a minute.

"I've got an idea," Freya said. She dialed the number for the Amos Hotel and waited. A moment later, she spoke. "Hi, this is Captain Sinclair. Is Gary working?" A pause. "Gary, hi. Good to talk to you again. Quick question—what kind of vehicle does Trent drive?"

Candy arched her eyebrow.

"No reason." She nodded. "Great, thank you." After

hanging up, she turned to Candy. "Apparently Trent just started driving a big black Dodge. At least we know what to look for."

"He doesn't have any vehicles registered to his name, so where did he get this truck?" She paused. "It could be borrowed. Or stolen."

Freya nodded her agreement and pulled her phone from her pocket then tapped the button to call Brad, who picked up on the first ring. "Brad, you're alive."

"Alive and well... maybe not well, exactly, but alive, sure. What's going on?"

"We have a suspect. We're putting a BOLO out on him for a twenty-five-mile radius. No way is this guy leaving the area, not when he's close to finishing this. And I need you to stay on Mary. I know it's not what you expected, coming upstairs to detectives, but she's the key. We have to keep her safe." All Freya and Candy needed was for Mikey to pop his head out from under his rock long enough to be spotted, and a BOLO would mean everyone with a badge would be looking for the guy.

"Not a problem. I'm on it. Just send me everything, and I'll get straight to it."

Brad ended the call, and Freya looked over at Candy, who was back on her phone.

"He stole that truck—I'd bet my job he did," Candy said. "The guy you called didn't mention loaning him the truck?" Freya shook her head and Candy sighed. "I hate that we can't put a BOLO out on the vehicle. Black Dodge pickups aren't exactly endangered around here."

"We're doing it anyway, just so we can keep an eye out. Officers will have to be studious when looking to pull over a truck," Freya said. "We have to be smarter than him. Now that we know what happened when the girls were in high school and we have him as our main suspect, we can close in on him."

Dispatch had sent over Trent's phone number, and while Freya was itching to call it, she knew what would happen as soon as she did. Trent would rip open the back of the phone, pull out the SIM card, and destroy it. Then he'd toss the phone, and any chance they had of finding him that way would be gone.

No, even though she wanted nothing more than to call him, she and Candy needed to be careful. They needed to treat Trent like the prey he was and move in slowly, making sure the man didn't see them coming.

It was only by being careful enough that they'd be able to catch him first. If Mary had been willing to work with them, then Freya could guarantee that the woman would be safe. But she didn't want that, and the only option was to race against the clock and hope Brad could protect her.

Freya stood, the movement so sudden Candy looked up in surprise. "I'm going to go talk to Mary," she announced, snatching her keys from her desk.

Candy stood too. "Want company?"

She shook her head. "No, you're on Trent duty. Handle the BOLOs for me. Find something."

FORTY-THREE

Freya was not expecting Brian Frost to open the door. She'd rung the doorbell, stepped back, and checked the time while she waited on Mary to come to the door. The day was slipping by faster than she would have liked. When she'd heard footsteps, she'd looked up, a smile already on her face to try to win the woman over.

But it wasn't Mary who appeared in front of her.

Brian was taller than she thought he'd be. He towered over her in that ex-quarterback way, his beefy hand gripping the door while he looked out at her.

"Can I help you?"

"Mr. Frost?" She shot him a winning smile. "I'm Captain Sinclair with the Fawn Lake Police Department. Is Mary home? I just need to ask her a few questions."

"You're the one who harassed her at the salon." He hadn't moved from the door.

"I wouldn't say harassed," she countered. "Is she here? I really need to talk to her."

For a moment, she thought he wasn't going to let her into the house. He stared at her a moment longer before holding up a single finger. "Wait here."

She did as she was told, even as he closed the front door on her. Even as she heard his footsteps recede. Even as Mary opened the door, the smile on her face not coming anywhere close to reaching her eyes.

"Mary, hi. It's good to see you again," Freya said. She gestured at the chairs on the porch. "Do you mind joining me out here to answer a few questions?"

Mary hesitated. Glanced over her shoulder into the house. When she looked back at Freya, she didn't make eye contact. "Of course not, Captain. My husband will be joining us." She pushed past Freya, holding the door for Brian, who carried a steaming cup of coffee. The two of them sat side by side, Brian reaching out to take Mary's hand.

"What can we do for you?" Brian asked. He held Mary's fingers tight in one hand; the other gripped his coffee mug like he was afraid someone would try to take it.

"I'm here to talk about Valerie Odem," Freya said.

Mary stiffened. Brian's fingers tightened on hers.

"Valerie?" Mary asked, her eyes flicking to Brian before she looked back at Freya. "I haven't heard her name in years. What's bringing this up?"

Freya eyeballed her. Mary was acting completely differently than she had been at the salon. There, she'd obviously been scared. It had come out in rudeness. Now, though, she looked terrified. Her mouth was tight, her cheeks pale. Even though she was clearly wearing a full face of makeup, it was obvious the blood had drained from her face.

"I'm sure you've seen the news," Freya said, deciding on a different tactic than the one she'd landed on when she'd arrived at the house. "Jolie Marin was killed in Clear Creek Forest. Annaliese Nowland was killed after her vehicle got stuck in the mud. Courtney Moore was just found murdered in Taylors."

"What does that have to do with my wife?" Brian asked. He

hadn't taken a sip of his coffee since sitting down and now leaned to the side to place his mug on a small table. Still, he didn't let go of Mary's hand.

"I have reason to believe you may be targeted next," Freya said, talking to Mary. "I know we've talked about this, but we need to discuss your friendship with Jolie, Annaliese, and Courtney. I need your help so I can keep you safe. Now's not the time to stay quiet."

"This is preposterous," Brian scoffed. "You can't honestly believe my wife may be in trouble because of the friends she kept in high school, can you?"

Freya waited for Mary to respond. When she didn't, she leaned forward, lightly touching the woman on the knee. "Mary, do you know any reason why your friends may have been targeted by a killer? If you know anything, you need to tell me."

"This is a farce." Brian stood up, pulling Mary with him. "Come on, darling—you need to get into the house. You know that too much sun isn't good for your skin. Let's go."

"Mr. Frost, I'm not done speaking with your wife." Freya stood up too, angling her body to make it impossible for Brian to pull Mary past her. "I appreciate your concern for your wife's health, but I need to talk to her. We can do it here or at the department. Her choice."

He was already shaking his head. "Mary is my wife, Captain, not yours. I know what's best for her. I always have. Right, darling?" He was squeezing Mary's fingers so hard now the skin was turning white. But before he could say another word, his phone rang.

Brian closed his eyes, his mouth pressed into a thin line. He had to release Mary to pull his phone from his pocket, then he scowled at the screen. "I have to take this. You get inside," he said to Mary. Before he'd turned away from her, he had his phone pressed to his ear. "This is Brian."

"Mary, wait." Freya followed the woman as she hurried into the house. They were in the foyer, the light from outside streaming in through the screen door. Brian was on the far end of the porch, but she could easily make out everything he was saying. "Jolie, Annalise, and Courtney all had matching tattoos, and the date of them was the night of the football game, the night Valerie died." She only had a minute alone with Mary. Every second was pushing her luck. "Why? What really happened that night? She was found in the quarry, and your friend group had a history of hazing girls by making them go there. You know something, Mary, and I want to help you, but I can't unless you come clean with me."

Mary reached out; touched Freya's arm to move past her. She pressed her face up against the screen door, caught a glimpse of Brian, then turned back to her.

"You can't be here asking those questions," she hissed. "What happened to Valerie was terrible, but it was an accident. We all moved on. You need to leave it alone."

"I can't," she said. "You know I can't. Someone is killing the women in your friend group. Aren't you terrified you're going to be next? Why aren't you taking this seriously?"

Mary ran her hand through her hair, tucking a stray piece behind her ear. "I am. I just—" Her voice cut off as Freya grabbed her hand, twisting it to the side.

"You have the tattoo too," she said, rubbing her thumb over the inside of Mary's wrist. She looked up, locking eyes with Mary. "Tell me what happened that night. What really happened to Valerie?"

There were heavy footsteps behind her.

"Unless you have a warrant to arrest one of us, you need to leave."

At the sound of Brian's voice, Mary jerked her hand back from Freya. She nervously tugged her sleeve down as she chewed on her lower lip.

Behind Freya, the screen door screamed on its hinges as it was yanked open.

She didn't have to turn around to know Brian was towering over her. She could feel his hot breath on the back of her neck. Anger rolled off him in waves.

"Where were you this past Sunday night, Mr. Frost?" she asked, turning around. Who cared how tall the man was? Who cared how big his hands were; that he still looked like he was in peak physical condition?

"Sunday night?" He glowered at her, his thick brows even more pronounced this close to him. "Work trip. I got back yesterday afternoon."

"Can you prove that?" Freya heard Mary shuffle her feet behind her but didn't turn around. "Now?"

"You want proof? Fine." Brian pulled his phone from his pocket and tapped on the screen, turning it to show her. "Plane tickets." Another tap. "Receipt from a restaurant in Boston Sunday night. How about this? I had two beers before my flight yesterday. In the Boston airport." He flicked his finger across the screen and pulled up another receipt. "Happy?"

"Thrilled." She did her best to smile at him. She didn't trust him. Not one bit. But his alibi looked good. Didn't mean he wasn't still a jerk, nor did it mean he wasn't abusive. It just meant he wasn't the murderer. "I hope you both have a wonderful rest of your day," she said, stepping to the side to slip around Brian.

He didn't make it easy on her. Her hip hit his; her elbow brushed his arm. A shiver raced up her spine.

Regret coursed through her as she walked down the porch steps. An officer sat in an unmarked cruiser down the street, and it was pretty obvious neither Mary nor Brian knew he was there.

She wasn't leaving Mary alone in the house with Jolie's

murderer. But there was something about the man she didn't like.

Something she didn't trust.

FORTY-FOUR

"Tell me everything." Candy stared at Freya over the desk. "Did Mary have any insight for you?"

"I wouldn't go that far. Her husband was there. Brian. He's the type of guy to bring up his high school glory days any chance he has, and he wasn't keen on me talking to his wife."

"That's the feeling I got looking into him. He's a real peach. Tell me more." Candy stretched then propped an elbow on Freya's desk, resting her chin on her palm.

"She has the same tattoo Jolie, Annaliese, and Courtney did. I told her she's in danger, again, but she still doesn't seem to care." Freya groaned and took a sip of water. "Brian doesn't want her talking to anyone, and that seems fine by her. But she was upset when I mentioned Valerie, so that's something. I'd be able to get through to her if I had more time—I'm sure of it."

"What's your read on him? Besides high school being the best four years of his life?"

"He strikes me as an abuser. The way he was gripping her fingers when I was trying to talk to her, how he spoke to her, how she looked at him. With just a little fear in her eyes, you know? Just like we thought."

"Could he be the killer?"

"He has a great alibi," Freya said, shaking her head. "Doesn't mean he's a good guy though. Just means he hasn't screwed up enough for us to nail him to the wall." She pressed print on her computer. "Now your turn to tell all. No word on the truck Trent's driving?" Behind her, her printer whirred as it spat out pages. This was the type of work she wished she could do on the road in her Jeep, but working at her desk made things a hundred times easier.

Candy shook her head. "I got dispatch to put out that BOLO on the vehicle with a note it would be driven by a man. They weren't super thrilled with the thought of how many false leads they're going to get called about, but maybe we'll get lucky."

Freya nodded then leaned back in her chair and stretched, cracking her knuckles. "The truck's not registered to him, so how do you think he got a hold of it?"

"He could have bought it from a private seller, paid cash, then not registered and insured it. Once the title is notarized and out of the seller's hands, they wouldn't know what happened with it."

Freya thought for a moment and nodded again. "You might be onto something."

Candy grinned, but the smile slid off her face. "No, that won't really work. Have you seen the prices of trucks recently? Even used ones? Not unless he had inheritance money.

"Okay, but if that's the case, why no house? Where does the guy live? Most people do one of two things when they come into some money: spend it all on stupid stuff like boats and strippers, or buy a house and settle down. No house that we can find on any tax records here or in surrounding counties, and we don't have an address for the guy besides the one that's now a parking garage. So where is he staying here in Fawn Lake?"

"In his truck."

"That's what I'm thinking. Or with a friend." Freya stood and grabbed the papers from the printer. "Think this through with me. Trent has nothing to live for but his sister, right?"

"You mean getting revenge for her? Unless you think he's totally delusional and believes Valerie is still alive? But his actions aren't those of a delusional man. They're calculated."

"Exactly. He's not acting rashly. He's taking his time, thinking things through. Killings like this? Following Jolie up the mountain? Hunting down Annaliese and Courtney after killing Jolie? No way he's acting blindly. Remember, revenge is a powerful motivator. I wouldn't be at all surprised if everything he's doing is because of what happened to his sister. It's driving him to kill these women, to get revenge for Valerie. We know she died in the quarry after that football game. And we know those four girls were the reason she went there in the first place. Sounds to me like he has them linked together in his mind, like he's already found them guilty."

"That all tracks. And the fact that they all have matching date tattoos from the night Valerie died? It doesn't look great for them in terms of proclaiming their innocence. But keep going—I'm with you."

"His entire family is dead, so there isn't anyone to talk him off the ledge, try to get him to see reason. People like that are the most dangerous, I've found. Without any conscience or person who can act as one, they go off the deep end. They do whatever they want and can do a really good job convincing themselves that they're in the right. That they're the sane ones."

"You think his parents were keeping him sane? They died a few years ago, so why wait?"

"I'm thinking that through." Freya took a deep breath and closed her eyes. Tried to picture the man she'd met at the hotel, not the one in the driver's license photo. The difference was stark, and there was something there.

It hit her.

"I think he's sick, like you suggested. Between when his driver's license photo was taken and now? Big changes for Trent, and not in a good way."

Candy nodded. "You know what happens when people get close to the end of their lives? They start tying up loose ends."

"Exactly," Freya said, her voice higher now. She was excited. Closing in on a perp and figuring out what made them tick was her favorite thing. She navigated to the Find a Grave website and started typing. "He's taken his time planning this all out, but now it's go-time. Trent doesn't have the luxury of waiting any longer, not if he's sick like I think he must be." The webpage loaded and she clicked around, her eyes wide.

"You have something," Candy said. She planted her hands on Freya's desk. "Spill."

Freya grinned. "How much do you want to know where everyone in his family is buried?"

"Please tell me right here in town and not three towns away. I swear, Freya, you can't go chasing down ghosts way outside of our jurisdiction. Chief can't handle you pushing him any closer to an early grave."

"Oh, he'll survive. Luckily for him, though, they're all here in town. His entire family all in a row."

Candy frowned. "Weird. Why? If they lived in Taylors, then why would they come back here to be buried?"

Freya clicked a map to enlarge it, then turned the computer for Candy to see. "Family roots run deep. Looks like Mommy and Daddy Odem moved to Taylors to start a new life, but when it all hit the fan, they moved back here to be closer to their parents. Losing Valerie probably tore them apart and they needed to get out of that house, get to where they could have more support. Bingo, they move back to town to live with the parents. Only now, everyone is dead."

Candy rested her chin on her hand. "How does it feel to be the luckiest person in the world right now?"

"So good." Freya started towards the door. "Keep looking for his truck, okay?"

"I will. It sounds like you're all-in on this Trent guy?"

She paused in the door. Leaned against it. She took a deep breath and shook her head. "Being all-in is dangerous. You know that as well as I do, but all signs point to this guy. I'm going to find him before he can get to Mary."

"We have people watching Mary. Right now she's about as safe as she can be as long as she doesn't do anything stupid. But I'm impressed, Freya. You sound confident for someone hunting down a guy in the wind."

"I am. There's one place I can think of where he might be."

"The cemetery. He thinks he's close to finishing this, so it would make sense he'd want to go see his family one more time."

"That's what I'm thinking. I can't guarantee it, but Mary's safe and sound with Brad watching her, so now's the time for me to make my move. He could be at home, wherever that is for him, but I have a feeling he's getting antsy. There's no way he'll want to draw this out any longer, especially if he has any inkling that we're on his trail."

"Getting antsy." Candy laughed. "You mean just like you are."

She nodded, suddenly somber. "Yeah, like I am, I guess. Three of the four women who were involved the night Valerie died are dead. Trent is close to finishing this—he has to be. He's emotional. He's been doing this for one person."

"Valerie. I have no doubt he'll want to see her one more time before this is all over."

"Exactly." Freya pulled her keys from her pocket. "Trent's on the move, but Valerie's not going anywhere."

FORTY-FIVE

Flipping his collar up against the chilly wind blowing across the flat land of the cemetery and rustling the leaves in the trees, he hurried between the tombstones. Most of the stones around him were new, with fresh flowers placed on them every week and someone coming along from time to time to clean off any moss that grew on them. The stones ahead of him, deeper in the cemetery, were darker with age and covered in lichen and moss.

Valerie.

A few birds called from the trees, but the cemetery was otherwise quiet. His feet crunched on some fallen leaves, the browns and reds and yellows a gorgeous carpet on the ground. The sun was low in the sky, and the headstones cast long shadows.

He didn't look around, instead keeping his eyes locked on where he was heading. The smell of freshly turned dirt caught his attention, and he paused, looking for the grave. There, off to the left: a small grave, one fit for a kid. The sight made his breathing grow shallow, and he forced himself to close his eyes against it.

Deep breath in, two, three, four. Let it out, two, three, four.

Kids didn't deserve to die.

But the four women he was hunting down?

He didn't care what the police said.

What they said.

They deserved everything coming to them.

FORTY-SIX

Freya took each curve of the road slowly. For the first time since Monday morning, she wasn't in a rush. She'd delegated, split tasks between Candy and Brad, gotten the road officers on the case, and now she just needed to bide her time.

Trent would show up. She had to be ready for him.

He'd been hiding, but she had a very good feeling he wasn't going to keep hiding for long. He was accelerating, and if there was something she knew about perps, once they picked up the pace, they made mistakes.

But she didn't. She wasn't planning on it.

Her hunt took her to the outskirts of town. In front of her on a hill stood the Fawn Lake cemetery. She stared at it for a moment, at the neat headstones all lined up, at the way the road through the cemetery curved and wound from area to area, then she pressed down harder on the gas and made straight for it.

The idea of catching the killer here, right by his sister's grave, was so clichéd that the thought of it was enough to make her laugh. Now that she'd figured out Trent's motivation though, she had to give it a shot.

He was killing for his sister, so why wouldn't he be at the

cemetery? It had made sense when she'd been talking it through in her office with Candy. She was sure this was where he'd be.

But where? The cemetery was huge, and it stretched far away from her.

She parked in a gravel lot, spraying small rocks as she slammed on the brakes then hopped out, wind whipping her jacket away from her body.

A small stone building to the right of the parking lot housed the records where visitors could come and look up where their loved ones were buried. The door was unlocked, and she flicked on the overhead light and closed the door behind her, grateful for some protection from the wind.

Her fingers trembled as she flipped through the old ring binder filled with names, dates, and locations. It was alphabetized, each person in the cemetery having their own sheet of paper with information about where to find their grave. It only took her a moment to find Valerie's information. She was with Trent's parents, but if Trent came to the cemetery, it wouldn't be to see them.

It would be to see her.

"Section B1," she muttered to herself, flipping the book shut and leaving the small building. After taking a moment to get her bearings, she hurried off in the right direction, only slowing down when she came to the grave.

She crouched, frowning as she looked at the stone. It was simple, completely undecorated, nothing written on it but her name and dates, unlike some of the other headstones that had carvings of flowers and tender inscriptions.

Freya stood, turning in a slow circle, looking for anyone who might be watching her. There was another parking lot on the far side of the cemetery, and she looked over there, raising her hand to shield her eyes from the sun.

The sound of a vehicle starting up made her stiffen. She leaned forward, desperate to get a better look at the far parking lot, but it was impossible thanks to the location of the sun. She swore, peeking out between her fingers.

The vehicle sounded big, much larger than a small car. Without taking her eyes off the parking lot, she pulled her radio from her belt.

"Dispatch, this is three-zero-one." Excitement was in her voice.

"Three-zero-one, go ahead."

"I'm at the Fawn Lake cemetery on the north side of town, in the gravel lot. There's a large truck leaving the other lot, but I can't get a good look at it. It's driving into the sun. I need someone out here to follow it."

A pause. "Three-zero-one, I don't have any units near you right now, but I can send some in that direction."

"Come on!" Shoving the radio back into her belt, she turned and ran for her car. A stitch in her side ached, but she refused to slow down.

She had to follow that truck.

Her feet slipped in the gravel, but she righted herself on her hood. The radio on her belt squawked, but she ignored it, throwing open the driver-side door and getting in. The pain in her side had built from a dull roar to a hot scream, and she gritted her teeth, slamming her door shut before cranking the engine and tearing out of the parking lot.

Gravel flew up, rattling in her undercarriage. She tightened her grip on the steering wheel but didn't slow down. She had no way of proving it was Trent Odem driving away from her, but she knew it was.

It had to be.

There were no coincidences, only truths you had to parse out.

Blowing through a red, she flicked on her lights to get other drivers to notice her. She didn't want to turn on her siren and warn Trent she was coming, but it was too dangerous to drive without some kind of alert for everyone else on the road.

Just a few more turns. Her fingers tightened on the steering wheel, and she winced as she cut off a car that was trying to turn onto the main road. Ahead of her was a red light, and even though she didn't want to, she reached up and hit the switch for the siren.

The sound ripped through the quiet afternoon. Cars got out of her way, angling off onto the shoulders, the cars who had a green light and the right of way pausing to let her through the intersection.

This was the worst way to go about it, because Trent would know for sure she was coming for him now and would drive in the other direction, but she didn't have a choice. She was going to get held up at every red light otherwise.

She pressed down on the gas.

"Three-zero-one, are you in pursuit? Is everything okay?"

Refusing to take her eyes off the road for a nanosecond, Freya mashed a button on the dash to connect to her radio. "Dispatch, I'm running code after this truck. Backup isn't needed right now, but I will need someone if I can't find the guy."

"Ten-four, three-zero-one. Backup is on the way but won't reach you for a few more minutes."

She wiped the sweat from her brow. It was chilly out, but she still cranked the AC, adjusting the vents to blow right on her face. Gulping in the cool air, she pulled into the parking lot, circled it, stopped.

There were two ways Trent could have gone.

"No!" Freya slammed her fist on the steering wheel. "Are you serious?"

She had a fifty-fifty chance of getting it right. Taking a deep breath, she left the parking lot, turned to the right, and mentally crossed her fingers that the truck hadn't gone the other way. Fear ate at her—fear that she'd made the wrong decision.

If Trent got away, he'd get Mary.

But no. Brad had an officer watching Mary. And she'd put a personal detail back on Esther after she was reinstated. Anyone who might be hurt by this psychopath was protected, and now all she had to do was find him.

She crested a hill. From here she could see most of Fawn Lake spread below. Main Street was a winding road in front of her, lined with shops and busy with cars. Other roads forked off to the left and to the right. Blue lights flashed as officers hurried towards the cemetery.

There was no large truck that she could see.

Sure, there were a few down on Main Street, but none of those could have been the one from the cemetery. Trent wouldn't have had the time to drive all the way down there yet. It meant one thing: Freya had taken the wrong turn.

She deflated, exhaling hard, blowing all the air out of her lungs. Above her, lights and sirens still flashed and roared, warning everyone to stay off the road. She was stopped at the top of the hill, completely blocking the single lane of traffic. She glanced in her rearview mirror. At least three cars were lined up behind her, but nobody dared to honk at her.

Her hand felt heavy as she reached out to switch off her lights and sirens. She'd had a fifty-fifty chance, and she'd blown it. Now she just had to hope nobody would pay the price for her mistake.

FORTY-SEVEN

It wasn't technically fireplace weather, but Freya needed something to look at that wasn't the news. She knew full well what she would see if she turned on the TV: photos of all the dead women and attacks on the police department, possibly herself personally, for so far failing to put the killer behind bars. So she opted for flames.

Instead of whiskey, she chose hot tea. It wasn't the same, didn't course through her body and help her relax the way alcohol would, but it also kept her from becoming despondent. Angry. *Sad.*

It had been a long afternoon hunting Trent and coming up empty-handed. He was a ghost.

She was exhausted, and going home hadn't been something she'd wanted to do, but she needed rest. Her entire team did.

Her phone sat on her leg; the ringer turned all the way up in case she fell asleep. The thought of missing any critical bit of information that might come in the night terrified her. From time to time, she checked the phone, tapping the side button to turn on the screen, just in case she had missed something important.

She hadn't. No calls or texts from Candy or Brad. Nothing from dispatch. No information from any of the road officers who were on the lookout for Trent Odem.

He'd gone underground after he'd got away from her at the cemetery.

Mary Frost had been bitterly rude to the officer watching her when she'd left the country club and found him there waiting for her, but it turned out he had surprisingly thick skin. She may not have wanted a police car sitting in her front driveway, but it was there anyway, watching. Waiting. Rather than parking down the street, it was front and center, a clear sign to Trent that Mary was being watched.

All they could do now was hope Trent slipped up. Freya knew he was going to be angry that his plans were being foiled, and angry murderers tended to act out. She hoped he made a stupid mistake that would allow them to catch him.

Then it would all be behind her. She could move past letting him out of her sight at the cemetery this afternoon. More than that, she wouldn't have to worry about another unsolved case following her around. Haunting her.

She took a sip of her tea. It had grown cold, and she put the cup down on the floor next to her, her eyes still locked on the fire. Flames danced and snapped, heat pouring from them, making her feel more relaxed than she had been in days. She closed her eyes.

Gasping, she jerked awake again. Something was happening; something had pulled her out of the deepest sleep she'd had in a very long time. What was it? Fumbling for her phone, she blinked at it in confusion. Any light from the fireplace was gone, the flames long extinguished after she'd neglected to feed them. The only glow that lit the room was coming from the device in her hand.

Freya squeezed her eyes shut, then wiped the back of her hand across them to try to clear them. More blinking. She forced herself to sit up in her chair, groaning as she did. Her hip screeched at her, pain radiating from it like someone had stuck her with a hot ice pick.

Roughly, she swiped her thumb across the screen, relaxing a bit as it unlocked. Just one missed call, from Brad. One was bad enough: two or three would have ended her. She called him back.

"Brad." Freya cleared her throat, trying to get rid of the croaking thickness in it. "What is it?"

"Mary left the house." Unlike her, Brad sounded wide awake. He was breathing heavily. "She left, but when the officer I put on her tried to follow her, someone had slashed his tires."

"What?" Sitting bolt upright now, she tried to wrap her mind around what the rookie was telling her. "Someone did what?"

"He fell asleep. He didn't mean to. I just talked to him and he's beating himself up. I'm getting in my car now to head in."

"Nobody's slept." She looked around the living room where she'd done the exact same thing. There was no way she could get mad at the officer for falling asleep when she couldn't keep her eyes open either. "We'll fix this. Where did she go? Did she walk or drive? And have you called it in yet?"

"I was about to when you called me back." Something slammed hard on metal, and Freya could easily picture Brad banging his fist on the hood of his car. "I'll call dispatch now— let them know. She drove, but the officer doesn't know which direction she went in after she left the neighborhood."

"Okay, I'm up." She stood, forcing herself to unfold from the chair. She was dizzy and a little dehydrated after falling asleep in the same room as the fire. "I'm coming, Brad. Call dispatch. Let them know. We need to figure out where she'd be going. Keep me posted."

She ran to the bathroom and splashed cold water on her face, the shock helping her wake up a little bit more.

"Where would you go, Mary?" she muttered, pulling her work boots back on. She'd fallen asleep in her work clothes. Lifting her arm, she sniffed herself and grimaced. Smoke. Sweat. But she wasn't about to waste time getting changed. "Why would you be so stupid to leave your house and go out in the middle of the night?"

Checking her watch, she groaned—2 a.m. She hadn't gotten enough sleep to fully recharge her brain, but it didn't matter at this point. She had to find Mary; had to stop the woman from getting herself killed.

She headed out to her car, her feet still not working the way she needed them to, but she pushed forward, unwilling to take any longer to wake the rest of the way up. She moved slowly, each step feeling like she was walking through molasses. Above her, bright stars decorated the black sky. She was far enough out of town not to have any light pollution blocking her view of the stars. The moon was full, casting an eerie glow.

Freya wondered where she should go once she got into town. Mary was in trouble, of that she was certain. Now, though, they weren't just looking for a serial killer. They also had to look for the next victim, one who was stupid enough to head out on her own in the dark.

And then it hit her. Where Trent would want to take Mary.

He'd want it to be full circle, poetic.

Valerie died in the quarry, and Freya had no doubt in her mind he'd take Mary there to end it.

She started the car, cranking the AC knob to the left to turn on the heat. Clearing her throat to get rid of the last few cobwebs, she picked up her radio. "Dispatch, this is three-zero-one. I'm headed to the quarry to look for Mary Frost and Trent Odem. I need backup."

"Ten-four, three-zero-one. You be safe out there."

She backed up and then pulled out of her driveway. *Be safe out there.* It was easy enough for the dispatcher to say that when she was sitting in the well-lit police department. Nothing bad could happen there. But that wasn't where Mary had headed off to in the early-morning hours.

No, someone like Mary Frost, who believed the entire world revolved around her, who believed she could get whatever she wanted simply by throwing enough money at it, wasn't going to listen to someone like Freya. She was obviously going to take matters into her own hands.

And it was going to get her killed.

FORTY-EIGHT

Trent shifted position, a cold rock pressing hard enough on his leg to make his foot go numb. He stood, shook out the limb that had gone to sleep to get the blood flowing again, then sat back down. Above him, the full moon made it easy for him to see exactly what was going on in the quarry. His vantage point not only afforded him a great view of the scene below him but also gave him enough cover that nobody would be able to pick him out among the rocks.

Dressed all in black, he was prepared for this. The knife he'd used to silence the other women had been perfect for slashing the tires of that stupid officer sitting in Mary's driveway. The man had been sound asleep—utterly useless. For a moment, Trent had toyed with the idea of killing him too. He could only imagine how broken the entire town would feel if an officer was killed.

But no. He was going to stay focused. That was what made him better than everyone else. Nothing was going to stop him now.

A figure dressed in dark pants and a white shirt carefully worked their way down the quarry. His breathing grew faster, and he leaned forward, holding on to a large rock to keep from slipping.

Why hello, Mary Frost.

She was far enough away that he couldn't hear her footsteps on the rocks, but he could see her flashlight bobbing in the dark. He watched as she picked her way carefully over a ditch that had been washed out over the weekend.

A cloud passed over the moon. He shifted, impatient, wanting to see more.

Finally, he could make out the bag slung over her shoulder. Even from far away he could easily tell it was heavy, stuffed full of money, exactly as he'd told her. She was his last phone call, then he'd destroyed his cell.

The police were on to him: he'd seen Freya's Jeep tear out of the gravel parking lot at the cemetery. He'd been faster though, going not through town but in the other direction, taking side roads, putting as much distance between him and his dead sister as possible. Then he'd heard the sirens, and he'd pulled off the road and hidden behind an old barn.

When Trent made a promise, he kept it. And he'd promised himself he'd get revenge for Valerie. Just like he'd promised his dad.

Just like his dad had taught him.

Down below, the figure stopped. He watched as Mary dropped the bag on the ground then held her flashlight up and shone the beam into the air, clicking it off and on three times. It was a ridiculous signal, just one more thing he'd told her to do to prove to himself that he could get her to do anything he wanted.

Then she sat, the flashlight in her lap, and waited.

It was time.

Carefully, so Mary wouldn't know he was coming, he worked his way down from his vantage point. Each time he took a step, he held his breath, putting weight on it as slowly as possible, making sure she'd never hear him. He'd look down, place his foot, look back up. She could try to run, but he was going to catch her. Sure, he was tired and weaker than ever before. But he wasn't about to let her get away.

Twenty feet away from her, he stopped, setting his bag down on the trail. He pulled his knife out, slipped it into the back of his belt. Mary didn't move. She was peering in the other direction, like she thought she'd heard him coming from there.

He smiled, licking his lips, even though his body was aching and his brain was screaming at him to go home and get some rest. How he wanted to take one of those pills the doctor had given him for the pain. The desire to pop one and get some relief from the headache he had brewing, the way he had to fight for every breath, was almost overwhelming.

No. Net yet. Stay focused.

He took another step. Then another. This was where they'd found his sister, slain and raped, her dried blood dark on the rocks. Years of rainstorms had long washed the scene away, but he could still see it when he closed his eyes.

So he kept them open.

In his growing haste to reach the woman, he kicked a small rock. It skittered away from him before coming to rest. Mary whipped around, fumbling with the flashlight as she stood. A beam of light cut through the dark, swiping across his chest.

"Hello?" Her voice shook. He felt stronger now, the pain he'd felt a moment ago receding. Was there anything like sensing their fear to make him feel better? Nothing could be more enjoyable than making this woman pay. But first, he needed answers.

"Mary Frost." Her name was bitter in his mouth. "You came."

"I came—" She briefly shone the flashlight at his face, then lowered the beam. "Sorry. I came. I brought the money. You can count it if you want; it's all there. I had to take it from my husband's stash; I didn't have time to make it to the bank. He'll know, but I—"

"There's something else I want." He could feel the pressure of the knife against his back. His fingers ached to pull it from its hiding spot and end this woman here and now, but he needed to wait just a little longer. Just until he got the name of the man who'd hurt his sister. Then he would kill her.

"What is it? I can get you more money, but not until the bank opens."

"Do you know where you are?"

For what seemed to him like the first time, she looked around. He saw the way her mouth dropped open a little bit as she realized exactly where she was standing. Her eyes were wide, and he could see the whites of them. Good.

"In the quarry." A quick recovery. "We're in the quarry, but why you wanted to meet here, I don't know."

"You're lying." He reached behind his back; grabbed the handle of his knife. She didn't deserve her tongue; didn't deserve to be able to speak. "You know why I brought you here, Mary. Tell me."

She paled, looked down, stubbed her toe into the ground. "Valerie. You brought me here because of Valerie."

God, yes.

Relief flooded through him. He had been afraid Mary was going to refuse to answer him. In that case, he would have held her down, cut out her tongue, made her suffer, but then she couldn't have given him the information he needed. No. It was best for him to take his time, let her think she had a way out of this.

"Who was the boy?"

She blinked; shook her head. "I don't know what you're talking about."

"Liar!" His voice echoed around them, the quarry distorting the sound, making it stretched out, higher pitched. "You're lying," he repeated, finally pulling the knife out of his belt and brandishing it at her. When he spoke, he jabbed the air for emphasis. "I hate liars."

She gasped; took a step back. Her hand fluttered to her throat, and in the soft light of the moon, he could see how her face was tight and her neck flushed red.

Defiantly, she lifted her chin. She was trembling but stared him straight in the eyes, unwilling to look away.

He shook with rage. His grip was so tight on the knife that it felt like the handle was going to crack. He took a step forward, then another. The gap between them was closing too quickly, but even though he didn't have all the answers yet, he couldn't stop himself from advancing on her.

"*Who did it?*" His voice was so loud that his ears hurt when the words bounced back to him. Another step and he was close enough to smell her, her expensive perfume so out of place in the quarry it was laughable.

She shrieked, no longer even trying to look brave. Huge tears coursed down her face, and she stumbled back, her foot catching on a rock. She sat down heavily, her face tilted up to look at him.

This was his chance. Anger, fear, hatred... the expression on her face was an intoxicating cocktail of emotions. Part of him loved it. He loved the chase, loved the sweet reward he was going to enjoy when he felt her body go lifeless beneath him in a few minutes.

He'd been too hasty with the other three women. He was going to be more careful this time.

"Please." She was crying so hard she choked on the word. "Please let me go. I'll go, I'll leave, you'll never see me again. I brought the money you wanted! You can have it! I won't tell anyone what you did, I promise." Huge sobs wracked her body, and she curled up into a tight ball.

He lunged at her. Even though she wasn't going anywhere,

he couldn't help himself from throwing his entire weight at her. He wanted to hurt her, wanted to carve into her perfect skin until she told him the name of the man who'd taken his sister from him.

He wrapped his hand in her hair and pulled it free from its bun. The strands got tangled, his fingers twisting in them, and he jerked her head to the side.

"You lied." Still screaming, he pressed his face right up against hers. His sweat rubbed onto her skin. She was screaming back, clawing at him, her hands slipping as she tried to get a grip on him. *"You lied!"*

She wasn't going to give him the information he wanted. He realized that in a moment of horrible clarity and stuck his finger into her mouth, trying to pry it open. He'd cut out her tongue. He'd do it; he had to finish her.

She fought back, her jaw tight, her teeth grinding together. They caught the edge of his finger, and he cried out, pulling back and smacking her across the face.

He raised his knife, the tip of it pressing into her skin, then pushed down, feeling the tension, then the release. The bubble of blood. The way it sliced through flesh, smooth and quick.

A sudden crack cut through the night, the sound so loud it drowned out the echo of his own voice. He stumbled forward, pain searing his shoulder. Even so, he kept his eyes locked on the woman in front of him.

Another crack. Someone yelling. He jerked forward, pain blossoming in his chest.

FORTY-NINE

Pebbles skittered out from underneath Freya's shoes as she slipped and slid down into the quarry. The smell of gunpowder filled her nostrils. It burned. Overhead, the clouds shifted. The moon barely shone bright enough for her to avoid the large rocks and sticks that were in her path. Some limbs had gotten washed down here during the weekend's storm; others remained from illegal campfires teenagers would start when they needed a break from home.

Nothing mattered right now except getting to her man. Trent Odem. Freya kept her eyes locked on him as she stepped closer, unwilling even to blink. So far, Trent had been an elusive shadow, there for just a moment before disappearing again, and she couldn't risk losing him now. Her flashlight bounced across him, making him turn to look up at her.

He couldn't see her. She knew that. There was no way, not with her flashlight trained on him, for him to make out her features, to know who was watching him, but a chill still raced up her spine. His mouth twisted in anger, and a scream ripped through the quarry.

She'd hit him at least once. Trent had stumbled forward, jerking in that way a human body does when a bullet slams into it, ripping through flesh, almost knocking them off their feet. But now he looked away from her, dropped his gaze from her, and it was obvious why.

Mary Frost was curled at his feet, her body in a tight ball like an old cat. Trent leaned back, balanced on one foot, then kicked her, the sound of his hard shoe slamming into her soft flesh making Freya's stomach twist.

Mary cried out. A sob tore from her throat as Trent kneeled next to her. Freya was running now, but her flashlight still caught enough of the scene for her to see him trying to roll Mary onto her back.

He was going to take her tongue.

He was going to slit her throat.

Her lungs burned from running, and her legs still felt like tree trunks. Each step hurt, but she ran through the pain. Left, right. Left, right.

Again and again.

Finally, she was there.

"Trent Odem, back away from her!" A vein stood out on her forehead as she screamed. Her grip on her gun didn't waver as she pointed the weapon at him.

Trent stood, turned. Blood was spreading across his shoulder and his chest. Rage twisted his face, making him almost unrecognizable. He staggered forward, bending at the waist, supporting himself on his thighs.

Something shone in his hand, the bright light from the moon hitting its blade. Freya's heart pounded in her ears as she stared at the knife Trent held. Its jagged edge perfect for slitting throats. The tip of it sharp and pointed, ideal for slicing out someone's tongue.

He glanced down at it. Looked back up at her. His fingers tightened around its handle.

She glanced at Mary. Once again curled up on her side, the woman didn't move. Red soaked into her shirt.

"Step away from her, Trent." He was still too close to Mary. Freya needed to get him away from the woman. More than that, though, she wanted to take him in alive. The need to know what he knew about the Fawn Lake Killer ate at her. If Trent died, any information he might have had about the person who tormented her dreams would die with him.

She'd do anything to take him in, get a confession.

Another step, then another. She toed a rock, then took a step, her ankle twisting on the shifting sand and pebbles. Freya tripped but kept her gun out in front of her, trained on her suspect.

"It's over," she said. "You're done, Trent. Do you hear me? You're done. Give it up."

The man wheezed. Only a punctured lung made that sound, that sucking wet noise. Freya winced hearing it, but her eyes never left the man's face.

"Trent Odem, you're under arrest! Down on the ground!"

He shook his head, moving slowly. When she raised her flashlight to shine in his face, the man didn't wince away. He stared at her, blood dripping from his shoulder.

"On the ground! Now!"

He didn't move.

Her finger tightened on the trigger.

"You need to step away from Mary," Freya said. She barely recognized her voice, the way her words carried so much power. "I'm giving you every opportunity I can for you to walk away from this in one piece! Take it!"

The man stumbled as he stepped towards her. Freya braced herself, sighting him, aiming right for the middle of his chest, but before she could pull the trigger, he dropped like a stone, the back of his head thudding hard on the ground.

His eyes were open, staring, his face turned to the sky.

Moonlight played along his jaw, his thin frame almost disappearing into the shadow of the large rock next to him.

His knife clattered against a rock and Freya grabbed it, then threw it out of the way. Just in case.

"I need backup at the quarry! *Where is my backup?*" Freya screamed the words at her radio as she held down the call button.

She stepped over Trent and kneeled beside Mary. "Mary, can you hear me? Are you alive?" Her gun was next to her on the ground, within reach. Her flashlight next to it, trained on Mary.

Mary shifted, finally uncurling, stretching out in Freya's arms. Blood poured from her mouth, soaking her chest, making her clothes stick to her body. It smelled fresh, coppery, thick. Freya could taste it on her tongue, and she swallowed, saliva pooling in her mouth as she fought to keep from throwing up. Mary kicked out, knocking Freya's flashlight. It grew brighter for a moment, then the beam faltered before it winked out.

"Mary, you've got to stay with me," Freya said, helping Mary lie down, keeping her hand behind the woman's head to make her as comfortable as she could on the hard stones. Her eyes were glassy, unfocused. Each breath she took was thin and rapid, her hands growing clammy in hers as she squeezed them. "Mary, you're okay. You're going to be okay."

Her radio squawked. "Three-zero-one, where exactly are you at the quarry? We have officers on site looking for you."

In one fluid movement, she snatched her flashlight and hit it against her thigh. It didn't turn on, and she thumbed the switch back and forth. "Come on, come on." Sweat dripped off her nose.

She got to her feet and turned, scanning the edges of the quarry for any sign of movement. "Come on, come on." Pulling her radio from her belt, she clicked it on. "I'm standing, but I don't know if you can see me. There's no light. Send someone to the edge of the quarry. I need an ambulance. Mary Frost is here; she's bleeding. I shot the suspect. I—"

Something grabbed her ankle.

FIFTY

Trent dug his fingers into Freya's ankle and pulled backwards. She fell, her chin catching the corner of a rock even as her hands flew out to catch herself. Pain shot up both arms. It radiated from her jaw.

She screamed, the sound echoing through the quarry.

Laughter greeted her ears. Trent was *laughing*.

Wheezing.

She gasped, kicking out with her free foot. The hand tightened, gripping her hard, and she rolled to the side before sitting up. The wind picked up; a cloud slowly started to reveal the moon.

For a moment, she could see Trent, his body stretched out across the quarry floor, his hand locked on her ankle.

Then the clouds shifted again, and they were plunged back into dark.

"Let me go!" She kicked out with her other foot, the sound of her boot making contact with his face sending a shock of pleasure through her. Still, all his fingers did was tighten. She lunged forward, her own hand closing around his wrist. "Let go!"

Mary was behind her, her breathing labored. She'd barely moved when Freya had touched her, but her breathing was constant, a rattling in and out, so painful Freya could feel it in her chest. But now her breathing wasn't the only thing she could hear.

Trent's laugh was metallic, pained and gritty. The hair on the back of her neck stood up, and she twisted her grip, trying to peel his hand off her.

"She killed Valerie!" he howled. Something hot and sharp and painful sliced into her leg. Freya screamed.

The sound echoed around them.

He laughed harder.

"She killed her!" he cried, letting go of her ankle for a moment. The clouds shifted again, and she could see he held something in his fist. She fumbled with the knife embedded in her leg. Its short handle was different from the serrated knife she'd tossed away from the two of them. He'd had it hidden on him, but that wasn't what she needed to worry about. He raised his other fist.

Brought a rock down on her hip.

The scream ripped from her, taking with it all the oxygen in her lungs. Bright lights exploded in her eyes as a wave of pain washed over her. Freya gasped for air, letting go of his wrist as she massaged her hip.

He knocked her hand away. Did it again.

"No!" Snot bubbled from her nose. She choked on it, gasping for air as the pain in her hip threatened to overtake her.

"This is what you get for trying to stop me!" Each of his words was labored, but he was still strong. Too strong.

Freya stared down at him. He was climbing her, pulling himself up little by little, using his knife as leverage, and she bucked him off, her hands on his shoulders. No matter how hard she pushed, however, he was stronger.

Adrenaline coursed through her body, but rage coursed through his.

Another sharp pain from her thigh and she screamed again, twisting her hips up and to the side as he gripped them and slammed her back into the ground.

Her hip landed on a rock. Pain radiated from the pressure, hot and bright, so overwhelming that she was forced to close her eyes, to try to breathe through it.

That was a mistake.

He slithered up her, using his knife as he went, stabbing it into her flesh to help pull himself up like he was rock climbing. The blade in his hand was short, not the serrated weapon he'd used to end the other women, but it cut deep enough that it made it hard for Freya to do anything other than try to breathe through the pain. She could feel the blood welling up, pouring out, soaking her pants and dripping onto the ground as he worked up her, puncturing her every step of the way.

"Do you think Valerie deserved this?" He was on her chest now, lying flat, his mouth right by her ear. "Shall I do to you what someone did to my sister? She told me not to tell that she went to the quarry, and I didn't!"

Freya gasped for breath. She couldn't respond, but the man didn't want one. He screamed the words at her, but it was almost like she wasn't there.

"She left to make those girls love her! And I stayed home. Even when my parents couldn't find her, even when they were worried, I kept quiet, like she'd asked."

He grabbed her throat and squeezed. "They couldn't find her. I finally told my mom she'd gone to the quarry, but it was the next morning, and she was gone. They killed her, and I didn't stop them! But now I have the chance to do that. I have the chance to make things right for her. You're not going to keep me from finishing what I started."

Freya was aware of him pressing down on her windpipe.

She could feel him crushing it, making it more and more difficult to take a breath. She also knew she didn't have long before
he did something stupid, before he slid the small knife he held
in between her ribs.

Mary didn't have long.

She didn't have long.

But neither did Trent.

She was aware of a lot of things, and one of them was that
she refused to die in the quarry, under the man she'd been
trying to catch.

Screaming pain ripped through her as she twisted her arm
to get it out from under him. Trent had pinned her arms down,
but now one was free, and she jabbed her fingers into the soft
tissue at the base of his neck.

He choked. Sputtered. Spit and blood sprayed against her
cheek as he tried to catch his breath.

She did it again, bucking up with her hips at the same time.
He released her, his hands flying to his throat, the small knife
still gripped tightly in his right hand.

Freya rolled to her side. Her firearm was right there, and she
reached for it, finally gripping it and lifting it in one fluid
motion, turning and pointing it at Trent.

He stared at her, one hand on his throat.

The other holding the knife.

When his eyes cut from her to Mary, when he started to
turn, angling his body towards the woman on the ground, Freya
knew she no longer had a choice.

She had so many things she needed to ask him. So many
things only he would know.

But she had to do it.

She pulled the trigger. The sound ricocheted around them,
filling the quarry before fading away. The clouds had disappeared completely, so she saw how his body jerked back. The
spray of blood from the center of his chest.

The grin on his face, still there when he tipped back.

How his head bounced on a rock, the sound hollow.

His legs jerked once; his fingers fell open. The knife landed on the ground.

Freya crawled towards Mary. Her legs streamed blood, each puncture wound pulsing with pain. Ignoring them, she pulled the woman's head into her lap. There was so much blood on Mary—down her face, down her neck, soaking into her shirt.

Freya worked her mouth open and was greeted with a pool of blood. Panic flooded through her, and she turned the woman on her side, tipping her face down so the blood could stream out. If it went down her throat, she could choke on it.

She had lost whatever other information Trent had. She wasn't about to lose Mary too.

A thick chunk of flesh flopped out of her open mouth. Her tongue, halfway cut. Mary's eyes were open, her fingers opening and closing on Freya's pant leg. She tried to sit up, a guttural sound working its way from her throat.

Her hot blood flowed down Freya's arms. It was sticky as it cooled, and Freya tilted her head back and screamed.

FIFTY-ONE

"Listen to me," Freya said, grabbing Mary's chin and forcing her to keep her face turned to the side. "You're going to make it. You're going to make it, Mary. Stay with me." Above her, on the quarry ridge, bright beams cut through the night. They illuminated the sky briefly, then lost the fight against the dark and faded away before they could reach where she kneeled next to Mary.

"Here!" Her throat was sore. "We're down here!" She waved her arms frantically, forcing herself back to her feet so the officers would be able to see her. "Down here!" Her leg burned, the stab wounds still open, blood still flowing down them.

A stronger beam of light swept through the quarry. It missed her the first time, then swung back, hitting her full in the face. Freya winced, covering her eyes. She dropped back down to her knees, placing her fingers on Mary's neck. The woman's skin was cool, clammy.

But there was a fluttering there, somehow, against all odds. Grabbing Mary, she pulled her up into a sitting position, then leaned her forward. She was still alive—for now.

Still keeping one arm on Mary, Freya shrugged out of her jacket, then wrapped it around the other woman. "You're going to be fine, okay? Just fine. Trust me on this—I'm not going to let things end like this for you. I need you to stay with me."

Mary gurgled. The sound was quiet, but it pounded in Freya's ears. Behind the two of them came footsteps, her team running to get to them. Beams of light flashed around them, sweeping across their bodies, but Freya didn't look up from Mary.

"You're okay," she whispered, brushing hair back from her forehead. The older Freya got, the easier it was for her to lie. Now the words slipped from her lips without her even having to think twice about it. "You're okay, Mary. You're fine."

"Freya, I need you to move." The voice was firm. In control.

She looked up, right into a flashlight. She blinked hard, and the light moved as someone kneeled next to her, bumping her out of the way. More lights clicked on, illuminating the scene in front of her as she stumbled to her feet. Pain ripped its way up her leg, and she gasped but managed to stay upright.

EMS was there. Freya's mouth fell open in shock as she took in the scene in front of her. Briseyda Hernandez had bumped her out of the way and was now bent over Mary Frost, her hands working quickly, her voice a low rumble as she commanded the rest of her team.

How long had she sat there next to Mary, holding her, willing her to stay alive? It only felt like a minute, but it had to be longer. When she raised her wrist to look at the time on her watch, the face was coated with blood.

She used her thumb to smear it away but still couldn't make out the time.

"Freya."

Candy's voice this time, and she turned, letting the younger detective pull her into a hug.

"Hey, are you okay? Oh no." Her eyes flicked down Freya's body, and she turned away. "I need help!"

"I'm fine," Freya managed. "I'm fine. I shot Trent. He... he stabbed me." She gestured to the side where the man lay, twisted, his unseeing eyes staring up at the night sky. "But he took Mary's tongue. Part of her tongue. There's still part left." She was babbling, the feeling of insanity clutching at her throat, and she forced herself to shut up.

Candy rubbed her hands up and down Freya's arms. "I heard the call go out when you radioed in to dispatch. I'm sorry it took so long to get here. I was speeding, but you beat me here. Oh, Freya."

Freya nodded. "Right. It's okay." She turned away from Candy, her head fuzzy. She felt light, like she might have to sit down.

A paramedic appeared at her side. "Captain, I need you to sit here." He pointed to the ground, looping his other arm around her waist as he did. "Nice and easy, that's how we're going to do it. I'm Jeremy Stone; I'm going to take care of you."

Freya sat like he told her to, then blinked up at him. "Jeremy. How is she?"

There wasn't any way to get a gurney down into the quarry, but two paramedics had loaded Mary onto a stretcher. They moved quickly but carefully, carrying her up out of the rocks. Another two men walked with them, shining lights on the path ahead of them so they didn't trip.

"She's going to be fine." Jeremy turned and looked at her. He pulled a flashlight from his shirt pocket and shined it in her eyes. "I'm a little worried about you, Freya. Talk to me. Is all of this your blood?"

She managed to shake her head. The scene in front of her kept moving even after she stopped.

"I'm more worried about Mary. And then there's Trent." Her voice trailed off, and she glanced over at the man's body.

"She looks like she was stabbed." That was Candy, her voice so full of concern that Freya's heart ached.

"Stabbed? This is your blood then," Jeremy said.

Candy must have gestured because the next thing she knew, Jeremy kneeled next to her. "I'm going to cut your pants off, Freya."

A ripping sound filled the air. Freya winced as the fabric pulled away from the wounds.

"Oh, boy. Yeah, I'm wrapping you up before we get you out of here." Jeremy turned to Candy. "Sit with her. I'm grabbing my bag and getting her a stretcher."

Candy took his place, slipping her hand into Freya's. When she squeezed it, Freya turned and looked at her.

"Don't worry about me." Her tongue felt thick in her mouth. That thought made her think about Jolie, Annaliese, Courtney, and Mary.

At least she still had a tongue.

"I want to make sure you're not going to go into shock."

"Over what? Killing that jerk?" It came out *jershk*. Still, she didn't pull her hand away. "The last thing I'm going to do is let him send me into shock, trust me. I'm fine."

"You're bleeding. He stabbed you over and over, Freya." Candy's voice held an edge it normally didn't. "I know this is really hard for you, but you have to let people take care of you every once in a while."

Jeremy reappeared before Freya could respond. "I'd love to give you the all-clear. But right now I'm going to wrap your leg so you don't bleed out. You need to go to the hospital to get checked out." He glanced over at Candy, and his face softened for just a moment. "I have no doubt you'll take care of Freya when this is said and done?"

"I've got her." Candy reached for a pack of gauze. Together, she and Jeremy dressed Freya's wounds. Jeremy treated each one then Candy wrapped, the sound of unwinding gauze the only thing Freya could focus on.

"Let's get you on the stretcher." Jeremy stood and walked behind Freya to grab her around the waist. He helped her stand, then Candy slipped under Freya's shoulder.

"I can walk," Freya said.

"No, Captain, you can't. Let us help you. Just... let us, okay? For once."

"I'll send some paramedics to carry the stretcher." Jeremy smiled at Candy. "Be right back."

"Candy," Freya said, turning to her. She took a deep breath to get her thoughts in order. "I swear to you, if you let me walk out of the quarry myself, I'll let you put me in the ambulance. But if you make me get on a stretcher, I promise you I will get in my Jeep and drive away as soon as we're out of here."

"You're in terrible shape." Candy dug her fingers into Freya's side to keep her upright. "And you can barely put weight on your right leg. What the hell happened?"

Freya thought about the rock Trent had brought down on her hip. Over and over, he'd slammed it right there, right on her old injury.

He'd known exactly where to hurt her. This entire time she'd been learning about him, carefully piecing together who he was and what he wanted, he'd known everything about her.

"Candy. Please."

The younger detective sucked in a breath. "Fine, but I'll be with you every step of the way," Candy promised her. "Don't make me regret this. I'm not giving you a piggy-back ride."

Freya snorted, and Candy pulled her closer, wrapping her arm tighter around her waist. Every step they took jolted her and sent shooting pains through her body, but she didn't make a sound. Small rocks skittered away under their feet, and Candy, walking next to her, tripped once, but they didn't stop until they'd crested the edge.

They were loading Freya into the ambulance when the radio on her hip buzzed.

"Sinclair." Chief's voice filled the air. "Come on by the department to debrief. I want to know exactly how tonight went down."

Candy reacted before Freya could, speaking into her own radio. "Chief, this is three-zero-two. Sinclair and I are on the way to the hospital. I advise you meet us there."

"Really?" Freya asked. "You want him to meet us there?"

Candy jumped into the ambulance and settled into the jump seat by Freya. "You know as well as I do that he can't handle not knowing everything that's going on." She eyeballed Jeremy, watching as he ran an IV to Freya's arm.

"Painkillers," he explained.

"I'm not in pain," Freya said. "Nothing hurts."

"Because you're in shock." His words were soft. Kind. "But you're going to hurt, trust me."

Freya barked out a laugh. "Fine. Although, as soon as Mary's stable, I have some things to ask her."

"Like what?" Candy reached out and took her hand.

"Trent could have killed her," Freya said. The words come out in a mumble. "But he didn't. Not right away. He cut her... tongue." It was getting harder to form words. "He thought she knew more. About Valerie."

She closed her eyes and took a breath. The ambulance jolted to life under her.

And she was out.

FIFTY-TWO

FRIDAY

"So... it's over?" Brad took a long sip of his coffee. His eyes were red and puffy, his skin sallow. Even his hair, which he normally kept neat and slicked back, was mussed up. He looked like he needed a shower and to sleep for a week, but debriefings waited for nobody.

Freya nodded. Even without looking in a mirror she could tell she looked just as rough as Brad did. She'd checked herself out of the hospital against medical advice that morning, just a few hours after everything had happened at the quarry but was still moving gingerly. The combination of stab wounds up one leg and being hit in the hip with a rock made everything hurt.

But the killer had been stopped. She still had a lot of questions, but sometimes you didn't get all the answers you wanted that would tie everything up with a neat little bow.

Brad was still looking at her dully, clearly waiting for a response, so she nodded. The movement felt mechanical. "It's over. He's dead. Mary's not. If y'all hadn't had EMS meeting us at the quarry, then she never would have made it. I'm still waiting for the go-ahead from the hospital to talk to her, but as soon as I get that call, I'm heading over." Her coffee sat untouched in front of her, next to a huge slice of coffee cake from Esther.

"So... what now?" Candy leaned forward, tapping the table to get Freya to look at her. "We still have questions."

"So many questions," Brad said.

Chief stood in the door, watching. Freya kept an eye on him and saw how he nodded in agreement at Brad's statement.

"Well, this is what we know." Exhaling hard to clear her head, Freya closed her eyes for a moment. "Trent Odem's sister, Valerie, was killed when she and the four girls were still in high school. It doesn't seem like the girls had anything to do with it besides hazing her and sending her to the quarry. Candy dug into the case last night, and they all had rock-solid alibis. She wanted to be their friend, so she had to go through their hazing process. The plan was for Valerie to sneak out and steal a rock from the quarry to bring to school the next day. She made it to the quarry but never made it home. Trent knew where she was going and what she was doing, and when he grew up, he decided to get revenge on all four of them because he blamed them for Valerie's death. Millicent was collateral damage, as far as we can tell. He was just working his way through the four women who hurt his sister, trying to get his revenge before whatever had him so sick got him."

"He was pretty sick," Candy offered, and Freya nodded.

"Right. He was running out of time. We found his doctor and got a hold of his records. Trent had cancer and was dying. He'd refused treatment, knowing he only had a short period of time left. But it's clear he wanted vengeance and, from the sounds of it, he got Mary to meet him at the quarry after calling her late last night."

"How did he get her number? We couldn't even get that." Candy reached for the coffee cake but changed her mind.

"Someone gave it to him. Someone had it, he got to them, and they passed it on, maybe for a price. Remember how the housekeeper had been so terrified to give us her number? Said she'd made the mistake once before and didn't want to do it again? We can push on her and Mary for the truth, but I bet she accidentally gave it to Trent."

They all fell silent for a moment.

"The money in the bag was probably because she thought she could pay him to go away," Brad offered. "I don't think it's all been counted yet, but there were tens of thousands of dollars in there."

"Yes, she thought she could just pay this guy off and not end up dead like her friends. From the little I saw of Mary Frost, that would fit perfectly." Freya sighed. "But it looks like Trent just wanted to get her alone, so she'd be easier to kill. It's hard to kill someone when they're in bed next to their husband."

"That leads me to our next question," Brad said. He stifled a yawn, then continued. "Where was this guy holed up? How was he operating so far under the radar? Someone must have been helping him. How the hell does someone exist without leaving behind any kind of a trail? It makes no sense."

"Tell me you have answers for that, Sinclair." It was the first time Chief had spoken up, and the three detectives turned to look at him before Candy and Brad looked back at Freya.

"Of course we do. We ran the tag on the vehicles we found at the quarry. It was immediately clear Mary was driving the Lexus, so we ignored that one. But one of our patrol officers found a truck parked a little way away, hidden where it wouldn't easily be seen by anyone at the quarry."

Candy stared at Freya. "So was he living in the truck?"

"We already knew he didn't own the truck. That was easy to confirm when we ran him through CJLEADS," Freya said, more to Brad and Chief than Candy. She shifted a little before flipping open a folder and spinning it around so everyone else could read what was inside. "When we ran the tag, it came back to Nicholas Hatch, eighty-two."

"Should we know him?" Brad grabbed the first photo and stared at the man looking back at him. He had thick glasses and wispy white hair. His mouth was set in a firm line, and he glared at the camera.

"Nope, and Trent didn't either. Nicholas was a bit of a recluse, from what we can tell, which made him the perfect mark for Trent when he moved back to town a month ago to enact his plan. Looks like he wanted to be close to the action. Nicholas lived at the end of a neighborhood in the cul-de-sac, high on a hill. Somehow Trent gained access to the house and killed Nicholas. He moved in and has been living there ever since."

"You found Nicholas's body?" Chief picked up the folder and flipped through it before dropping it back on the desk. "In the house, I assume?"

Freya nodded. "Exactly. I'm sure we'll get more answers as time goes on, but right now this is all we have. From what I can piece together using The Last One to check prior addresses, he moved to Tennessee for a while, then headed back here when his cancer progressed to the point of no return. He hitched his way here to Fawn Lake since he didn't have a vehicle, picked a house to move into, killed the owner, and started his reign of terror."

"It still doesn't give us all the answers from Valerie's murder though. The four girls sent her to the quarry, but then she was killed and raped. Do we have any idea who that man was?" Brad asked.

"I aim to find that out as soon as I can talk to Mary. She knows more than she's letting on. I'm certain of it. Trent stalked the other three women, going to them. But Mary was the one he coerced to the quarry. Yes, you could argue it was because we had a detail on her, but he was sneaky. I think it was more, and I think she has the answers we need," Freya said, finally standing up. Everything hurt, and she moved slowly. "But that's a problem for me, okay? Both of you go home, get some rest. I don't want either of you back in the office until this afternoon, and I want you to be well rested and ready to work."

Candy opened her mouth to complain but closed it again when Freya shot her a look. She and Brad stood, the rookie grabbing one last piece of coffee cake before the two of them left Freya's office. She watched them go, then finally locked eyes on Chief, who was staring at her.

"Well? Are you here to lecture me, tell me I should have tried harder? Should have moved faster to prevent him from getting to Mary?" Freya crossed her arms and leaned against her desk. Getting defensive with Chief never worked, but her attitude slipped out.

"I thought you'd want to know that the SBI will be here any moment. You'll have to talk to them of course." Chief's face softened for a moment.

Of course the SBI would be on their way. The State Bureau of Investigation were called in anytime an officer was involved in a shooting, and she'd just killed a murder suspect. There wasn't any way they would feel comfortable with the Fawn Lake officers handling the investigation themselves, even though it was clear-cut.

"Well, I kept the SBI out of your hair until now, so I think I made good on my promise." Freya forced a laugh.

"That you did." Chief paused. "Good job finding this guy and figuring out where he was going, Freya. I know you wish you'd gotten there sooner, but there's only so much we can do."

"I just hope the SBI sees it that way."

"They will. I'll make sure of it. But right now, I want you to go home and rest up before you talk to them. You're about to have a few very long days, and you need to get your energy back. Besides, Trent's dead. The SBI can wait for a few hours to talk to you. They'll be crawling all over the quarry looking for any additional evidence, so that will keep them busy for a bit. I know you want to talk to Mary as soon as possible, but I guarantee you, she's not going to be up to having visitors for a while."

Freya bit back an argument. Nothing she could say right now would convince Chief to let her stay in the office, and besides, she'd just kicked Candy and Brad out to do the same thing. Grabbing her keys from her desk, she followed Chief out the door, turning and locking it before heading to the stairs.

Chief was right about one thing. The next few days were going to be very long.

FIFTY-THREE
A WEEK LATER

She wasn't used to being on this side of an interrogation table. Rarely had Freya sat where the perps did. She looked up at the little camera staring at her. Everything was being recorded, and anything she said or did now would later be analyzed.

Agent Collins sat across from her, his long slim fingers tented together, a slight, professional smile on his face. He was thin, almost gaunt: his suit hung on him as on a clothes hanger. The man had been nothing but kind since they'd sat down together. Around his neck he wore a lanyard with a badge declaring him a visitor, although the SBI had more than made themselves at home in Fawn Lake.

Freya had first met him the day after she'd shot Trent Odem. The SBI had been in town for a week now, going over what happened, looking for evidence, making sure nothing had been missed. Now they were about to pack up and head out, and she was happy to see them go.

Of course, everyone in town knew what had happened, and they'd all found her innocent of any wrongdoing. Fawn Lake wasn't a super small town any longer, but everyone stood by her. But public opinion didn't matter if Agent Collins told her they believed she'd done something wrong. She needed the SBI to support her too.

"Captain Sinclair, is there anything else you want to tell us about that night?" Agent Collins picked up a pen and clicked it, holding it above the notebook in front of him, obviously waiting for some kind of earth-shattering revelation.

Freya shook her head. "You know it all by now. I've told you everything. If I'd gotten there sooner, I might have stopped Trent from attacking Mary, but there was no way for me to arrive any faster. And the only reason I shot the second time was because the suspect was right next to the victim, holding a weapon. I believed he wasn't going to stop until he'd killed Mary."

Blinking to clear away the cobwebs in her mind, she stared levelly at the agent.

"You did the right thing." He clicked the pen again and put it back down on the table. "I just wanted to make sure there weren't any other details that you'd remembered and wanted to share with us, but everything checks out. Thank you for your cooperation, Captain; you're a real asset to this department."

A wave of relief washed over her, crashing down so heavily that her shoulders slumped forward. She took a shaky breath, held it for a moment, then released it. Even though everyone around her, including Chief, told her that she had been in the right and that nothing was going to happen to her, she had still been terrified throughout the entire investigation. She hadn't slept and had hardly eaten anything, much to Esther's chagrin. Esther had come over to her house every day after she closed the bakery, whipping up meals that normally Freya would have inhaled, but she couldn't seem to make herself take a bite.

But having Esther around made Freya feel safe. The woman made her feel like she was protected, she was loved, that she could get through this.

Agent Collins continued as if he didn't see the relief on her face. "The case is closed. As to the original Fawn Lake murder, we rushed the DNA. It wasn't a match. You'll find this interesting though: Trent Odem didn't murder Michelle Hawsey, but there was a familial match."

It took her a moment to process what the agent was saying. "I beg your pardon?" She scooted to the edge of her seat.

"Your original Fawn Lake Killer was somehow related to Trent Odem. We can't tell if it was his dad, a brother, an uncle, a grandfather... But there is a relationship there—we do know that much. We looked into his immediate family, but his parents are dead, as you know. It's been impossible so far to track it back any farther than that; there aren't any other family members currently living in the area."

"Huh." Freya sighed and sat back in her chair. The hard back cut into her hip, and she shifted to relieve the pressure. Her mind raced as she tried to think about what all that information meant for her cold case. If Trent and the original murderer were related, it could explain how he'd known about the letter the killer had sent Freya. She'd originally believed it must have been the same perp, back to torment her, but that wasn't the case. The thought that Trent had learned from someone made her sick. She cleared her throat. "And no hits on the original DNA in the national database?"

The agent shook his head. "None. Of course, if the guy rapes again, then we'll be able to tie it back to the Fawn Lake Killer, but otherwise it's cold."

"And who raped and killed Valerie Odem in the quarry? Any idea there?"

Again, he shook his head. "I'd love to say we knew, believe me, but we don't have a match. Again, if the guy reoffends and leaves his DNA behind, then we'll nail him. You hate to hope that it will play out like that, but it's the only way we're going to catch him. Unless you think Mary will suddenly remember more than she has for the past decade." Collins arched an eyebrow.

"That's where I'm going after this. She's... well, she's been unwilling to talk to us so far. I can't say I blame her, but it's been a week now. The doctor's giving her the all-clear. We need answers, and she's the only one who can give them to us."

"Then we'll go ahead and get out of your hair," he said, standing up and picking up his notebook. "You should be proud of your work, Captain. I know you're not happy with the outcome right now, but if anyone can get the truth out of Mary, I have no doubt it'll be you."

Freya nodded and followed him out of the room. Chief was waiting at the elevator and shook the agent's hand.

"I can't say it's been a pleasure to have you here, but you made this as painless as possible," he said. "So thank you, Agent Collins."

Chief's back was straight as he shook the agent's hand. Freya watched the two of them, noticing how Chief stood as tall as possible and how Agent Collins didn't seem to notice.

"Anytime. If Captain Sinclair ever decides to move on from a local department, give us a call. We're always looking for women like her." Agent Collins turned and shot Freya a look. "I'm serious, Captain. If you ever want a change of pace, reach out. We could keep you stationed here in Fawn Lake so you didn't have to move. We don't have anyone covering this part of the state right now. We could use someone like you."

"Thank you." Surprise filled Freya's voice. "Seriously, I appreciate that, but right now I'm happy where I am. I need to wrap up this case with Mary."

Chief cleared his throat, and Agent Collins glanced at him. "Of course, we don't want to step on any toes. I just wanted to make sure you knew the offer was on the table."

"Thanks for making that clear." Chief nodded at the SBI

agent, then turned to Freya. "Are you headed to the hospital now?"

"That's exactly what I'm doing." She patted her pocket to check for her keys. "I'll let you know how it goes with Mary. I think she's finally figuring out I'm going to get this information from her one way or another. She might as well make it easy on herself."

"Good." Chief exhaled hard. "Don't leave the hospital without an answer from her, Sinclair. This is ridiculous. She's lived a cushy life up until now, and if she knows more about what happened to Valerie than she's letting on, I want to know. Find out everything that happened last week at the quarry, what Trent said to her to get her to come out, everything."

"I'm on it." Freya waved at Agent Collins then took the stairs quickly, hurrying out into the parking lot. The afternoon was cool, a bit of an autumn chill nipping through the air. Gone were the long hot days of summer, at least for a while. Leaf lookers were sure to start flooding the town, all of them hoping to see gorgeous fall colors before heading back to their cities.

But until they did, Fawn Lake was relatively calm. Freya drove quickly through town, parking in the front row of the parking lot and hurrying into the hospital.

"I need to see Mary Frost," she said to the woman at the welcome center. Normally Freya would scoot right by her on her way to Mary's room, but Mary had moved rooms a few times during her stay as she stepped down from more intensive care to less. The woman helping her had a tight gray bun and tapped her keyboard for a moment before speaking.

"Looks like she left earlier this morning." Another keystroke, followed by a few clicks of her mouse. "You missed her by just a few hours."

"Wonderful. Thank you." Freya tapped the counter and turned away, already pulling her phone from her pocket. Before she could call Candy or Brad to let them know what was going on, someone stopped her.

"Please tell me you don't have any more bodies for me." Lance grinned at her, then took a sip of coffee. His mug read *Support Your Local Medical Examiner—Die Strangely!*

"Not right now, but I can't make any guarantees for later. I'm looking for Mary Frost, but she pulled a runner. My bet is she's at home, licking her wounds."

"Can't say I blame her."

"When everything falls apart, hiding at home always feels like the safest option." Freya knew that one from experience.

"Well, good luck talking to her. I hope you can get the info you need."

"I'll need it." Freya reached out and tapped his mug. "This is classy by the way."

"You like that?" Lance lifted the mug a bit for her to get a better look. "My brother-in-law sent me that. He's a plumber. You should see the one I sent him first."

Freya laughed. "I can imagine. Alright, I'm on Mary patrol. Be good."

"It's the only thing I know how to be!" Lance chuckled to himself and threw her a salute as she pushed through the double doors back into the crisp fall air.

Surely Mary wouldn't leave town when she knew Freya needed to talk to her, right?

That's the thought that echoed in her head as she hurried back to her Jeep. After throwing it in reverse, she sped out of her parking space, then drove as quickly as possible to Mary's house.

FIFTY-FOUR

When Freya pulled up into Mary's driveway, she hit the brakes so hard the wheels locked up. After slamming her door, she hurried onto the front porch, ignoring the impressive fall display of pumpkins and corn stalks someone had used to decorate.

All the way over from the hospital she'd been terrified Mary would be gone. What if she missed her? What if she pulled up to talk to her and Mary had left Fawn Lake, never looking back?

No. She couldn't let that happen.

She pressed the doorbell then stood back, waiting for a moment before yanking open the screen door and knocking. "Mary Frost! This is Captain Sinclair. I need you to come out here so the two of us can talk!"

Yes, her voice was loud. And yes, the neighbors were sure to hear it, sure to start talking, to lift their curtains and stare out of their windows. But that didn't matter. Mary's brush with death had been headline news for a week now, and if the neighbors wanted to watch, Freya was more than happy to give them a show.

Whatever it took to get Mary outside to talk to her.

"Mary! Open this door!" She pounded the door with the side of her fist, then stepped back. She was breathing heavily and brushed some hair off her forehead. The day was heating up, a fine line of sweat beading on her forehead.

She was raising her fist again when a click from the other side of the door made her pause.

The door swung open, and Freya blinked, leaning forward a bit to see into the dark. Even though the door was only open a crack, barely enough to look through, it was clearly Mary Frost on the other side.

"Mary, thank you for opening the door." She stepped forward, putting her foot in the door to keep the woman from closing it on her. "You checked yourself out of the hospital, and I need to talk to you."

The woman didn't respond, which wasn't surprising. According to the doctor, Mary Frost was lucky she hadn't bled out in the quarry. Whether or not she'd ever be able to speak again with what little bit of her tongue she had left... that remained to be seen.

She was thinner than she had been before, which seemed impossible as she'd been all angles, collarbone, and elbows. Still, she was dressed the same, in a navy jacket and tan slacks. Diamond rings sparkled on her fingers, and the gems dripped from her ears. Even though she was still in her foyer, oversized sunglasses hid her expression.

"Can I come in, or do you want to talk out on the porch?" Freya gestured at the chairs behind her.

Mary took a deep breath. After a moment, she stepped out onto the porch. Freya moved her foot out of the way, still holding the screen door wide.

It wasn't until the two of them were settled, Mary in a rocking chair with blue pillows, Freya sitting next to her on a bench, that Freya spoke again.

"I wanted to make sure you're okay. What happened in the quarry, it's terrifying, Mary. But I'm glad you made it out alive."

Mary sniffed, but she didn't respond.

Freya's face was turned out to the yard, but she glanced at Mary out of the corner of her eye. The woman shifted position, then began slowly rocking.

"Trent wanted to know who killed and raped his sister, didn't he?"

A slow nod.

"Do you know?"

Mary didn't respond.

"If you do, tell me. I can stop this guy. I can put him in jail for what he did to her."

No response.

"You have to give me something, Mary." Freya turned to her, unable to keep the frustration out of her voice. "Valerie deserved more than what happened to her. You see that—I know you do."

Mary sucked in a breath. She held up one finger, tears streaming down her face. When Freya nodded, the woman hurried into the house, the screen door slamming hard behind her.

Freya took a deep breath and waited.

A moment later, Mary was back, a pad of paper clutched in her hand.

"Good." Freya nodded at her as she settled back against her pillow. "Tell me who hurt Valerie."

A pause. Hesitation was written all over Mary's face, but a moment later, her jaw tightened. She clicked the pen she held and scribbled something on the pad of paper, lifting it for Freya to see.

"*I wasn't there. I don't know,*" Freya read, then shook her head. "Let me get this straight—you and your friends sent Valerie out there to scare her a little, am I right?"

A nod. Mary wiped away the tears. For a moment, she looked like she probably had in high school. Scared. Unsure of what was going to happen.

"Whose idea was it?"

Scrawling. *Courtney.*

"None of you went with her?"

Shaking her head, she tried to speak, the sound twisted and guttural, then angrily scribbled something on the paper. This took a long time, and Freya forced herself to relax as she waited for Mary to finish.

I regret this every single day. Valerie was amazing. Beautiful. Courtney was threatened by her, but I liked Valerie better.

"You all got matching tattoos after, didn't you? To remember what happened?" Freya asked.

Yes. Courtney's idea. To tie us all together, remind us we all were part of it.

Freya sighed. "What did Trent say to you to get you to come out?"

Bring money and meet me or I'll kill your husband.

"And you believed him?"

A frantic nod.

"Who gave him your phone number?"

Mary's mouth tightened.

My housekeeper. I fired her.

Freya sat in silence for a minute. "Mary, take off your

sunglasses." It wasn't strange for the woman to have them on outside, but she'd answered the door wearing them.

Mary reached up and touched them but didn't comply.

"Mary. I need you to take off your sunglasses. Now. That's an order." She had no real power over whether or not the woman removed her sunglasses, but Mary didn't know that.

Mary sucked in a breath. Fingered the arm of her sunglasses, then pulled them off. She folded them and placed them on a small side table next to her, then tightened her jaw and stared at Freya.

The shiner was so new it hadn't had time to really settle into a deep purple. Over the next few hours it would, the color growing richer and more intense, but right now the bruising was minimal.

The hair on the back of Freya's neck stood up. "Did Brian do that?"

Mary lifted her chin. For a moment, Freya thought she was going to deny it, that she'd argue with her about it, but then she gave a single nod.

"Why?"

Mary paused, tapping her pen against the paper.

Freya felt her gut tighten as the truth hit her. "Trent was convinced you knew who hurt Valerie. He wanted you alive at the quarry so he could get it out of you. You know who it was, don't you?"

Freya leaned over to the woman and put her hand on her knee. She was so thin, like a fragile bird just on the cusp of breaking. When she gave her knee a gentle squeeze, Mary finally looked at her.

"You know that living with an abuser won't ever work out for you. Let me guess—Brian found out you took the money to pay Trent off and gave you that as a little gift. Only he wasn't nearly as upset as he could have been, was he? Because he knows nobody will ever know the truth."

Tears ran down Mary's cheeks, but she ignored them.

"Who was involved with Valerie's death?"

Mary lifted her right hand and touched her wedding band.

"I thought so." A pause, while she tried to find the right words. "You knew, didn't you? But you felt like you didn't have a choice but to keep quiet."

Mary nodded. She took a shuddering breath and started to write.

Brian knew about the hazing. Valerie had just broken up with his best friend, and he went there to talk to her.

"He said he just went there to talk to her?" When Mary nodded, Freya continued. "And you believed him?"

Mary locked eyes with Freya. In them, she saw everything. The fear of who she was married to, the hope it was over, the anguish of living with this secret for so many years.

"Did he confess to you?"

Mary looked away, and Freya spoke faster. "Mary, listen. You can't live like this. Brian hurt you. You think he's going to stop at one black eye? I doubt this is the first time he's gotten angry and taken it out on you. You've taken a few trips to the hospital for various injuries. Work with me. Help me get justice for your friend."

Mary was still crying.

"I'm going to arrest your husband for Valerie's rape and murder," Freya said. "I'll need you to make a statement. Would you be willing to do that?"

Mary's shoulders rolled in. She looked like she was going to collapse in on herself. She was crying so hard that tears dripped off her chin, but she didn't move to wipe them away as she wrote.

"*I'll do whatever it takes*," Freya read. "*Valerie deserved better.*" She looked at Mary. "You're right—she did. We can't go back in time and change what happened, but we can hopefully get justice for her. I'm going to need your help."

Mary nodded, then pressed her hand against her heart.

"Good." Freya stood. "Is he home right now?"

Mary shook her head. Mimed driving and typing.

"He's at work. Great. You're coming with me to the station. We're going to keep you safe, okay? Get your purse. Lock up the house. We're leaving. Now."

Freya leaned forward, stretching out her leg to work out the pain in her hip. She'd wait outside while Mary got her things together.

And then? Then she'd finally get justice for Valerie, the justice her brother had wanted so badly. She'd lock up Brian. Mary had been covering for him for years, but it was clear he was abusive and she was terrified of him.

That would play a role in what happened to her.

The screen door slammed open, and Mary locked the front door. Her purse was hitched high on her shoulder, her lips pressed into a firm line.

Freya watched as she reached for the sunglasses sitting on the table, then pulled her hand back, leaving them where they sat.

Good. Let everyone see what kind of a person Brian was. What happened to Valerie was a tragedy, and people needed to heal. Arresting Brian was the first step.

Freya loved her hometown. Even when she'd fled, her tail between her legs, there had been people there that hadn't turned their backs on her.

And she wasn't about to turn her back on them.

EPILOGUE

Freya paused outside Esther's home, a sack of takeout Mexican food in one hand, a bundle of flowers in the other. Esther might act like she didn't love it when Freya brought her flowers, but Freya knew the truth. Esther liked being taken care of in little ways, and one of them was with fresh flowers. Not roses, thank you very much, so she held a bundle of sunflowers.

Just as she was going to knock, the door swung open. Esther stood in front of her, her hands on her hips. Her eyes flicked down to the sunflowers, and she grinned, then hugged Freya.

"Thank you for coming to lunch."

"Thanks for having me." Freya hugged her back, then led the way into the kitchen. Esther already had the table set, so Freya quickly flipped open the Styrofoam containers with cheese-covered chimichangas, extra cups of salsa, and chips. "I was feeling cheese and chips. How does that sound to you?"

"Sounds amazing." Esther took the flowers from Freya, chopped off the bottoms of the stems, then plunked them in a vase before setting the whole thing on the table. She sat down across from Freya with a sigh, then grabbed a chip and dug in. "Tell me, darling," she said a moment later, "how you've been."

Freya opened her mouth, but Esther pointed at her with a chip. "Hold on. Before you give me some pat answer like you'd give your chief, I want you to think things through. Be honest. I know when you're not telling me the truth."

That gave Freya pause. She took a bite of her chimichanga, then washed it down with some water. Finally, she felt ready to answer. "I'm much better than I thought I would be, Esther. This case is wrapped up and, what's better, Brian Frost is in jail."

Esther arched a brow. "Permanently?"

"Not yet. We still have to have his trial. Mary's willing to take the stand, to tell everyone what he's done."

"She's quite brave."

Freya took another bite while she considered how to respond. Was Mary brave for standing up against Brian? Sure. That took a lot of bravery, a lot of support, and a lot of hope that people would support you for doing something so scary. But, at the same time, where was that bravery when Valerie was killed? Mary had lived with her friend's killer all this time, had put up with his abuse, and only when it all came to a head had she been willing to put her foot down.

"She is," Freya finally decided. "Though a lot of heartache could have been avoided if she had come forward when Valerie was killed."

"She was scared. Just a teenager." Esther was watching her, her keen eyes fixed on Freya.

"I know, and I'm not saying other people wouldn't have done the same thing. But imagine if she had come forward then, not just now. Three more women would still be alive. Maybe Trent could have gotten the help he needed to deal with his sister's murder. Their parents would have gotten closure. It's a terrible situation all around, and I don't know that anything would have made it all better, if I'm honest."

"Not everyone is as strong as you," Esther remarked.

For a moment, Freya felt quiet. "And not everyone has you in their corner."

They ate in silence after that, but it wasn't uncomfortable. It was two women who had been brought together by circumstances outside their control having a meal. Breaking bread. Just enjoying each other's company.

It was only after, when they were washing dishes together, that Esther brought it back up. "How long do you think he'll be in prison? That poor girl, and it was so long ago, he deserves to pay for what he did to her."

"Honestly, Esther, I have no doubt he'll be in prison the rest of his life, and his wife is going to be the one to slam the door on him. There's no statute of limitations for murder. He can't hide from his actions, not any longer. You may think you can get away with hurting people, but the ugly truth will always come back out."

"Good." Esther finished drying a plate and set it in the cupboard. "I'm really glad to hear that, Freya. Thanks for what you did."

Freya frowned. "It's my job. Anyone would do what I did."

Esther eyeballed her, and Freya closed her eyes. What she didn't need to say, but Esther apparently knew, was how she still saw Trent at night. She was awake every night, her legs in pain, screaming as she imagined the man clawing his way up her, stabbing her over and over, desperate to kill her for almost stopping him.

No way could she ever admit to that. Showing that much weakness, even in front of someone like Esther, wasn't something she could do.

"Oh, darling. You think you can hide what you're feeling from me, but you can't." Esther pulled her into a hug. "Now, as much as I'd love to let you hang out here all afternoon, I have a new cookie recipe to work on."

"Oh? Do tell." Freya leaned against the kitchen counter and waited.

"It came to me last night in a dream," Esther said, grabbing a handwritten recipe from the fridge and handing it to Freya. "Chocolate cookies with a crisped coconut topping and caramel drizzle. Sounds divine, doesn't it?"

"It honestly does," Freya groaned. "What time do I need to come back by to taste test the first batch for you?"

"I was hoping you'd ask that. Paul and Marla will be over around four this afternoon, so why don't you come back then? The three of you can try them out—offer any suggestions you might have."

Freya's first instinct was to argue with Esther, tell her she didn't want to meet up with Paul and Marla in just a few hours, but she bit her tongue. Thought about it. She didn't have a lot of friends outside the police department, but why not? Why not spend time with Esther's neighbors now the case was finally over? One bad guy was dead; another was in jail. She could relax. For the first time since Jolie and Millicent's bodies had been found in the forest, she could take a deep breath. Put her feet under the table. Laugh without feeling guilty.

"You know what? I'll be here. And I'll bring the milk," Freya said, surprising herself.

Even Esther looked surprised. "Alright, darling. I can't wait."

"Me either." Freya hugged her and let herself out. Four wasn't that far away, and she had a few things she wanted to do. First, she needed to swing by the library and check out a book. It had been years since she'd had time or the inclination to read for pleasure. Next, she needed to buy some milk. She also wanted to swing by Mary's house and check in on the woman. With Brian's trial coming up, more and more pressure was going to be put on her shoulders. She couldn't get rid of the pressure for Mary, but she could remind her that she wasn't alone.

As she started her car, her phone rang. An unsaved number. Freya answered it as she pulled away from Esther's house.

"Captain Sinclair, Fawn Lake Police Department. How can I help you?"

"Freya Sinclair?" The voice filling Freya's car sounded young. Familiar.

"That's me. Who's calling?"

"Hi, this is Lorna. I work at the Amos Hotel. You gave me your card if I ever wanted to make a change."

Lorna. The young woman working the front desk. Freya tapped her brakes and pulled over to the side of the road. "Lorna, of course. What can I do for you?"

The girl inhaled, then exhaled hard. "I want a change. This place? You were right. It's no good. I saw something online, that you're hiring dispatchers. I thought maybe..." Her voice trailed off.

"You know what? I can head by the department right now. If you have time, why don't you meet me there? We can get you set up with an application, see when you can come in for your interview and polygraph."

There was a pause. Freya drummed her steering wheel as she waited. "Lorna?"

"You know what? Yes. I'll do it. I'll head there now. Thanks, Captain."

"Freya. Please. I'll meet you there shortly."

She hung up and pulled back onto the road. *Change of plans.* She'd get Lorna set up at the department, then head out to see Mary. If she remembered correctly, Sandra was working dispatch, and that woman loved taking people under her wing. Lorna would be fine.

A smile played on her lips. For the first time in weeks, she felt in control.

Anything could happen of course. But she was prepared.

A LETTER FROM EMILY

Dear reader,

Thanks so much for joining me back in Fawn Lake in *One Liar Left*! If you enjoyed Freya and her team, and want to keep up to date with all my latest releases, just sign up at the following link. Your email address will never be shared, and you can unsubscribe at any time.

www.bookouture.com/emily-shiner

One Liar Left was everything I wanted it to be, and going back to Fawn Lake was a dream come true! I had a wonderful time writing this book and spending time with the entire team. Hopefully you enjoyed reading it as much as I loved working on it! If you did, I'd be very grateful if you could write a review. Not only do I enjoy hearing what my readers think, but reviews make a huge difference helping new readers discover one of my books for the first time.

I truly love hearing from my readers and personally respond to every message I get. Please feel free to reach out to me via my email at emily@authoremilyshiner.com, or you can get in touch through social media or my website.

Thanks,

Emily

KEEP IN TOUCH WITH EMILY

www.authoremilyshiner.com

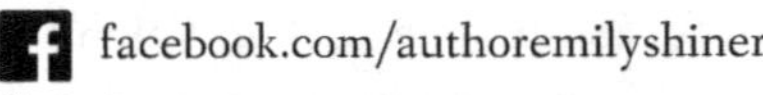

facebook.com/authoremilyshiner

x.com/authoreshiner

instagram.com/authoremilyshiner

ACKNOWLEDGMENTS

Getting to go back to Fawn Lake was like going home, and I couldn't have done it without the incredible Bookouture team! Thank you to everyone who has read, edited, and loved this book as much as I have, especially Kelsie Marsden, editor extraordinaire.

To my older sister, Ashley, for reading all of my books, finding typos, and happily pointing them out.

A very special thank you to the rest of my family for reading this book and talking about it over dinner. There's never a dull moment when I'm writing certain scenes.

To my friends who pulled me away from edits when I was too close to losing my mind and who celebrate every milestone with me.

And, of course, thank you to my readers! Y'all are everything. I can't thank you enough for tagging me, sharing my books, and reaching out to let me know what you think. Writing is my dream, and having so many incredible readers is more than I ever could have asked for.

Copyeditor
Donna Hillyer

Proofreader
Laura Kincaid

Marketing
Alex Crow
Melanie Price
Occy Carr
Cíara Rosney
Martyna Młynarska

Operations and distribution
Marina Valles
Stephanie Straub

Production
Hannah Snetsinger
Mandy Kullar
Jen Shannon

Publicity
Kim Nash
Noelle Holten
Jess Readett
Sarah Hardy

Rights and contracts
Peta Nightingale
Richard King
Saidah Graham

www.ingramcontent.com/pod-product-compliance
Lightning Source LLC
Chambersburg PA
CBHW061631190726
48289CB00006B/1561